STONEWALL GOES WEST

A NOVEL OF THE CIVIL WAR
AND WHAT MIGHT HAVE BEEN

R.E. THOMAS

BLACK GOLD MEDIA

BLACK GOLD MEDIA
Copyright © 2013 by R.E. Thomas
ISBN-13: 978-0988892200
ISBN-10: 0988892200
stonewallgoeswest.com
facebook.com/stonewallgoeswest

To my father,
my first and best example
of a man pursuing his dreams

INTRODUCTION

The death of Lieutenant General Thomas J. Jackson stands as the great "what if?" of the Civil War. The only event during the war that comes close to producing the same amount of speculation is the battle of Gettysburg, and many scenarios for a Confederate victory at Gettysburg are based on the survival and presence of Stonewall Jackson.

Southerners probably first began wondering what might have been if their beloved Stonewall had lived in the wake of Lee's defeat at Gettysburg. Indeed, in Michael Shaara's landmark novel, *The Killer Angels*, they began wondering after the first day of that battle. Shaara put the following words into the mouth of the irascible Isaac Tremble, summing up the sentiments of many:

> "General Ewell, we have got to take that hill. General Jackson would not have stopped like this with the bluebellies on the run and plenty of light left and a hill like that empty."

Yet the difficulty with sending Stonewall Jackson to Gettysburg has always been one of realism, since it demands Jackson emerge from the violent and confused clash in the dense, second-growth forest around Chancellorsville with either light wounds or no wounds at all. That was most unlikely. The friendly fire incident that claimed Jackson's life also killed several of his aides, and Jackson was struck by no fewer than three bullets. Major General A.P. Hill was himself wounded upon replacing Jackson, and Lieutenant General James Longstreet was wounded in another friendly fire incident at the Battle of the Wilderness a year later, just a few miles from where Jackson was shot.

All of these officers were killed and wounded doing what good officers did during the Civil War, namely overseeing things personally and exposing themselves to danger in the process. As it turned out, the Virginia Wilderness around Chancellorsville was a particularly lethal place to do that.

So imagining Stonewall Jackson as escaping Chancellorsville unscathed misconstrues the kind of man he was, as well as doing a disservice to the particularly horrific combat that took place in the Virginia Wilderness in 1863 and 1864. However, the injuries Jackson suffered need not have been mortal. The majority of patients who endured amputations such as Jackson's survived.

If Jackson had recovered from his wounds, his recovery would have come too late for him to have participated in the Gettysburg Campaign, but what might have happened after that? It is from that question that *Stonewall Goes West* springs.

As a consumer of military history, one of my pet peeves is a book lacking maps, since regional and battlefield maps greatly simplify following the course of events. This is so much the case that I have often been forced to sketch out crude maps of my own when the author and publisher of a given book have failed to provide them.

Sadly, publishing constraints forced me to commit the sin of omitting maps from *Stonewall Goes West*. Instead, I have drawn a set of maps and made them available on my author's website (stonewallgoeswest.com) and my author's Facebook page (facebook.com/stonewallgoeswest).

Another issue affecting clarity in this novel was how to name the various military units in a way that wasn't a burden to the reader, but at the same time didn't sour the tenor of the narrative. My solution deviates from the nomenclature of the period to some degree, but I felt it necessary and shall explain my method.

At the top, the North preferred to name field armies after rivers ("Army of the Potomac"), whereas the South preferred territorial designations ("Army of Northern Virginia"). This is a crucial distinction in Stonewall Goes West, as it separates the Federal Army of the Tennessee (named for the river) and the Confederate Army of Tennessee (named for the state).

The Confederate Army often referred a given corps, division or brigade after the man permanently assigned to lead it. Hence Archer's Brigade, Heth's Division, and Hill's Corps at Gettysburg. I have adopted this system to refer to both Federal and Confederate units, and chose to do so for two reasons. One is that referring to a unit by the name of the man leading it reinforces its connection to that character, and makes it easier for the reader to follow what that character is doing in the story. The other is that the Federal method, which might refer to the above arrangement as 3rd Brigade, 2nd Division, 3rd Corps, produces stumbling blocks in the text that only those who are intimate with military terminology could easily navigate.

The exception to that rule is the corps of the Federal Army. These were identified using Roman numerals ("II Corps"), a system still in use today. I have kept that system because I found it visually distinctive, and it highlighted the differences between the Federal and Confederate armies without becoming cumbersome and confusing.

ACKNOWLEDGEMENTS

A book may have only one parent, but always has many midwives. Writing a work of alternate history is a daunting task, because when well-done it is still at its heart still historical fiction, and therefore carries the special burden of accurately weaving accurate details into what is otherwise a fictional story. I am therefore thankful that I had a huge volume of readily accessible material to work from, and that so many people proved helpful in bringing this tale to life.

A few individuals personally contributed to my research, and therefore deserve special attention. Kathy Niedergeses at the Lawrence County Archives was instrumental in helping me construct the landscape for the Battle of Lawrenceburg. Edwin G. Frank, a professor at the University of Memphis and President of the West Tennessee Historical Society, steered me in the right direction on several crucial matters, as did Ann Toplovich at the Tennessee Historical Society.

I must also extend thanks to the people who assisted me with the nitty gritty of making this book happen. Several years of publishing experience gave me a firm foundation for producing this novel, but I could never have done it all alone. On the editorial side, I owe some thanks to Amy Brown, Scott Peters, and Elena Pavlova. On the artistic side, Cindy Flora turned my vision of a one-armed Stonewall Jackson giving orders to Patrick Cleburne and Nathan Bedford Forrest into reality, while my former Wilson Center colleague Lianne Helper did the cover design. Without the help of all these people, crafting this book into shape would have been impossible.

I must also acknowledge the support that came from my family. My mother and father-in-law were my biggest fans as I plowed through multiple drafts of *Stonewall Goes West*, while my sister was the one who reminded me that my father, J.K. Thomas, would have been the first to approve of what I was doing. Finally, I must thank my wife, who has never wavered from supporting me in spending however much time was necessary (including the diversion of some of our precious vacation time) to finish this project.

PART I
OLD DOMINIONS

OCTOBER TO DECEMBER 1863

CHAPTER 1

October 13, 1863
3 p.m.
Lee's Headquarters, Army of Northern Virginia, CSA
The Warren Green Hotel
Warrenton, Virginia

Jackson tightened the grip on his reins by reflex, the sole outward sign of his irritation. His orders were to halt on the northeastern outskirts of Warrenton, to rest his men, and permit them time to cook rations. He thought the stop a mistake, hadn't agreed, had even argued against it, but he had obeyed faithfully. Obedience was a soldier's duty, and that was that.

So the men had fallen out, built their fires, boiled acorn coffee and foraged white cabbage, and fried hoecakes. They would have food in their bellies, Jackson thought, but they should be pressing on, as soon as possible. The army was losing time, and he would happily trade the full bellies of the men to get that time back.

He stopped in front of the Warren Green Hotel. Horses were tied up all up and down the street, and a dusty courier sat in a rocking chair on the front porch, strumming out the notes of "Bonnie Blue Flag" on the strings of his fiddle.

Jackson fumbled his dismount, stumbling off, caught in the stirrup. A man caught him, set him aright, and asked "Are you well, sir?"

Turning, Jackson saw it was Lee's chief aide, Major Walter Taylor. Jackson had known Taylor since before the war, as his former student at the Virginia Military Institute, and thought he had grown into a slim, dapper young man, but one who looked more like a banker than a soldier, what with his well-combed hair and neatly trimmed goatee.

"Yes, Major" Jackson stammered. I shouldn't be this tired or this sore, he thought. It's making me careless.

Might have been softness from months of bed rest, or might have been the wounding and the loss of his left arm that went with it, but whatever it was had left him feeling weaker, compromising what he thought of as his already precarious health.

Worried as he might about it, health didn't matter so much Jackson, not when compared to his duty. Whatever the cause, he reckoned he should be overcoming his frailties, and doing so more speedily. He had already spent the entire summer recovering from his wounds, and was as impatient to return to his old strength as he had been to return to duty.

Straightening first his cap and then his coat with his one hand, he said to Taylor "I'm reporting as ordered."

"General Ewell is already here, sir" Taylor replied. "Follow me, please."

Jackson nodded, motioned to a pair of his aides, and then followed Taylor into the hotel. The Warren Green was still in presentable condition, in spite of the war. Armies had marched and counter-marched across northern Virginia for three years now, Warrenton was a crossroads town, and the Warren Green had been used as quarters and headquarters by both sides many times over. Jackson's West Point classmate and the one-time commander of the northern Army of the Potomac, George B. McClellan, had said his goodbyes on these steps. Perhaps it was a shared sense between the armies that they would all pass this way again that spared it from ransacking.

Taylor showed Jackson and his party into the dining room, now serving as a map room. Jackson went to the table, while behind him his men quietly exchanged pleasantries with Taylor. Dick "Old Baldy" Ewell, with a wooden leg and a rooster's face, stood on his crutches next to General Lee and studied the map, Ewell's own staff officers standing behind them.

Jackson strode up to his commanding officer and saluted. Lee took a step forward, and with a look of concern, asked quietly "General, I do hope you are well."

"Well. I'm well, sir." Jackson replied flatly. I must look still worse, he thought ruefully.

Lee nodded and stepped away.

Ewell stepped awkwardly forward, and extended his hand. Jackson took it for a firm handshake, and Ewell grinned and stammered "Erm, Thomas," still finding it awkward to address his old chief as his equal. "How the heh… how are you? Holding up?"

Jackson smiled warmly. Ewell had been a bachelor and a profane man for most of his life, but after he lost that leg he found both love and God from his sickbed. Still, old habits and all.

"About as well as you are," he replied.

After Jackson's wounding at Chancellorsville, Lee promoted Ewell and gave him a corps, while A.P. Hill became the acting commander of Jackson's old corps. So it was that Old Baldy Ewell, Little Powell Hill, and James Longstreet all led infantry corps to Gettysburg, while Jackson lay in bed and recuperated. With Jackson returned to duty, Hill had gone back to his division. Longstreet was detached to Tennessee, which left Lee's army in the hands of Jackson and his former lieutenant, Ewell.

Lee brought the pleasantries to an end by calling on Major Taylor to start his presentation. "Gentlemen, four days ago this army marched with the objective of reaching around the Federal right flank, taking advantage of their detachment of the XI and XII Corps to Tennessee. While we disengaged from the Rapidan and made for the Federal flank with some success, General Meade wasn't fooled long, and pulled back."

Taylor indicated positions on the map. "We know the bulk of the Federal force lies to the southeast of our position, about ten miles away, in the vicinity of the Orange and Alexandria rail line. General Stuart reports that Kilpatrick's cavalry and the III Corps, under the command of William French, with perhaps as much as 25,000 men altogether, are several miles north on the Warrenton Turnpike, shielding their right flank."

Jackson's brow furrowed at the mention of French. Lee noticed this, and recalled the bad blood between the two men, back in the Old Army.

Taylor paused for a moment, and then said "Union numbers are thought to be at least 85,000 men. Perhaps as high as 95,000."

Lee spoke up. "Gentlemen, Meade has no intention of stopping here. Those people are still retreating, even as we speak, indeed may continue retreating into the night. After we catch our breath, this army will march again for the Federal flank and rear. Your thoughts?"

Ewell murmured "Meade has conducted a skillful withdrawal, and that's a fact. He kept his army together, put a strong rear guard in all the proper places. To reach his flank again, we must march much farther than he. I fear he won't give us any opportunity."

"Yes, the Yankees have always been very good at retreating," Taylor said. Everyone laughed at that. Even Lee chuckled.

Everyone except Jackson, who instead looked up from the map at Taylor and asked flatly "Have we any reports of an enemy presence at Thoroughfare Gap?"

Taylor looked back quizzically. Thoroughfare Gap was at least 10 miles west of French's position. Maybe a cavalry patrol had been out that way, but only maybe, and there were no reports about it one way or the other. "No, General Jackson, we have not. Although I would describe our knowledge of what goes on at the Gap as scanty at best."

Jackson nodded. "Good, good. I propose to send a brigade of cavalry at once to occupy Thoroughfare Gap, by way of Georgetown village" he said, pointing to the map, tracing his finger along his desired route. The twang of the Virginia hill country seeped into his voice, just as it did whenever Jackson became excited. "After passing the Bull Run Mountains, the cavalry turns north and moves on back roads and overland, leaving guides as they go, emerging unseen at Thoroughfare Gap. I then follow with my entire corps. Once clear of the Gap, I march east and fall upon the enemy flank."

An awkward silence followed. It was Lee's habit to allow his chief subordinates to chew matters over, but Ewell was clearly too accustomed to taking orders from Jackson to readily question him at a council of war. Longstreet was gone, and there was no one else of such standing there. Speaking up was therefore left to Major Taylor.

"That is a march of some 20 miles," Taylor eventually said, skeptically. "When do you propose to be in position to attack?"

Jackson imagined the roads, the country, both of which he already knew firsthand, and the time it would take to move all those horses, men, guns and a minimum of wagons. "If the cavalry is sent at once, I will follow immediately. I can clear the gap by day-dawn, and in position to attack by 10 o'clock tomorrow morning."

That was optimistic, Lee thought. Very optimistic. I doubt that, doubt it very much. Noon sounded better.

"Why not advance directly, General, on the Warrenton Turnpike?" asked Colonel Chilton, Lee's chief of staff.

Jackson looked directly at Lee and shook his head. "The enemy expects it. Even if we escape notice during the night, we will surely be observed at first light. We must attack where least anticipated, or the enemy will pull back all the quicker for it."

Lee finally spoke up. "I believe you should give yourself more time, General."

Jackson replied "As you say, sir. 11."

Lee imagined Jackson's plan unfolding. Those people only had a few ways north, across Broad Run. Milford and the railroad bridge at Bristoe Station were closest. Even if the Federals should march through the night, many of their troops would still be south and west of Broad Run at noon. Jackson's Corps would then smash their flank, push across their line of retreat, and in so doing, cut off one or two of their corps. Of course, it would improve matters greatly if the Federal retreat was delayed...

Lee suddenly recalled that Stuart, his cavalry chief, was with Hampton's Division, far away and probing the Federal right. I must supply Jackson with cavalry from elsewhere, he thought.

"There is no reason for delay" Lee said matter of factly. "Major Taylor, send a courier to Major General Lee," referring to his nephew, Fitzhugh Lee, who commanded the nearest cavalry division. "Give him my compliments, and instruct him to select a brigade for detached duty. Send its commanding officer here for orders."

"Yessir!" Taylor saluted and left.

"General Ewell," Lee continued. "At first light, your corps must be ready to move directly upon the enemy, in the direction of Cattlet Station. Wherever you find the Federal army, there you shall attack it with the utmost vigor. Force those people to turn and fight you. When Meade stops or turns, General Jackson will strike their right."

Ewell hesitated. "It's risky, sir. A very risky plan. It divides our army in the face of the enemy, and places our two corps at least 10 miles apart until after mid-day. We won't be able to support each other, General Lee, for at least the entire morning. Meade could easily hold off General Jackson or myself with only one or two of his corps, and crush the other with the rest. Or he could turn in the morning and attack my corps with the bulk of his army. He could come between us, and defeat us in detail."

Lee looked at Ewell, studied him, shielding his disappointment behind dignified impassivity. Ewell had shown great promise under Jackson, yet at Gettysburg, the man had been indecisive, dithering. Lee could see Ewell remained focused on what the enemy could do, not what the enemy would do or what Ewell himself could do to the enemy.

Old Baldy was right, of course, if in a pedantic way. The absence of Longstreet's Corps, off in Tennessee where it had helped win victory at Chickamauga, was keenly felt.

Yet there was nothing to do about that, Lee knew, except make do with what they had. Long odds demand great risks. The Seven Days, Second Manassas, Chancellorsville, these past battles proved that. And when has the Army of the Potomac ever shown as much aggression as that? To turn around and concentrate on us! Why, they have my army outnumbered by at least two to one, and here they are, backing away from a fight.

"Those people, General Ewell, are retreating" Lee said in a polite, but flat tone, his cue that the discussion was over. "And they will continue to retreat. General Meade may come to stand his ground, but he will do it closer to Washington, and he will not suddenly turn to strike us." Lee said.

"Yessir." Ewell replied.

I must stay with him, Lee thought, slowly rubbing his hands together, as was his habit when thinking things through. I'm feeling a little better, strong enough to ride a horse and not in that ambulance, like a feeble old man. I can stay with Ewell, make sure he pushes hard tomorrow. He needs very little, only nudging.

"That will be all, gentlemen. General Jackson, if you and Mr. Hotchkiss there will wait here with me, I wish to discuss your proposed route with you in greater detail. Very well. General Ewell, you can expect your written orders shortly." Lee turned and left the room.

Ewell shook hands with Jackson again, and hobbled out. Lee watched, thinking they were quite a pair, these two corps commanders of mine. Eccentric and always worried about ailments that Lee thought were real and imaginary in equal measure. Jackson without his left arm, Ewell without his left leg.

Lee was broken from his reverie when Jackson barked to one of his aides "Captain Smith, ride back to headquarters. Tell Sandie to have Early's men up and ready within the hour. Johnson and Hill ready to follow at 5 p.m. Then you collect those picked guides, and have them ready for dispatch upon my return. Understood?"

11:30 pm
Jackson's Corps, Army of Northern Virginia, CSA
Behind the Bull Run Mountains

Jackson watched in the dark as the teamsters whispered a countdown, and men and mules strained together to free an ambulance from the mud. He sat in his saddle with his right arm bent at the elbow, thumb sticking up, as had been his practice ever since First Manassas. He had been shot through the hand then, ruining the circulation and causing his thumb to swell up painfully sometimes. It was more important than ever for his circulation, holding that thumb up, what with his left arm gone.

The main column of Early's Division trudged through the mud beyond him, and the urge to intervene, to make things happen, gnawed at him. The march had begun later than Jackson had intended, and when darkness fell, it was into an inky black, moonless, drizzly night. Even with well-placed cavalry guides showing the way, the march had slowed to a crawl once the head of his column turned off the main road and behind the Bull Run Mountains.

A man couldn't see ten feet in front of him now, and the damp ground was sodden again. The route behind the Bull Run Mountains was a patchwork of roads, tracks and open fields. Only a few of those fields had dried-up cornstalks still standing, leftover from the harvest and holding the soil in place. The rest had swiftly become a bog, churned up by the passage of men, horses, guns and wagons. The roads and tracks were only marginally better. Each passing regiment or battery made the route worse for all who followed.

Giving up on trying to see beyond more than a handful of men at a time, Jackson crooked his ear and listened. The men were silent, as commanded by their night marching orders, but there was still plenty of noise. Creaking wagons and gun carriages, the muffled, sucking sound of a horse pulling its hoof from the mud, and the endless toots and groans of flatulent men as they walked by in their thousands.

Jackson shook his head and muttered "Cabbage."

It was a fine mess, and the slowness made Jackson restless, but there was nothing to be done about it. These were his boys. They knew what to do, even if he seldom admitted it, because he had trained them to do it. Many had been with him since the Shenandoah Valley, and slogging in the dark through miles of muddy fields was old hat. No sense in chastising a man who was already doing his duty, so Jackson sat, watched, and fumed.

I must not be so impatient, he thought. The rain was, like all else in nature, the doing of Providence. Providence blessed the cause, and Jackson knew that if he was slowed by the weather, it must be to His willful purpose. All great events in this world were the work of Providence. Perhaps the enemy was slowed more. That thought warmed him.

Then Jackson heard a "hee-yah!" shouted from farther back. He snatched up the reins and pounced, spurring his horse and galloping back down the column, leaving his staff in his wake. The yell was followed by a few more.

"Who broke silence?" Jackson hissed, arriving at where the sound had come from, a mired battery. The men stopped what they were doing and stood to rigid attention. Even if they couldn't really see him, every man knew that was an angry Old Jack.

Jackson's staff slogged up behind him. Not taking his eyes off the offending battery and the passing infantry that had paused to help them, he quietly, flatly said "Sandie?"

Major Sandie Pendleton, his chief of staff, paused for a moment and studied the faces and the cannon in front of him. "Milledge's Battery, I think, sir. Georgia boys."

A man stepped in front of Jackson's horse and saluted. Jackson couldn't see his face, but the man whispered "Captain Milledge, sir. This is my battery."

Jackson leaned forward over his horse's neck. He could see him now. Milledge had been pushing a cannon himself, and was caked in mud. "Captain, the general orders for a night march command silence. Absolute silence. If you cannot keep these men quiet and move this battery, I will find someone who can."

Milledge stood at rigid attention. "Yessir. Even my horses shall not whinny, sir," he said in hushed tones.

"Good, good." Jackson turned in the saddle and said "Major Pendleton, send for Colonel Nelson. I would remind him of the necessity of silence on a night march."

Sandie was barely a month into his 23rd year, a thin boy endowed with a cherub-like face that suggested perpetual innocence, completely at odds with his role as chief bureaucrat and aide in Jackson's Corps. It was an honest mistake, he thought, but Old Jack had not a whit of tolerance for disobedience to his orders, honest, mistaken or otherwise.

Sandie replied quietly "Yessir."

October 14
6:30 a.m.
Lee's Headquarters in the Field, Army of Northern Virginia, CSA
Southeast of Warrenton

Lee sat in his saddle, enjoying the crisp morning air and musing on how nothing in war ever went as planned, not ever. Just a little apart from General Ewell and their assembled staffs, he watched Ewell's troops march by, waving hats but otherwise staying quiet, and reflected on the overly complicated plans he had once attempted, how everything about them went awry. He knew better now. Simplest was always best.

One of their European observers, the engineer Captain Scheibert from the Court of Hohenzollern, explained it best. One night at the campfire, Lee overheard Scheibert speak of a Prussian book on the philosophy of war, which described even the simplest things as being ground to a halt by "friction," like gears grinding away in sand, and the most obvious things as being confused by a "fog." No Jomini that Clausewitz, Lee thought, but he clearly knew this business first hand.

His plan started predictably enough. Fitzhugh Lee sent Wickham's Brigade for service with Jackson, along with a thoughtful note explaining that many of that brigade's 4th Virginia troopers were from hereabouts, and would prove most useful. Then Lee's chief aide, Major Taylor, and the mapmaker Hotchkiss explained to Colonel Owen, in temporary command of that brigade, what Lee wanted done and how, and the brigade was on the road by dusk. The first of Jackson's divisions, Early's, followed shortly thereafter.

After seeing them off, Lee and Taylor returned to the Warren Green and worked until midnight, at which time Lee went to bed. No sooner was he under the covers then friction set in. After 1 o'clock, a message arrived from Stuart. It was politely phrased, with all Stuart's usual cavalier pleasantries, but the contents were alarming for all that: Stuart, accompanying Hampton's Division of cavalry, was cut-off behind enemy lines. He was well-hidden, he wrote, and could stay that way until after daybreak, but was nonetheless trapped between the Federal II and III Corps. Could Lee send him some assistance? Stuart asked.

Sending that assistance meant rewriting Ewell's orders, diverting Wilcox's Division to move farther east than originally planned, marching overland to Stuart's relief. It was still the broad net Lee had hoped to cast, and he remained confident that some part of Ewell's Corps would make solid contact with the Federal II Corps. That done, Ewell would pitch in with everything he had. Simple.

Lee observed Old Baldy chatting, and noted how confident and animated he was, quite a change from his hesitant demeanor the previous afternoon. When Lee had ridden to join him, he had delighted in reminding Lee that he was raised on a farm not far from here, knew the ground well, and would have no trouble finding the Union lines.

It was good to see Ewell so relaxed, Lee thought, but he still bore watching. I can trust Jackson to conquer whatever obstacles might lie in his path, to find a way to attack. No cause to worry about that. That leaves me free to focus my attention on supervising Ewell, who had started his corps forward at 5 o'clock, before first light. There had been some shooting, Lee thought, some scattered musketry, but nothing of substance. And no information.

6:30 am
II Corps, Army of the Potomac, USA
Auburn

General Gourvener Warren took the tin cup of coffee that was proffered to him, and thanked the orderly who brought it. With his II Corps on the road since 4 o'clock, well before dawn, and he himself attentive to his business, he hadn't had time yet for breakfast.

Warren was handsome, a man of visible intelligence and prospects. He started the war a lowly lieutenant in his early 30s, but rose quickly to the post of chief topographical engineer in the Army of the Potomac. It was in that post that Warren saw the importance of a hill at Gettysburg called Little Round Top, critical to anchoring the Federal line, and on his own authority diverted the troops to defend it.

As a reward, he had been promoted again and given temporary command of the II Corps in place of General Hancock, severely wounded in that battle. Warren knew if he played his cards right, he might be in line for permanent corps command.

Of course, his men had missed breakfast too, and many of them were now making up for that, clustering around little fires and boiling coffee of their own. Warren grinned and sipped from the cup, and instantly became more wakeful. If there was one thing you could count on from a foot soldier in the United States Army, it was that given any opportunity, any at all, that man would collect some sticks, start a fire, and make some coffee. Other branches of the service mocked them for it, labeling them "coffee boilers."

Warren sipped from his cup, and studied the surrounding village. Auburn was a little place, only a few homes, a post office and a blacksmithy near as he could tell. The air was still misty, especially around Cedar Run, which passed by just to the south. Auburn itself was quiet, with the few civilians present staying indoors and away from the hated bluecoats. The only real noise came from his own staff and field kitchen.

Caldwell's Division and some of the artillery were perched on a neighboring hill, just behind the village. Webb's Division was even nearer, and Hays' Division had already crossed Cedar Run and was marching southwards. The corps wagon train led the way. To the north was the III Corps, under plodding old French, and together French and Warren faced the Rebels as the Union right wing. Behind them were Sykes and the V Corps.

Thus far that morning, there had only been a little musketry off to the west, Gregg's cavalry and his own pickets skirmishing with the Rebels just a bit. The light contact was reassuring.

So it was that the sudden boom of artillery jarred Warren from his pleasant morning reverie, and he almost spilled his coffee in the process. "What the devil?" he exclaimed. "That's coming from the east, the east and almost behind us by God!" Warren looked around, confused, and shouted "My horse! Where's my horse!"

His horse brought up, Warren mounted and rode out of Auburn and up the low hill, his staff hurrying to follow him. When Warren reached the top, he could see Caldwell was already moving his boys over the top of the rise, away from the fire on the east slope and to the sheltered west slope. The three batteries of artillery that had been parked with Caldwell, some 18 guns in all, were unlimbering to return the Rebel fire.

Warren studied the scene below, peering through his field glasses. It looked like sometime during the night, Rebel cavalry had slipped between his right and the left of French's III Corps. Jeb Stuart's bastards had gotten into his rear, cut him off from his nearest source of support, and were now shooting him up with what looked like several horse guns down there.

A courier galloped up. Saluting Warren, he said "General Hays begs to report that he has put out skirmishers, and is advancing on the Rebel position with both his brigades."

Outstanding, Warren thought. He had suspected Hays was a man of initiative. On the last day at Gettysburg, Hays had come out from behind the stone wall and counter-attacked the assault on Cemetery Ridge, scattering the Confederate left. Suspicion confirmed.

The courier inquired if he had any further orders for Hays. Warren said "No, but tell him to keep me informed." He then went back to studying the country to the west, as oblivious to the bursting shells as to the departure of the courier.

Hays was doing the proper thing, Warren thought, but best make sure no one else goes tearing off on their own. I'm new to this corps. I don't know these men very well, and they don't know me.

Turning to an aide, Warren said "Send to Webb. Tell him to continue breakfasting his men, with my compliments, but once he has finished he is to unstack his arms and be ready to move. Then find Colonel Baxter—Webb ought to know where he is—and tell him to keep that wagon train rolling, as ordered. No change there."

7:00 am
III Corps, Army of the Potomac, USA
Greenwich

William French felt much more than his 48 years in his back and thighs. Meade had put French's III Corps to marching and counter-marching for days, and now they were retreating back to Centerville. The retreat suited him just fine. Getting up well before dawn and spending an entire day in the saddle, day after damned, live long day, did not.

He sat on the other side of Broad Run, puffy-eyed and sore, adjusting his paunch, watching as his last division marched past. Kilpatrick's cavalry screened them from the other side of the river, and there had been no reports of Rebels yet. If Lee and Jackson had stirred, they weren't coming his way.

French said absently to his new aide, a fresh-faced teenaged boy he had taken on staff as a favor, "Well, lieutenant, you won't meet the elephant today." Feeling chatty, French continued "Did you know I used to command Stonewall Jackson?"

"No, sir," the aide croaked. Of course, he had heard all about it. The boy had caught up on all the staff gossip during his first week at headquarters. Still, army life was all very new to him, and French had never spoken to him in such familiar terms before. "That's very interesting, if I may say so, General."

French continued, almost as if the boy wasn't there. "Yes. An intemperate man, obstinate, insubordinate. He was my post quartermaster, and he made a fine mess of it. Crackbrained. I wanted the man court-martialed, but it was all swept under the rug."

"I ran him out of the army, though" French said, brightening. "Yes, I did. Jackson tucked tail, resigned, ran off to become a professor. A proper soldier would have persevered, stuck it out and stayed in the army."

Glancing at the boy, he added "Met him again at Gaines Mill, then White Oak Swamp. Stopped him too, held him fast. Yes, if you ask me, Thomas 'Stonewall' Jackson is an overrated man. He beat a gaggle of third-raters in the Shenandoah, it is true, men who were no soldiers, but the brains and the guts of the Rebels is Lee. Jackson just does what he's told. Don't you believe what the newspapers tell you about Jackson, because Robert E. Lee's the real ticket."

French pulled out his pocket watch. The tail of his corps had left the Greenwich crossroads at a quarter after seven, he thought. No one would call him tardy today.

8:00 am
II Corps, Army of the Potomac, USA
Auburn

Warren had only just finished watching Hays drive back the last of the Rebel cavalry from his immediate rear when the musketry to the west, which had been crackling lightly all morning, tore open rapidly. He rode over to the west slope of the hill to find that Caldwell's boys had started a whole new set of fires, and were finishing their breakfast of coffee and hardtack.

Examining the woods about half a mile west of Auburn, he saw enough butternut lurking about to think that the forest must be crawling with Rebel skirmishers. That thick screen of butternut was pushing his own picket line back, and some were already running back on Caldwell's position.

Bearing the message, Warren thought. He rode down to John Caldwell, a burly man of about the same age as himself, and found Caldwell looking through field glasses, studying the Rebel-infested woods.

"Well, General, it looks like you're going to have your hands full in just a little while" Warren said.

Caldwell nodded, "It might come to nothing, sir, but I'd best prepare all the same. I'll put my division into line above the foot of this hill. I reckon I could use some artillery support."

"The action to the east is pretty much over," Warren said. "I'll put all three of those batteries on line here. If any Rebs come out of those woods, we'll really get a good twist on them. Put down fire on them so hot, they'll each get a score of blisters."

Warren gave the orders, and then pondered his next move. He was only supposed to stop here for a couple of hours, shield the army's flank and rear, and wait for the traffic to clear on the creek crossings, especially Broad Run. If he withdrew now, that Reb cavalry would come right back and nip at his heels. Then that Reb infantry massing to the west would come up quick and smash his rear.

I could order Caldwell to send out a reconnaissance in force, he thought, to see what really was brewing to the west. No, that would be one more thing to pull back in when I march out of here, more time lost. I also can't put Webb on the march yet. His division is my only reserve, so it stays right here, with Caldwell and Hays.

That made up Warren's mind. What he needed to do was stay about Auburn until he either put the Rebel cavalry to flight or gave whoever was massing behind that wooded ridge to his west a bloody nose. Preferably both.

The two generals dismounted, waited and watched, chatting idly over more coffee. They soon received confirmation by a written message from General Gregg of the cavalry, dated roughly an hour before. Warren read it and showed it to Caldwell: two strong Confederate columns were pressing on Gregg from the west, and one more had swung past him to the northwest. Warren and Caldwell agreed that the latter was what was behind the woods to Caldwell's front.

Warren had half-hoped for an engagement of some kind, since he knew if it went well, it would boost his case for a permanent command. On the other hand, he had only 10,000 men with him, and from the looks of it, an entire Confederate corps of 20,000 or 25,000 would be at Auburn before the morning was out. He had a good position here, but not that good.

"Why don't those bastards just hurry it up?" Warren muttered unhappily. He summoned a courier, wrote out a message to explain his delay to General Meade, and waited for either Hays to say the Rebel horsemen were gone or for a grey line of battle to come out of those woods.

8:30 am
Jackson's Corps, Army of Northern Virginia, CSA
Thoroughfare Gap

Jackson stood on the banks of Broad Run, across from Chapman's Mill, watching as the head of Early's column cleared Thoroughfare Gap. The sun rose in a fog so thick he could not make out the men on the other side of his four-abreast column, but it was slowly thinning now, and turning into a gloriously crisp mid-October morning.

"This is something I love about Virginia," Jackson said to himself. My home, he thought. The foothills of the Blue Ridge on a morning like this one. The crisp, cool autumn air, the golden sunlight. I can't see it all, but I know the hills are alive with colors, green and red, yellow and orange. The Almighty blessed us in making this place, truly.

Jackson dutifully turned his mind back to the task at hand. By his accounting, they were three hours behind schedule, and most of his corps remained snaked back around behind the hills. But they were finally here, and he was confident the enemy remained in ignorance of his movements. Greenwich and the enemy right flank were just four miles east of their position.

CHAPTER 2

8:40 am
II Corps, Army of the Potomac, USA
Auburn

Warren lowered his field glasses, looked to Caldwell, and said "Dammit, what took them so long?"

The Confederates were in a line of battle, men marching almost elbow to elbow in two densely packed lines, filtering their way through the low, thinly wooded slopes on the edge of the forest. They stepped out onto the muddy fields, followed by a battery clattering out to the left, its four guns unlimbering alongside them. The butternut mass paused, ordered itself, and went forward.

Warren took a dry swallow. "I'd say they have as least three brigades over there, wouldn't you say?"

Caldwell replied grimly "Yes. There might be another brigade or two back in those woods there. I reckon if there is a whole Confederate division here, they must have at least another brigade tucked away about here in some place or another."

Warren nodded, and then turned to Captain Ricketts, posted nearby with his Pennsylvania battery. "Open the ball, Captain."

Ricketts gave the order, and the Federal cannon boomed out, one gun after another. Each gun crew then set about reloading and firing at will, lobbing shell at the Confederate line roughly 900 yards away.

The butternuts had almost no cover, only a stand of trees about halfway down the field and alongside Cedar Run or the odd depression in the fields, so they had to cross over half a mile's worth of open ground under fire. Exploding shells burst over their heads, raining down jagged iron fragments, or in the muddy ground, sending up plumes of earth. The Rebels left a trail of wounded and dead as they advanced. When the grey line came up to 300 yards, the gunners changed from shell to canister, each shot flinging dozens of inch-wide iron balls into the Rebel ranks, cutting their targets down in swathes.

Warren could see that the Confederates had Caldwell's small division outnumbered by a margin of about three to two. When they got here, he thought, their line would extend from Cedar Run and lap around the hill, beyond Caldwell's line. And then there was that reserve, menacing and unseen.

He yelled to his aide "Send to General Webb. He is to bring his division up to behind the crest of this hill and stand in reserve. He is to exercise every precaution to avoid being observed from the west."

Riding over to Ricketts's and Ames's batteries, Warren issued more orders, telling them to concentrate their fire by the right, putting two-thirds of the artillery down on the danger.

Warren looked on as Caldwell trotted behind his line, and when the Confederates came up to 150 yards, he drew his sword and shouted "Give them the blazes - fire! Fire!" Down the line, regiment after regiment leveled their muskets and fired a crashing, rolling volley. Caldwell shouted encouragement, but what he said was smothered by the din, as his men followed up the volley by firing at will.

The butternut and grey line still came on. Too soon, Warren thought. Caldwell fired too soon. I would have waited until the Rebs were closer. The rifled musket might kill at a quarter mile, but most of the boys couldn't hit anything anywhere near so far as that.

The Confederates marched another few dozen yards, stopped, leveled their muskets, and returned fire. The lines were now partially obscured by the pall of smoke clinging to the foot of the hill, but Warren could see the dozens of men falling out dead or wounded on his side well enough, along with the skulkers instinctively cringing from the danger, backing off up the hill and towards the rear. The latter were mercifully few.

Warren watched the stand-up fight ensue as bullets flew all about him, his staff, the gunners, and the skulkers, over-shot misses from the Johnnies. Neither side was entrenched, but his men had the high ground, and they also had the artillery. This will be bloody for us, he thought, but bloodier for them. He looked to the right of his blue line with relief, for not only had Caldwell pulled it back and refused it to face the threat, but he saw that a green flag stood fluttering there. That was the Irish Brigade, and those stubborn micks weren't going anywhere.

Even so, through the smoky haze Warren could see the Confederates inch closer, especially on the right. He went back to Ricketts.

Warren leaned down over the neck of his horse and yelled over the din "Captain, double shot your rightmost pair of guns and hold them back. When you see those Rebs over on the right get close, getting ready to charge us, fire. Tear them apart. You understand?"

"Yessir!" Ricketts saluted and sprang into action. Warren watched with approval. Ricketts hadn't been to West Point, but he was a fine gunner nonetheless.

The lines continued to blaze away at each other, the Confederates moving step by tentative step closer. The distance between them was down to 50 yards, even closer on the critical right. The loud crash of a pair of guns firing in salvo came down, as Ricketts blasted double canister into the flank of the Confederate assault. Through the smoke, it looked almost as if the entire grey regiment posted there had been swept clean away.

A piercing chorus of shrieks went up, as the Confederates on the right gave a yell and charged forward. Although he had heard it many times before, it still gave Warren a sensation of dread. How the rankers felt about it, he didn't know, but he guessed the Rebel Yell didn't hold much terror for at least some of them, as the Irish screamed in turn and leapt forward to meet them, stopping the Rebel charge almost as soon as it started, clubbing, stabbing, shoving and chasing the butternuts off the slope. The charging Rebels recoiled, almost tumbling back down to the foot of the hill. Caldwell sent down his own local reserve, the Irish quickly withdrew back into line, and together they fired at will, shredding the Rebel flank.

The Rebels were soon in full retreat. More of their artillery had come up, and it now covered the butternuts as they skedaddled back to their starting line.

Warren breathed a sigh of relief. The fight might have lasted only an hour, but it had been a real brawl for all that. He guessed as much as a fifth of Caldwell's men were down. Yet whatever he had suffered, for the Rebs it must have been worse. He hadn't even needed to put Webb in, which meant he still had a fresh division if there was any more trouble. He motioned for the corps chief of staff.

"First, send to General Webb. He is to put his men on the road to Catlett Station as quick as he can. He leads the march. General Hays to follow, and General Caldwell to bring up the rear. Tell Caldwell he has my compliments, but I expect he has less than an hour to gather up his wounded."

11:00 am
Jackson's Corps, Army of Northern Virginia, CSA
Greenwich

Having left Early's Division and the head of his column, Jackson rode into Greenwich, a small crossroads at the Warrenton Turnpike and the namesake for the Greenwich Road. It was a little place, marked only by a church and a few widely spaced farmhouses. He expected to find Colonel Owen and Wickham's Brigade, and he was not disappointed.

"The Yankees left here about three hours ago, sir" reported Owen. "I have sent scouts to the south and west. I told them myself they were to take every care to avoid being seen."

Good, good, Jackson thought.

Owen continued "My scouts say there are no Yankees within a few miles to the south of us, but there is at least a division of them above Milford, on the other side of Broad Run."

"Have your men been as far as Cedar Run yet?" Jackson asked.

"No, sir. But they should either find Yankees or reach thereabouts soon."

Jackson imagined the lay of the land, thinking the left of Ewell's Corps should have passed by way of Auburn, only four miles south, give or take. With no battle noise, that meant there was no sizable Federal presence south of him. Owen's horsemen should find Old Baldy, not blue. Milford and the bridge at Bristoe Station were ahead and only a mile apart. That was where the Federals were crossing Broad Run.

Jackson's eyes lit up brightly. Ahead are rolling hills and woods, he thought. Good cover. We shall deploy here.

"Sandie, draw up written orders to this effect. General Early will come into town, turn south on the Greenwich Road, and deploy to the southeast, two brigades out front, two brigades in reserve, placed so as to put his right flank in contact with Kettle Run. General Johnson will come into town, turn north and deploy to the northeast. Two brigades in front, two in reserve, his left flank on Broad Run. Hill is to come into town and halt until he receives further instructions."

Pendleton watched his chief closely, nodding that he understood.

Jackson went on. "Early will press on until he meets the Orange and Alexandria line. Johnson is to post one brigade to cover Milford, and push on to Bristoe Station."

11:30 am
Lee's Headquarters in the Field, Army of Northern Virginia, CSA
Auburn

Upon arriving in the village of Auburn, Lee found that every building in the modest village had become an improvised hospital, crammed with the moaning and screaming wounded from Wilcox's Division. The acrid hint of gunpowder still hung in the air. Withdrawing to a quieter place near Cedar Run, he sent for General Wilcox himself.

"We moved here as directed," Wilcox began, "to press the Yankees and relieve General Stuart. The head of my column got here a little after 7:30, sir, and found a strong Federal force concentrated. There was at least a division posted on the west slope of that hill, yonder, with plenty of artillery, 18 guns by my count. More Yankees were situated nearby, and these were attacked from the northwest by a force I can only assume was General Stuart's. I ordered the boys to deploy and sent back to General Ewell for confirmation, that I should attack such a superior force in a strong position, sir."

Wilcox was a professional soldier, a West Pointer and Mexican

War veteran, who had written infantry tactics manuals before the war. He looked the part too, what with his barrel chest, burly mustache and neatly combed hair. But today he was a little shaken, and more than a little distraught.

Lee replied softly "Do go on, General."

"Yessir. It was my intention to attack with my whole division once I had it ready, as per orders, even without Ewell's confirmation. I had three brigades in line when word came to go in at once with whatever I had, that I was to force the enemy to stand his ground. Really kicked the hornet's nest with that, sir. We stood in with those Yanks for an hour, but I am sorry to say, I was forced to withdraw. Very sorry."

"How long have those people been gone?"

"The last of them left not more than half an hour ago. They marched on Catlett's."

Lee pondered that. He had a message from Jackson, dated 8:30 from Thoroughfare Gap. The head of Jackson's Corps ought to have reached at least as far Greenwich by now.

Lee asked "Were you able to identify those people?"

Wilcox nodded. "Yes, general. They were the clover leafs, the II Corps. I saw the guidon myself."

Lee checked his watch, sat down at a camp table, and wrote out a message.

Auburn, 11:50 am, 14 October 1864
H'quarters in the Field, ANV

Lt. Gen'l T.J. Jackson,

The Federal II Corps was engaged at Auburn this morning, and retreated towards Catlett's Station at 11 o'clock. Move on Bristoe Station to cut it off. Ewell's Corps will press them from the rear.

R. E. Lee
Gen'l, CSA

Lee dispatched his message by courier. Turning back to Wilcox, he asked "What about your casualties, General?"

"I don't have the exact numbers, but several hundred, at the least. Lane's North Carolina boys, who were on our left and tried to get around the enemy flank, suffered worst of all. Lane guesses a third of his men are down."

Lee nodded. What he had seen with his own eyes told him it had been a bloody repulse. Several hundred men down from just three brigades in only one hour, but the attack had to be made. Ewell had followed his orders, had done the right thing. If part of the Federal army stood here for most of the morning, then that part might have become separated from the rest.

1:15 pm
V Corps, Army of the Potomac, USA
North of Milford

Even while enjoying a little dinner of hardtack, cheese and coffee in a camp chair under the shade of trees, George Sykes sat in an erect, military posture. He thought of himself as regulation as regular army came, fit at 41, and with a beard trimmed to an almost geometrical precision. Yet despite his attention to what he thought of as a stern, professional bearing, he nervously checked his pocket watch for the half-dozenth time in the last half an hour.

Sykes had brought his V Corps to the Broad Run ford at Milford crossroads, on schedule at 11 o'clock, relieving Sedgwick and the VI Corps. Sedgwick marched on with the rest of the army, while he waited here for Warren and the II Corps to come up.

More than two hours now, he thought. Here I am, badly exposed, no word from any damn one about any damn thing, and that puppy Warren is late. What the devil is keeping him?

It wasn't all that surprising, Sykes mused bitterly. Warren had a brigade under him back when he was a division commander in this same corps, and goggle-eyed old George Meade was their corps commander. They had all moved up in the world, but none faster than Warren, who was one of those far too ambitious, far too clever fellows. He had been a good brigade commander and a good engineer, Sykes admitted to himself, but Warren had never handled a division, let alone a corps. Now he was out of his depth, behind schedule, probably muddled up in a jam with his wagons, and it was showing.

A lieutenant galloped across the river and rode up to where Sykes and his staff had set up a temporary headquarters. "General Sykes, may I report, sir?"

Sykes stood up and snapped "Yes, yes, yes. What is it?"

"I've seen a column, infantry and wagons, coming down the Orange and Alexandria. It's II Corps, sir."

At last, Sykes thought. "Very well," he said. Turning to his chief of staff, he continued. "We're relieved. Sound the bugles. We are moving out."

The officer looked back at him, paused, and said cautiously "General, should we not wait until the head of Warren's column reaches Bristoe Station? Or at least send someone over to have a word with those boys? See who they are, what the situation is? Bristoe is only a mile or so from here. The whole thing won't take 20 minutes, sir."

Sykes scowled slightly at the suggestion. "No, no need for that. If we wait for II Corps to arrive here in force, it will stuff up the roads. Warren's boys have arrived, and you have your orders."

The man saluted and went about his business. Within minutes, the camp furniture was being collected up, bugles were sounding, and a band was playing "Old 1812" to start the march.

Only two miles away, Colonel Baxter crossed the wagons under his care over the Kettle Run railroad bridge. The rest of II Corps, delayed by the morning action at Auburn, had been left far behind him.

2:00 pm
Early's Division, Army of Northern Virginia, CSA
Milford

Jubal Early looked through his field glasses, down from his perch on a low, wooded hill. His front line was on the slope beneath him, advancing into empty air. Cracker boxes and other Yankee leavings were scattered all around the railroad embankment before him, but not a single blue belly was in sight.

Early was a wiry, scraggly man in his mid-40s, but it was widely agreed he looked much older. He pulled off his hat, shifted the plug of chewing tobacco in his mouth from one cheek to the other, and rubbed the bald forehead revealed by his thin, receding hair.

He mulled over his situation, of which he knew very little, because that was the way things were in Jackson's command. Old Jack told you what to do, but never why, never a word about what might be transpiring elsewhere, and expected you to do exactly what you were told. Yet Jackson demanded some initiative of his generals as well, and that was the maddening thing, so simply occupying the Orange and Alexandria line and waiting for further orders wasn't an option.

Damn the man, Early thought. Secretive son of a bitch. Most likely we've swung and missed, but damned if I know. If there are any blasted Yankees around, they must be coming up from the southwest, along that railroad.

Early studied the ground, already familiar to him from the Battle of Kettle Run, and liked what he saw. He had helped defend this place as a brigadier under Ewell the year before, and he knew its advantages. Above Kettle Run sat a pair of low hills, perfect for observation and placing artillery. Below the creek was nothing, just low, rolling county, and while the creek itself wasn't much of an obstacle, it had steep, muddy banks for most of its course. Infantry could cross it anywhere, but guns and wagons couldn't cross it at all, so the Yankees needed that railroad bridge.

He made up his mind, ordered his lead brigades to wheel and assume defensive positions on either side of Kettle Run bridge, sent the rest of his men to the rear, and called up his artillery. He had just finished making his dispositions when Jackson rode up, trailing staff officers behind him.

After a moment spent studying the situation for himself, Jackson turned to Early, his eyes shining. "General Early, you are to advance your division towards Cattlet's Station." Jabbing with his one hand for emphasis, he continued "There is at least one enemy corps there. Move forward and attack any Federals you find."

Early shifted in his saddle, shifting the tobacco plug in his mouth at the same time. "Sir, if I may, I have good ground here. If the Yankees attack me in this place, they ain't getting by. But if I move out and fight them in the open, I got just one division against a whole Yankee corps!"

No, no, Jackson thought. It won't do. If they aren't attacked, the enemy might move away unhindered to the east, and there would be only about a mile and a half between Johnson's line, facing north, and Early's line facing south. The enemy must be fixed, and his men needed more room.

"I have already ordered Hill's Division to move down on your right," Jackson snapped. "You have your orders, general."

"Yessir," Early replied. He was about to spit some tobacco juice, but glanced at Jackson, who bristled at him with disapproval. Early swallowed the juice instead, suppressing a grimace.

Turning to an aide, he said "Tell Hoke to get his North Carolina pig fu..." then stopped himself in mid-curse. Early had gotten out of the habit of minding his tongue during Jackson's convalescence. "Tell General Hoke to cross Kettle Run on the bridge and advance. General Gordon to follow, resuming his place on Hoke's left. The rest of the division will follow behind them."

The aide was about to gallop off when a light crackle of musketry was heard from the southwest, down the railroad line.

Early called out "Lieutenant, never you mind. That'd be our pickets. The bluebellies are here."

3:15 pm
II Corps, Army of the Potomac, USA
Kettle Run

Warren galloped to the head of his column in search of Alexander Webb and the source of the firing. Behind the corps, Gregg's cavalry was dogged by Reb cavalry, and Ewell's Corps was surely behind that. He had just arrived when the boom of artillery joined the crackling of musketry. Finding Webb, Warren demanded a report.

"We just drove in a Johnny picket line, sir. More of them are across the creek, where they have started to dig in, and are supported by at least two batteries of artillery on those hills behind it," Webb told him, pointing forward. "They have more artillery coming up. I'm deploying both of my brigades forward, one on each side of the railroad."

Warren nodded. While the railroad's solid embankment was a ready-made breastwork, it was worse than useless in their present circumstances. If they put men behind it, their flank and rear would be exposed to enfilade fire from across Kettle Run. But if the Rebels put men atop that embankment, they would rake Webb's left from a stoutly protected position. The only choice was to extend the line, along the creek and beyond the railroad, even if that railroad divided them.

The two generals looked at each other for a moment. Webb was a promising West Pointer and from a prominent New York family, much like Warren himself, but even younger at 28. He too was in an acting command, serving in place of another man wounded at Gettysburg, the steely John Gibbon. Outwardly, they both appeared calm, in control. Yet they both knew they were in a bad spot. They nodded at each other and went about their business.

Warren withdrew his field glasses from their box and studied the terrain, especially to the east. If there was a way out of here, it was that way. Buford's cavalry was over there somewhere, and that was something. The problem was getting there. Ewell was behind him, and Warren was now certain Jackson was gathering across his front. He was cut off. To march away to the east, he knew he would have to deploy "rear guards" north and south, because to do otherwise would invite a Rebel advance. They would catch him on the march and slaughter him.

Warren decided his only way out was to attack, knock the Rebs back, stun them and gain some breathing space, then retreat to the east as night approached. Attacking Ewell was no good, since it took him further away from Meade and support. That left Jackson.

Warren made his plan and issued his orders. Webb would hold his ground. Hays was next in the column, and go onto Webb's right, extending his line to the east. Caldwell would send one brigade to stiffen Gregg's horsemen and hold off Ewell for a while, and the rest of his division would support the attack. They'd unlimber the guns, suppress those Rebel batteries, and attack in force.

3:15 pm
V Corps, Army of the Potomac, USA
Bull Run

"What in the blue blazes?" George Sykes was observing his column cross Bull Run when he heard the dull booming of cannon coming from the south. At that moment, a courier rode up and handed him a message from General Meade.

Noon, 14 October 1864
Headquarters in the Field, Army of the Potomac

To Major General George Sykes, V Corps

II Corps was attacked at Auburn in divisional strength at 9 this morning. Expect the arrival of General Warren and his corps to be delayed. Continue to hold your position at Broad Run in support of II Corps, as per previous orders, until they arrive.

George G. Meade
Major General, USA

Sykes felt the bottom fall out of his stomach, and screamed at the courier "This message is three hours old! Where in damnation have you been?!"

He wanted to smack the man. Instead, he yelled "Colonel! Colonel! Reverse this column. Counter march to Broad Run! At once, do you hear me! At once!"

4:00 pm
Early's Division, Army of Northern Virginia, CSA
Kettle Run

The artillery roared louder as the Federals tried to silence the Confederate guns overlooking Kettle Run. Early wasn't concerned. While he counted two dozen Yankee guns in position, he had 16 cannon posted on better ground. What was more, his boys had used the last hour to pile rocks and shovel earth as best they could, establishing a low breastwork about 20 yards back from the creek. It wasn't much, but it was better than nothing.

Thing was the damn Yankees were extending beyond his left. Early sent to Jackson for reinforcements, only to have that request flatly rejected. Determined to hang on to one full brigade as a reserve, Early had been forced to sidle out to the east, spreading his men thinner than he would have liked.

Jackson returned, and studied the Federal line while telling Early "All's quiet on Johnson's front, General Early, but it won't stay that way. He will likely have half the Army of the Potomac on him before nightfall, and needs every man. Hill will come up on your right before long."

Early spat tobacco juice, not caring what Old Jack though about it anymore. "Yessir."

Jackson ignored Early's discontent, and continued to peer through his binoculars, saying "You will hold, General Early. I know you will hold."

The enemy had lined up about 200 yards beyond the creek, five brigades strong. They began their attack by shouting in unison "Our clubs are trumps! Our clubs are trumps!" referring to their corps emblem, the clover leaf-shaped playing card symbol. Then the men of the II Corps cried "Huzzah! Huzzah!" and stepped forward.

The skirmishers rejoined the ranks as the advance came on, each man finding his place in the line. The westernmost brigade, beyond the railroad, held its ground, anchoring the Federals' open left flank. Jackson and Early both watched as a sixth blue brigade moved up behind the advancing line, swinging out beyond their own left.

Early growled at an aide "See those bastards back there on the left? Go tell Nelson I want fire placed on those God damned syphilitic whoresons. Chop them down."

Jackson snapped "General Early, I have little tolerance for profanity, and none whatsoever for blasphemy!"

Early mumbled "Yessir."

Jackson let it pass at that. Old Jube always forgot himself in battle. He was a bad egg, and Jackson was certain a suitable place in Hell waited for Early. But he was a good fighter, a cruel killer, and he obeyed orders. That was that. Providence worked in mysterious ways, and who was Jackson to quibble if He decided to use sinners so.

Watching the Yankee attack unfold, Early stood up in his stirrups and declared "General Jackson, the Yankees are going to turn my line if I don't put my reserve in, and all I've got is Pegram's Brigade. I need reinforcements."

Jackson didn't reply, merely shook his head in refusal. Early sent orders for Pegram to take half his Virginians to the support of the Confederate left, thereby leaving just two regiments in reserve.

The Johnnie line opened up when the Federals came up to 70 yards, firing a hard, almost simultaneous volley down the ranks. The blue line went on unfazed by the men who tumbled out of its ranks, advancing a few dozen more yards as each Confederate reloaded and fired at will, coming up very close to Kettle Run. The Billies halted, leveled their own muskets and returned a tight, disciplined volley.

The two lines took to firing away at each other from across the creek at a distance of only 50 yards, the grey moderately better protected than the blue. Then the last Federal brigade fell into place at the end of the line, opposite the Confederate left flank. It gave a loud, deep-throated roar, and shot forward at a run.

Early had sent forward his reserve too late. The last brigade in the Federal line, the hard fighting Irish Brigade from Caldwell's Division, surged across Kettle Run, scrambled up its muddy banks, and rose on the other side almost unopposed.

Once across, the Irish wheeled to face the Louisiana Tigers on the Confederate left, as well as the three Virginia regiments then being led up by Pegram. The Irish ignored the shot and shell falling on them as they dressed their ranks, and then fired a massed volley into the approaching Virginians. Many of the Irish carried old percussion smoothbores, and their buck and ball wreaked havoc at that murderously close range. The Rebels staggered in shock, and General Pegram fell from his horse, his guts perforated with buckshot.

Warren watched with satisfaction as the next brigade in line charged forward, leaping down and over the creek, and scrambling up the other side. This time, however, the men who climbed out of the creek bed were met with a steady rain of musket balls from the Louisianans, and were soon forced back down and behind the cover of the creek bank. Each brigade in turn surged forward, but each got only so far before taking cover in the creek bed. By the time the rolling, en echelon charge had reached the last brigade by Kettle Run bridge, those men didn't even try to push past the creek, and instead immediately took up positions to return fire from behind its banks.

Warren cursed and swore as his attack ground to a halt before the makeshift Confederate earthworks, but Webb reached out and grabbed his arm.

"Wait, sir, look," Webb pointed to his men, who were lying and kneeling in the creek, and firing back at the Rebels. "The Johnnies can't fire down into the creek from where they are. They're too far back. Our men now have the better cover!"

Warren could see Webb was right. Except for the odd Rebel shell that hit the creek bed, sending up a geyser of water and silt, his men looked well-protected, the Rebs more exposed. They could stay in that creek and fire away all afternoon if need be. He turned his horse and rode back to where his reserve, his very last uncommitted brigade, was posted, just outside of Rebel artillery range.

"General Caldwell," Warren shouted. "I want you to bring take your last brigade forward to support the Irish Brigade. When you are in position, signal back to me and I'll send the entire line forward. Once they are committed, strike from the right, and roll that line up. You lead the attack in person, General."

Caldwell saluted, drew his sword, and called on his men to follow him. Warren then rode forward to find General Hays, who was supervising the center, and give him his new instructions.

4:30 pm
A.P. Hill's Division, Army of Northern Virginia, CSA
The Greenwich Road

A.P. Hill stood alongside the Greenwich Road, watching the progress of his column as it continued off the road and on its overland advance to what was supposed to be the Federal left flank. Short-but-leonine, he always cut quite an appearance dressed up for battle in his bright red shirt, and his men cheered as they turned off the road, passed him and marched on.

Hill was in high spirits. He was in touch with Old Baldy now, and away from the overbearing Jackson on the sort of independent mission he craved. Artillery was audible in the distance, battle had been joined, and soon he and his men would pitch in.

An aide from his lead brigade galloped up and gave him a verbal message: the advance guards beyond the head of the column had seen Yankees, lots of them.

Hill sent him back with a simple order: "Attack at once."

5:00 pm
Kettle Run

It was now or never, Warren thought. A message from Gregg arrived just five minutes before, reporting infantry on his front. More Rebels were emerging from the woods on his left. Webb went over and helped see them off in person, but they would be back, and in greater numbers. Warren reckoned if he didn't break loose soon, he would be surrounded before nightfall.

On the other side of the lines, Early sat grimly, bracing himself for the renewed Yankee onslaught. Behind him, Allegheny Johnson was now under attack too, and Jackson had gone to look into the situation on that front. Early grumbled under his breath that he still hadn't been reinforced, although it looked like some of Hill's Division had at last begun to arrive

The line has taken a beating these last two hours, Early thought. Fucking yeller bastards carrying the wounded to the rear, never coming back up to the firing line only makes it worse. But the damn Yanks must be tiring too. I just need to hang on a little longer. Hang on until nightfall or when Hill gets here in force, whichever comes first.

A courier arrived with a short, scribbled message from Jackson:

I expect you to hold.

T.J. Jackson

Early crumpled up the note, threw it away with malice, and

muttered "Shee-it."

On the opposite side of the field and peering through his glasses, Warren saw the signal. He sent word to Hays, and within minutes the deep-throated shouting of several thousand men drowned out all the other noise on the battlefield. The bulk of II Corps rose from the creek bed, ripped off a thunderous volley, and charged forward.

Early's men tore hard at the attackers, gunning them down and sending parts of the blue line reeling backwards into the creek. Other Billies charged home, and sent the butternuts flying from their breastworks. On the end of the line, Caldwell brought three Union brigades, Irish immigrants, New Yorkers, Pennsylvanians and Delaware men, smashing into the Louisiana Tigers and dead Pegram's Virginians. Early watched as Pegram's leaderless boys streamed to the rear, but most of the Louisianans held, and resisted stubbornly.

Early ordered the last of his reserves, that slender pair of Pegram's remaining regiments, out to plug the Yankee penetrations in his center, and then galloped away to shore up his left. He rode among the broken Virginia throng, once his own brigade, waving his sword and even striking some with the flat of his blade, calling out "Cowards! Bastards! You shame Virginie! Get your yellow asses back in there and kill them fucking blue bellies!"

Most stopped and turned around, shamefaced and angry. Early didn't bother with putting them back into order, but instead led them at a dead run as a mob, back into the fray. Caldwell's attack was swept back into the shelter of the creek.

On the western side of the battlefield, Hill was feeding his men into the attack piecemeal, committing each individual regiment into the fight as it arrived. Leading the Federal left, Webb had steadily adjusted to the growing pressure, but now he had two full brigades facing his firing line.

Early's westernmost brigade, posted on the other side of the railroad embankment and all but forgotten by him, was heretofore engaged only slightly. It came forward on its own initiative, and joined in the assault on Webb. Vastly outnumbered and attacked on three sides, the Federal left caved in, sending men fleeing over the railroad embankment, who then turned and ran headlong for the rear.

Hill's soldiers advanced in the wake of the fleeing Billies to the top of the railroad embankment. Once there, they halted and poured fire down into the Union troops sheltering behind the banks of Kettle Run, causing great slaughter. Blue-coated troops instinctively began to move around, looking for protection from the crossfire, and finding none. Hays desperately tried to refuse his line and shield his left, but was shot down amid the fusillade, and his effort came to naught. Men abandoned the creek bed, first singly or in pairs, then in larger groups, and ran away from the carnage. The II Corps line visibly teetered on the brink of a collapse.

Early rode up behind his line, shouting "Forward! All regiments forward! Charge!" His soldiers gave a piercing yell, jumped over their pile of rocks, fence rails and dirt, and charged forward. Men in blue were shot, stabbed and clubbed down, and standards seized. In a matter of minutes, the center of the II Corps dissolved into a rout. The exultant men of Hill's and Early's Divisions chased, killed and captured in the light of the setting sun.

Jackson returned to the scene. Finding Early, he declared "You see, general. I told you. I knew you would hold."

CHAPTER 3

Confederate newspapers were not quite accurate in crowing that the Yankee II Corps had been "annihilated" at the Second Battle of Kettle Run. Caldwell had led away the three brigades on the corps' right wing in good order, escaping after nightfall. Baxter's Brigade was off guarding the wagon train and was never even engaged, and while Gregg's Division of cavalry had been mauled, it had escaped destruction.

Yet the claim had enough truth to it to raise depressed spirits throughout the South. Second Kettle Run cost the Army of the Potomac roughly 7,000 dead, captured or missing. Warren was captured, Webb wounded and captured, and Hays killed. The losses in Lee's army amounted to one-third that figure, and many of these were wounded who would eventually return to duty.

Whereas the summer of 1863 brought the South defeats at Vicksburg, Gettysburg and Middle Tennessee, the autumn saw the Yankees under siege at Chattanooga and whipped in Virginia. Stonewall Jackson had returned, and perhaps the war was not lost after all.

In the North, the witch hunt began from the day after the battle. Republican radicals in the Congress howled for the scalp of General Meade, but the facts of the case swiftly shifted attention to General Sykes. The V Corps commander was charged with disobedience and dereliction of duty, court martialed, and dismissed from the service in such quick succession that the entire business was over before Christmas. Disgraced, Sykes committed suicide in February.

Following the battle, Meade's army entrenched and remained in Centerville, its morale at low ebb. Lee retired back to his starting point on the Rapidan unmolested, destroying the Orange and

Alexandria as he went. Prodded by the War Department, Meade eventually followed, slowly and laboriously, rebuilding the railroad as he went.

Yet the tide of the war turned again, and it became the turn of newspapers in the North to trumpet victory, and those of the South to offer thin explanations and bitter recrimination. Less than two months after Second Kettle Run, the siege of Chattanooga was lifted, and the Confederate Army of Tennessee sent packing. It was the war's now three year old formula: while the Confederacy won victories and held the Union at bay in the East, it steadily lost the war in the West.

General Braxton Bragg, with his spirit broken by defeat and poor health, and long harried by his own senior officers, resigned command of the Army of Tennessee on November 29.

December 2, 1864
Evening
Richmond, Virginia

Jefferson Davis rode home, stiffly erect in the saddle. He always preferred a formal, military posture, as it suited both his character and his painfully severe features. Yet in trying times, he retreated even further into such poses, taking his natural bearing to extremes, and so he rode home looking very much like a bronze equestrian statue.

His private meeting with James Seddon, his Secretary of War, had not gone well. Seddon had not attended the Cabinet meeting held earlier that day to discuss a replacement for Braxton Bragg, the ex-commander of the country's second major field army, choosing instead to remain at home and tend to his ailing children.

That discussion had focused mostly on the Confederacy's two available full generals: Joseph E. Johnston and P.G.T. Beauregard. Davis was disgusted with both choices, and his Cabinet indecisive about picking one or the other of them. Worse, the Secretary of State, Judah P. Benjamin, refused to offer any opinion at all. Davis had gone to consult with Seddon, who had nothing to offer beyond the unpalatable pair of Johnston and Beauregard. It wouldn't do.

Davis was bound and determined that Beauregard would never again hold an important command. The frenchified peacock had thrown away the victory Davis's dearest and most admired friend, Albert Sidney Johnston, had died earning at Shiloh, and then had to gall to reward himself afterward with sick leave at a spa. The Louisianan was arrogant, vain, always proposing ludicrous schemes, and then sitting back smugly and criticizing what others did when his flights of fantasy were not adopted. He was utterly unfit for the western command, so Davis was content to let him stay in the Carolinas and rot.

The alternative, Joe Johnston, was secretive, quarrelsome, obstinate, and just as vain as the frenchified peacock. Instead of proposing outlandish schemes, the Virginian was fond of either doing nothing or retreating, and then blaming the disasters that resulted on the failure of Davis and the War Department to supply him with reinforcements that simply didn't exist. He was at least as overrated as Beauregard, and just as unsuited for command of the country's second largest army.

Of the Confederacy's other generals of suitable rank, Samuel Cooper was too old and infirm, and Robert E. Lee was not interested in a transfer to Georgia. Even if he had been, sending Lee west would only shift the problem of finding a new commander from the Army of Tennessee to the Army of Northern Virginia.

If only Hardee had accepted the job, Davis thought, things would be greatly simplified. William J. Hardee was a respected professional and the senior corps commander within that army, so in lieu of sending a more senior general, promoting Hardee was the most logical course. Yet Hardee had begged out of commanding the Army of Tennessee.

Davis's thoughts were interrupted by his arrival at the Executive Mansion, a white, stuccoed building in the neoclassical style. He handed his horse over to the groom, and was met at the door by his private secretary, Burton Harrison.

"Mr. President, Secretary Benjamin is here to see you. He has been waiting more than half an hour. I know he doesn't have an appointment, but he said it was urgent and that he would wait for your return."

Davis nodded. "I'll see him in my office. Wait 10 minutes and then bring him up." Even though he longed to see Varina and the children after such a long, tiresome day, Davis went straight to his office, where a plush chair for Benjamin was already set up before his desk. He inspected and straightened his clothes, sat down behind his desk, assumed a severe pose, and waited for his Secretary of State.

Benjamin, a plump, round-faced man with the happy, ruddy features common to men of that build, was shown in. He was the most loyal member of Davis's government, which was part of why Benjamin had survived so many tribulations as Attorney General, Secretary of War and now Secretary of State. The other part was his imperturbability and thick, leathery skin, two virtues essential to the fortunes of anyone born as a Jew in the British Caribbean and making his way in the politics of the South.

Davis greeted him by leaping from behind his desk to shake his hand, but still addressed him as "Secretary Benjamin" before inviting him to sit down.

Benjamin sat, laying his slender, gold-handled cane across his lap. He was accustomed to Davis's peculiar mixture of the generous and amiable on the one hand, and the stiffly formal on the other.

Davis started. "I had assumed I would be seeing you, Mr. Secretary, although perhaps not so soon. It is most unusual for you to remain so silent in Cabinet."

Judah smiled. "Mr. President, I wanted to consider this business more carefully before I offered my opinion to you. Also, I believe what I am about to propose might strike some as a sensational, perhaps even controversial act, and wished to take precautions and ensure it did not appear prematurely in the papers."

"I take it you have a proposal to make for replacing General Bragg, then?"

"Yes, and I think it is the only option, both viable and palatable to us: Thomas J. Jackson."

Davis remained composed and reticent, although he was surprised to hear this coming from Benjamin. "I had considered Jackson already, and discounted him for two reasons. First, he is clearly ranked by both Generals Longstreet and Kirby Smith, and some others probably think they outrank him, including some very senior men out West. Vaulting Jackson over all those heads will surely cause some resentment and dissension, and I think we have already had enough of that in the West. Furthermore, Jackson has the reputation for being at least as secretive as Johnston, and at least as difficult to work with as Bragg. You remember Romney, do you not?"

How could I forget? Benjamin thought. Jackson planned and led a minor-but-successful expedition into the mountains of western Virginia in November 1861. Afterward, he left his senior subordinate, one W. W. Loring, to garrison the town of Romney in winter quarters. Loring didn't care for being left in Romney or for serving under Jackson, and promptly circumvented Jackson by writing to Benjamin, complaining that his men were suffering badly in the icy weather and should be withdrawn.

Benjamin brought the matter to Davis, who agreed, and Benjamin ordered Jackson to withdraw Loring, a stupid blunder as Benjamin now freely admitted. That was because while Stonewall obeyed, he also tendered his resignation, sparking a major political flap.

"I remember it all too well, Mr. President, because I stumbled quite badly and brought on the whole thing." Of course, he had done no such thing. Davis had made that decision, just as he made so many of even the most picayune decisions of the War Department, but Benjamin had fallen on his sword in that instance, and was not about to pull himself back off that sword now. "In retrospect, I think that if proper channels had been strictly followed, that unpleasant incident would never have happened."

He suspected Davis gave the order because the President knew Loring better than he did Jackson, having made Loring a colonel in the old United States Army during his tenure as the U.S. Secretary of War. Davis often made such decisions on the basis of personal relationships, which explained why an incompetent schemer like Leonidas Polk was in command of Mississippi and Alabama, among others.

All of this was before the spring of 1862 and Jackson's prodigious feats in the Shenandoah Valley. They had no idea Jackson would prove a genius and become a national hero, while Loring would turn out to be a very ordinary division commander.

Benjamin continued "I can hardly blame a man for standing on principle. Can you, Mr. President?"

Davis said unthinkingly "Of course not," conveniently ignoring that he routinely questioned the motives of everyone and anyone who disagreed with his own principles.

"As for the personal frictions besetting our western army, perhaps the best way to rise above them is to appoint an outside man, a man with a clean slate. Even were that not the case, Mr. President, it is my firm and considered opinion that Thomas Jackson is, after Robert E. Lee, our best general. That is the only consideration that matters. Do you doubt that Jackson will give us victories where Johnston or Beauregard would not?"

"No, I do not doubt it," Davis admitted.

"Then he should be given the job. With the support of this government and the Southern people, Jackson will give us our best chance for sustaining the independence that is ours by right." Judah paused, and then added "And he cannot help but enjoy the support of our people, Mr. President. Is he not the most venerated officer in the army, the equal of General Lee in the popular imagination? You remember how the entire nation held its breath after his wounding?"

Davis replied "Yes, of course I do." Benjamin had a point, there was no denying it. Jackson was, after Lee, the only other proven field commander the country had. Yet promoting him meant setting aside all notions of seniority, and officers in general were very touchy about matters of rank and seniority. But it wasn't as if promotion on the basis of merit was illegal, unprecedented or unwarranted.

Davis turned his chair away from Benjamin, clasped his hands under his chin, and thought it over. His enemies in the Congress would begin agitating for the appointment of either Johnston or Beauregard as soon as Congress reconvened on Monday, December 7. Newspapers critical of his government were already printing such tripe, seasoned richly with invective directed against him personally. The promotion and appointment of Jackson was sure to be so popular with the people, no one in the Congress would dare to oppose it. Especially if he submitted Jackson's name on Monday, by surprise, before his chorus of critics could choreograph their carping.

In fact, he reasoned, there might be an opportunity to accomplish something more here. "What if I go beyond merely making Jackson head of the Army of Tennessee? What if I reorganize Tennessee, Mississippi, Alabama and the bulk of Georgia into a 'Department of the Center,' so to speak, and name Jackson to its head? Something like what Washington did for their General Grant, putting all the middle of the country under one man?"

Benjamin saw at once what Davis meant. "You intend to reorganize General Johnston out of his job?"

Davis smiled. A twinkle appeared in Davis's eyes, even the blind, filmy one. The malice of it almost made Benjamin shift in his chair, despite himself. "I have no intention of removing General Johnston, but he has often complained that his command in the West is impractical for one man. In my opinion, his poor performance vindicates that view, and I therefore propose, Secretary Benjamin, to lighten his burdens."

"And what if Congress balks at leaving Johnston shorn so?" Benjamin chuckled. "He has many supporters."

Indeed he does, Davis thought. My critics and Johnston's supporters seemed to always be the same people. "I'll make this a question of standing either for or against Jackson. Can you imagine anyone in the Congress daring to vote against the elevation of Stonewall Jackson? And I won't give them the time to introduce an alternative bill. This is war, and the Army of the Tennessee needs a permanent commander as soon as possible. I'll horsewhip any opposition with the urgency of the matter."

Benjamin nodded. He had suspected that Davis had already considered Jackson, but needed a little persuading to work his way through the bureaucratic legalisms the President so often entangled himself in. He had not, however, thought about using Jackson to settle scores with the administration's enemies, but that worked just as well. Johnston would give up the whole country in retreat were he given a free hand to do so. The sooner he was shelved, the better.

"Then, Mr. President, I suggest we dispatch a confidential messenger to the Army of Northern Virginia at once."

Davis replied "Yes. Assuming he accepts the promotion, I will reconvene the Cabinet on Sunday, put the matter to them as a formality, and submit Jackson's name to the Congress on Monday morning."

December 3
Evening
Lee's Headquarters, Army of Northern Virginia, CSA
Winter Quarters, Orange County Virginia

Jackson ducked under the tent flap and entered Lee's headquarters. He was surprised to find there not only Lee, but also Lee's eldest son, George Washington Custis Lee. A brigadier general at 31, George Lee served as a top military aide to President Davis. So, whatever this was about, Jackson knew it came from Richmond, not army headquarters.

Jackson snapped a salute. "Reporting as ordered, sir."

"At ease. Thank you for coming, General," Lee replied. "General Lee has something to tell you. From the President."

A stickler for discipline and protocol though he was, Jackson wondered if he could ever be as formal, pleasant but formal nonetheless, with his own offspring as Lee was.

George Lee showed he had not fallen far from the tree, by saying "Thank you, sir."

Turning to Jackson, he said "General Thomas J. Jackson, I have the honor of informing you that our President, Jefferson Davis, wishes you to accept promotion to the rank of full general, and assignment as the commander of the Army of Tennessee, now positioned in Dalton, Georgia."

Jackson blinked. He slowly extended his right hand to accept the letter proffered by George Lee. After an awkward pause, Jackson said "What of General Johnston? General Beauregard? Surely they…"

George Lee answered "The President feels that you are best qualified to take this command, General Jackson."

Jackson was numb. It was no secret the President's relations with Beauregard and Johnston were poisoned. Even so, Jackson had thought the command would naturally go to one of them. The possibility of it being offered to him had never occurred to him.

Jackson said quietly "I… I accept."

Lee, still seated behind his camp table, looked down. He knew Jackson as endowed with a modest, dutiful nature, but also with industrious ambition. There had never been any doubt in his mind that the offer would take Jackson by surprise, just as he himself was unsurprised by Jackson's acceptance.

Still, Lee felt slightly displeased, although he did not show it. Half-expect Jackson's promotion though he did, Lee had not wanted to hear of it. It meant the loss of one of his best lieutenants.

George Lee, on the other hand, smiled brightly with an assignment successfully completed. "Very good, General Jackson. I am to instruct you, on behalf of the President, that nothing is to be said of this matter by either yourself or General Lee until the promotion and appointment become official. The bill will be placed before Congress on Monday morning."

Lee stood up. "Now, General Lee, I have business to discuss with General Jackson. But if you would be so kind as to wait, and return when we are finished? Perhaps we could have supper together?"

"Of course, sir." George Lee saluted and left.

Lee said quietly "Please, sit down." After a pause, he added "May I call you Thomas?"

This was another surprise, although not as shocking as the offer of promotion and command. Lee rarely referred to anyone in the army by their Christian name, even in private. Even Jackson referred to his subordinates in given, informal terms more often than Lee did.

After Jackson assented, Lee said "Well then, Thomas, may I offer you my warmest and most sincere congratulations on this happy occasion? You have achieved a signal accomplishment in your career, and I can think of no officer in Confederate service who deserves it more."

Jackson blushed and stammered "Thank you, sir." After a pause, he continued "It has always been my pleasure to serve."

Lee nodded, and asked softly "When you were wounded at Chancellorsville, do you recall the message I sent? That while you had lost your left arm, I had lost my right?"

Jackson reddened. "Sir, I believe we have won victories through the grace of divine Providence. It was Providence that saw fit to give us you as our leader in our time of need. What part I have played in that has merely been as a lesser instrument."

"God favors our cause and graces us with victories, yes," Lee agreed, "but your role has not been so small as that. The good Lord blesses us each with our own talents, and yours have always been especially well-suited to command. May I give you some advice?"

Jackson replied earnestly, "I am honored, sir."

Lee spoke slowly. "The President has sometimes suggested to me that I assume command of our western army. I have always refused, for a variety of reasons. One is I believe I would not receive the cooperation of the officers there. We have always been a proud, spirited people, Thomas, but that is at least as much a burden as it is to our benefit. As many of our people are cursed with hot tempers and an empty, prideful stubbornness as are blessed with courage, dignity and those other virtues belonging to a true gentleman. And greed is far from being solely a sin of the Northern man."

Jackson nodded, aware of the bitter feuding between the western army's former commander, Braxton Bragg, and his generals. Both as a former teacher and as an officer, Jackson was quite familiar with the sinful character flaws of which Lee spoke, and he agreed completely. He also thought of these failings as part of the reason the war had dragged on at such dear cost.

While Jackson was absolutely certain in his conviction that God recognized the Confederacy, with all its flaws, as the true heirs of the Revolution and of His blessings of liberty, and wanted it to prevail, he was equally certain the nation was atoning for each and every one of its sins along the way. God wanted them to suffer, wanted them penitent, so they would emerge from the war a better, purer country.

Lee paused again, and silently decided that he would not point out that Jackson was one of those hot tempered, too stubborn men as well, as he had considered doing. It was not his place to chide Jackson so. Instead he chose to limit himself to one word of advice, something less personal.

Lee said "I have had to deal with many such people in this army, as have you. Some of our officers have talents of such promise that I overlook their personal shortcomings. I know you understand."

"Yes, yes" Jackson said. He thought of A.P. Hill's disobedient, impatient temper, or Ewell's former and Early's current profanity and blasphemy.

Lee went on. "There are other officers, however, who sadly have enjoyed no such redeeming traits. Men who were either not suited to their duties, or else were so ill-tempered that they caused us more problems than their merits could ever outweigh. Daniel Hill, for example."

Jackson nodded in agreement, but shifted uncomfortably. Daniel Harvey Hill had been an outstanding fighter and division commander in Lee's army, but the man was short-tempered, easily irritated and fond of finding fault with just about everyone, including his superiors. Consciously or not, D.H. Hill had been a font of contention and disunity.

He was also Jackson's brother-in-law. Lee had consulted Jackson about Hill's reassignment to North Carolina, and while Jackson had not liked it, he had concurred. Hill had made his own bed. If Jackson had been in Lee's place, he might have preferred charges over a polite transfer.

Lee's tone shifted, rising and stiffening from pleasant conversation into kindly lecture. "One of the strengths of this army has been the many excellent officers with which it has been blessed. Yet I did not begin with an army led by so many worthy men. I had to send away many, many unsatisfactory officers. You know this, but what you might not be aware of is I never could have done this, nor been allowed to follow my own plans as I have done, if I did not enjoy the confidence of the President."

"There have been past misunderstandings between yourself and President Davis," Lee continued. "In this army's operations, you have always been reclusive, secretive about your plans, with your subordinates and sometimes with good reason, but never with me. Now you must be as open with President Davis as you have ever been with me. You must confide in him, let no past grievances come between you. If I enjoy my own discretion in my commanders and my plans, it is because Davis trusts me. As do our people. You already have the one, Thomas. Part of your duty as an army commander is to cultivate the other."

If any other man had said this to Jackson, he would have ignored him or rebuked him for his presumption. But not Lee. Jackson had never modeled himself on Lee, for he recognized and accepted they were men of two very different temperaments, yet he still admired him as no other living soul.

Jackson sat silently, registering no emotion, but Lee could see he had absorbed his advice, and said "Now, I do not need to tell you that your company will be dearly missed here. I am not sure what fare can be found on such short notice, but I would be delighted if you and General Stuart would join me for supper. On some night in the next few days."

Jackson smiled. Despite their many differences, the flamboyant Stuart was his best friend in the Army of Northern Virginia. "Sir, I would be pleased and honored to join you and General Stuart. Send word of when, and I shall be there."

The conversation continued for some time after that. Jackson asked how much of his military family, the staff who had served him since the Valley, he would be allowed to take to Georgia. Lee insisted on retaining the services of Jed Hotchkiss, stating that the mapmaker's mastery of the Virginia landscape was crucial to the coming year. Jackson argued for a time, but ultimately conceded. Lee then thanked him, congratulated him again, shook his hand, and sent him on his way.

Upon returning to his tent, Jackson sat down and thought about what to do next. There would be the transition, both he and his people would need to hand over the corps to his successor, probably A.P. Hill. He would almost certainly be called to Richmond, to confer with the War Department and President Davis.

The thought gave him a warm sense of anticipation. All this made Christmas in Richmond a very real possibility, and that would make his wife Anna very happy, especially as soon afterward he would be posted farther away than ever. The only redeeming feature of his summer-long recuperation in Lexington, Virginia was that he spent it in his own home, with his own family. He knew very well that this would be his last chance to spend time with his wife and daughter for at least a year.

Jackson turned his thoughts to his military family. Those people who were coming with him would all receive leave before taking up duties in Georgia, of course. Jackson sadly realized he would likely have to part with Jim Lewis, his servant and cook, and long since a dear friend and companion. He was a hired slave, and Lewis's elderly master would likely not let him go to Georgia.

I will not buy him, Jackson thought, not even to keep him with me. I have no desire to acquire any more slaves, not under any circumstances. I should send him to home to Lexington, to help Anna care for little Julia. Yes, that will do.

Jackson sent for Sandie Pendleton. The boyish chief of staff had been requesting leave to marry his sweetheart, Kate Corbin, since summer. Sandie entered Jackson's tent moments later, for he was never very far from corps headquarters if he could help it.

"Sandie," Jackson said, "You had best write to Ms. Corbin and her family, and make your wedding plans. I'll grant your leave shortly. I doubt you will have another before the end of the war."

December 9
Late afternoon
The Executive Mansion
Richmond

Davis waited in his office for the arrival of Thomas J. Jackson, newly minted as the Confederate States Army's seventh full general, feeling completely satisfied with the way things had turned out. He had gotten his way, and his enemies in the Congress were utterly routed.

The most effective of those enemies had been Senator Wigfall, the blowhard from Texas, the *antebellum* friend who had betrayed him in the name of petty politics. Predictably, Wigfall praised Jackson, while condemning Davis for "vindictively humiliating that great soldier, Joseph E. Johnston, leaving him with an empty title and no role in the war proper to his dignity and commensurate to his prowess."

Wigfall had always had a talent for fiery oratory, Davis had to give him that. Yet Davis's political enemies, Wigfall included, always suffered from one key weakness: they were no organized party as such, united only by their opposition to Davis and his policies. They quarreled with each other as much as they quarreled with him.

Davis's own partisans in the Congress spoke out on the need to not shackle a man of Jackson's demonstrated ability, to give him the proper scope to win victories, and of the need to act quickly. With the thinly veiled threat to veto any bill that was not Davis's own lurking in the background, no alternative bill was presented, and Jackson's appointment passed unanimously, with his promotion dated to October 14, the date of Second Kettle Run. Even the President's bitterest opponents did not dare vote openly against the Confederacy's foremost hero, choosing instead to skulk away in abstention.

And so the War Department summoned Jackson to Richmond, where knew he had reported first to Mechanics' Hall, the seat of the War Department, to receive orders and to meet with Secretary Seddon and Adjutant General Samuel Cooper. Those were mere formalities, however. As Davis well knew, it was the first meeting between himself and his newest commander that mattered most.

Davis began to dwell memories of the Romney fiasco, which had never been far from his thoughts since deciding upon Jackson's promotion. Since that unpleasant misunderstanding, relations between the two men had been decidedly cool. Because of that, Davis had chosen to ignore Jackson as much as possible, but after Jackson's wounding at Chancellorsville, he had already come to regard that choice as one of his very rare mistakes. Starting with Jackson's convalescence, Davis had made some gestures at repairing the breach. Now it was time to finish the job.

"I bent over backwards and swallowed my own bile for months, placating Johnston in futility," Davis muttered to himself. "Will I do less for Stonewall?"

Davis sighed. He had been to West Point and came out of the Mexican War a successful leader of men, covered in glory. His dearest wish in the this conflict was to command an army in the field himself, not to be chained to office and the petty politicking that went with it, no matter how high the office might be.

The President's preoccupation came to an end when a clerk informed him that General Jackson had arrived. Burton Harrison ushered Jackson into Davis's office.

Jackson was wearing his best uniform, which while clean and freshly ironed, showed some signs of weathered fading and wear. Jackson drew himself up and offered a stiff salute.

Davis saluted back, and motioned for Jackson to be seated. "Would you care for some coffee? Or perhaps tea?" he inquired.

"Only some water, thank you, Mr. President," Jackson replied, sitting with his one thumb sticking up. Davis nodded at Harrison, who left to fetch it.

Taking his seat, Davis asked "How was your journey? And that of your family? I trust they are well. I understand you are staying in General Lee's house, on Franklin Street?"

"My family is very well, thank you, and yes, we are guests there.

Although I fear we might be too much of a burden on Mrs. Lee, I believe she and her daughters appreciate the company for Christmas."

Davis nodded. He knew Mary Lee suffered badly from arthritis.

Jackson asked "And your own family, Mr. President?"

Davis smiled pleasantly, thinking of his hellion brood and their high-spirited antics. "We manage. I confess I find fatherhood a state uplifting and trying, and both in the extreme."

Jackson nodded, but said nothing. Davis decided it was time to begin their real business. "General Jackson, I understand that you are a stranger to the western army, to the western theater. You will need some time to take the reins, to become acquainted with the army, the situation. However, I was hoping that you might have some general ideas on how the coming campaign should be conducted."

Jackson said emphatically "Yes, yes. I do. The army must endeavor to threaten and reverse the enemy's gains in East and Middle Tennessee."

"Some have advocated a more Fabian policy" Davis replied, testing Jackson with an idea he did not really endorse. "Since the most important Yankee objective in the west is now Atlanta, that counsel is to concentrate at Dalton, forestall the enemy advance, and make them pay a high price for every yard of Georgia's soil."

Jackson shook his head in disapproval. "No, no. We must seize and retain the initiative, and that can only be accomplished by advancing. The alternative is, as you say, to fall back upon Atlanta, fighting to delay and in hope that the enemy will make a mistake. Even if the enemy should blunder and provide such an opening, a victory would, in all likelihood, only force a retreat no farther than to Chattanooga, which by all reports is now a fortress and well-stocked with supplies. There would then be no repetition of this past autumn's siege of that place, Mr. President."

"I believe," Jackson continued, "that victories are won by the party blessed with audacity, celerity and surprise. In this way a weaker army, and our armies will almost always prove weaker in numbers than those of the enemy, might concentrate against only a part of the stronger, and inflict defeat in detail upon it. Many such victories build confidence, and make an army invincible."

"How do you propose to accomplish this?"

"That I cannot say," Jackson admitted. "As you have said, Mr. President, I am unfamiliar with both the army and the terrain." Pausing for a moment, he added "I can say that I believe the west offers greater opportunities for maneuver than the east. It is a vast place, compared to Virginia, where our contests with the Army of the Potomac all occur in the rectangle formed by the Blue Ridge, the Chesapeake, Washington and Richmond. That rectangle is bisected by several rivers, not much more than a hundred miles wide for the most part, and makes a severely constrained place for two large armies."

Jackson went on. "I also believe that we must take the war to the enemy, and by that I mean we must bring the war into the homes of the civilian population of the northern states. If we hope for them to discontinue their efforts to subjugate our people, we must break the Yankee nation as well as the Yankee armies. Unfortunately, in the west, I believe this is impractical at the present time. Too much occupied territory separates our base from the northern heartland. But if we can reoccupy Tennessee? I would make Ohio and Indiana howl."

Davis recalled Jackson's proposals, from early in the war, to send strong raiding parties into the North, with orders to lay waste to farms, tear up railroads, and destroy factories. Davis was unsure if such measures would break or stiffen Yankee resolve, but he had been certain that raising the black flag at that time would have alienated European support.

He inquired "But from the sound of it, that is for much later, yes?"

"Yes, yes, it is neither here nor there. For now, the focus must be on Tennessee."

Davis was pleased, even enthusiastic about what he heard. Johnston would have backed away, skillfully to be sure, but still backed away from any fight until he had reached Florida, and then blamed the government for endangering his army, the loss of the entire southern heartland, and not providing him with transportation to Cuba. Davis was certain of that.

Worse than Johnston, Davis thought, Longstreet wanted to put his entire army corps on mules for a raid into Kentucky, even though there were obviously not so many mules available in all of the Confederacy. Beauregard's wild, vainglorious schemes scarcely deserved mention.

Davis had taken his fill of plans that were defeatist or unrealistic. The man before him spoke of advancing northward, but tempered with some sense of the possible.

"General Jackson, let us begin these labors forthwith. What can this office do to aid you, right here and right now?"

Jackson had not been prepared for that. Taken aback for a moment, he considered his wants. "Well, Mr. President, I am taking my Valley staff with me to Georgia. Many of these men do not hold rank commensurate with their former duties in my corps, let alone the Army of Tennessee. My chief of staff is only a major, whereas I understand the job he is taking is currently occupied by a brigadier general. I have filed for promotions with the War Department..."

Davis interjected "I will push that through. When your men report for duty in Georgia, they will all hold suitable rank."

"Thank you, Mr. President. Another thing is that at least some of my key subordinates should be men I already know and can work with. I must have John Bell Hood. He is recuperating in Richmond now, I am told, and if he can mount a horse, I must have him."

Davis was glad to have a request he could grant so readily. He had been thinking of promoting Hood to corps command for months now, and the only vacancy was in Jackson's soon-to-be army. As Jackson had just said, it was only a matter of how soon and by how much Hood would recuperate.

"Done," Davis said.

The president continued discussing trivial bureaucratic matters with Jackson for some time, until Jackson finally grew impatient enough to ask that their meeting be adjourned until tomorrow, so that he might return to the War Department and make some requests before that office closed and the clerks went home.

After working in the department's offices at Mechanics Hall until well after dark, Jackson made a brisk nighttime stroll around the lovely, spacious green of Virginia's Capitol, trying to shake off a day spent sitting down. He then walked to the Lee's house on Franklin Street, let himself in and found his family and Mary Lee in the parlor.

He motioned for them to stay where they were. "Please, don't get up. I shall join you shortly." He doffed his overcoat and his boots, and returned to the parlor, where he spent the remainder of the evening quietly reading from the Bible to his sleepy five year old daughter Julia, who sat on his lap. Anna and Mary chatted, Anna enthralled with Mary's old family yarns about George Washington.

When Mary decided to retire, Jackson and his wife put Julia to bed, and then went to bed themselves. It was only once they were alone together, and under the covers, that Anna said to him "We haven't spoken of it, Tom, but do you want us to come to Georgia? We could find lodgings in Atlanta."

He smiled, and ran his fingers through her dark hair. "I have thought of that, but I am told that Atlanta has become a ... well, an unsuitable place. It is a factory town now, with rowdies and women of ill repute. I will not have our daughter brought up there, even if only for a year or two."

Jackson sighed. There would be no repeat of last year's winter quarters, when he was free to spend so much time with his small family. In addition to his low opinion of Atlanta, he also expected that taking charge of the Army of Tennessee would prove such an enormous task that he would not have the time to see them, even if they were in Atlanta. His duty to the country came before his duty to his family, as his family was part of the country he sought to defend. The former merited his full attention, while the latter should not suffer the slight of inattention.

"No, Lexington is our home. That is where we all belong. I will be there soon, Providence willing."

Resting her head on his chest, Anna asked "You will remember what you said to me? In Lexington?"

Jackson lips twisted slightly, as he suppressed his annoyance. He had given his word, had he not? Of course he remembered.

But she worried, and she meant well. "Yes. I will. Yes," he reassured her, softly.

During that long summer convalescence, Jackson had struggled hard with his wounding, and what it meant for his family and his duty to army and country.

Leading that nighttime reconnaissance at Chancellorsville had been nothing but vanity and foolishness, Jackson had realized from his sick bed, vanity that had resulted in the deaths of several of the fine young men on his staff, and cost the army his leadership at a critical moment. The situation that night had been so disorganized and confused that A.P. Hill had gotten wounded in the legs shortly after replacing him. Finally, it had kept him from Gettysburg, where by all reports he would have been of much service.

Jackson had concluded he had no business riding around between the lines in the dark, and should have instead focused on regrouping the elements of his corps. He deserved censure for his childish antics, and the praise that was heaped on him instead only made him feel guiltier about the whole business.

Then there was his family. He might still be called to God during the war, that much he knew, just as he knew that if he was killed it would be the work of Providence. Even so, he wondered if his wounding wasn't perhaps a sign that he should mend his ways, and he regretted the grief and worry it brought into his home. Julia was still too young to really understand, and Anna was too good to speak of it directly, but the pain was still there for them both all the same.

So, without Anna asking, he told her that he had been mistaken to do what he did that night at Chancellorsville, and swore to avoid such foolhardiness in the future. It was a promise he repeated to Lee upon returning to duty with the Army of Northern Virginia, as Lee had long cautioned him about going too far forward.

Still, he didn't like being questioned about it. At Second Kettle Run, there hadn't even been need for him to go forward, so he didn't. He had learned his lesson, and that was that.

December 18
Late morning
St. Paul's Episcopal Church
Richmond

Sandie Pendleton stood by the altar, waiting for the last guests to file through the church doors and to find their places. He was utterly serene, without even a hint of the wedding jitters. *Everything has gone well, everything will go just fine,* he thought. *And if it does not, I don't need to worry a whit about it.*

He glanced over at his groomsmen. There was Dr. Hunter McGuire, Jackson's medical director and personal physician, and Captain James Power Smith, Jackson's chief aide-de-camp. Both were good friends and close colleagues, and he would put his life in either man's hands without a second thought. There was also Colonel Edward Willis, a former member of Jackson's staff and now commander of the 12th Georgia Infantry; Sanide's cousin Dudley Pendleton; and Kate's cousin, Jack Wellford. All good men, so if anything was less than perfect, he could count on them to take care of it.

Sandie then glanced over his shoulder, up at the altar. There stood his own father, who looked oddly fidgety, whereas his son was calm and composed. Dear old Papa, Sandie thought. He isn't this nervous going into battle.

William Pendleton was not just an Episcopal priest, but also Lee's chief of artillery. St. Paul's own Reverend Charles Minniegerode had graciously stepped aside so "Parson" Pendleton could preside over the wedding of his own son.

Another thing lending Sandie complete confidence that everything would be wonderful was the smoothness with which his wedding plans had come together. First was the intervention of Robert E. Lee and Jefferson Davis, both parishioners, in securing the use of the leading church of Richmond, St. Paul's. It was a stately example of the Greek Revival style, the red upholstery of the ornate pews vividly contrasting with the stained glass and the brilliant, austere white walls and ceiling. Adjoining the state capitol's green, its exterior was just as lovely.

Aside from providing a beautiful setting, St. Paul's was also one of the largest churches in the Old Dominion, and that quickly became an important issue in the planning. The wedding of Sandie Pendleton and Kate Corbin immediately became Richmond's most prominent social event preceding Christmas. This was because all of Richmond's upper crust knew that the reclusive Stonewall Jackson would attend. Receiving a wedding invitation, and with it a chance to meet the great man, immediately became the most desired ticket in town.

Sandie smiled at the thought. Old Jack had politely, but firmly turned down every invitation to dinner that came to him from any stranger, no matter how highly placed. As he put it, he had enough to attend to with friends, family and his duties, and any spare time he had saved went to Sunday and the dour Presbyterian services that Richmond's high society regarded as unfashionable.

From the start, Sandie had realized the invitation list might pose a problem. Kate came from a prominent Fredericksburg clan, but Sandie was pleased when she resisted the temptation to allow well-heeled gawkers onto the invitation list, and that without the slightest prodding from him. The wedding plans had proceeded on sensible lines and with no discord, and as far as Sandie was concerned, that was as good a start into married life as a man could ask for.

Finally, Sandie had the self-assurance of a man who had just been promoted two steps to full colonel, and was set to assume the administration of the country's second largest army at the age of 23. With the arrival of the last few guests, he stood relaxed, but at attention, and waited calmly for his bride to walk in through the church doors.

Observing his young protégé from his seat in the last few pews, Jackson beamed with pride. In his mind, Sandie was not so much the son he had always wanted, but more like a cherished nephew.

People were whispering, gossiping around and over Jackson, annoying him. Catching snatches, he discerned it was over why he and his family had chosen to sit in the back. They had been offered a place in the front, and it was Anna who declined, fearing Jackson's propensity to fall asleep and snore loudly in the middle of religious services. Jackson preferred to sit in the back for that very reason as well, and had made no protest.

Jackson turned his thoughts away from Kate Corbin's gossipy kin and towards Sandie's guests, who were mostly military in nature. Lee himself had been unable to attend, Jackson noted with some sadness. He already missed the grand old man.

Still, he was pleased that Lee had released many familiar faces from his old corps. Old Baldy Ewell and Allegheny Johnson were there, as were some of his staff officers, such as commissary officer Wells Hawks, the mapmaker Jed Hotchkiss, and the foul-mouthed, mule-driving quartermaster, John Harman. These men were counted among Sandie's friends, but were much older and therefore not close enough to join the groomsmen. They thought highly enough of Sandie to postpone their journeys home on leave for his wedding.

Pausing on Hotchkiss, Jackson's sadness at losing such a talented and valuable man returned, for Hotchkiss and his skills would remain in Virginia with Lee. When all of them met at the church earlier that morning, together again for what they all knew would be the last time, the happy day took on the air of a teary farewell.

Also present were some of Jackson's former staffers. He could see Sandie's predecessor as chief of staff, the preacher Robert Dabney, and there was Congressman Alexander Boteler was well.

Finally, he could see General John Bell Hood. With an arm mangled at Gettysburg, his right leg lost at Chickamauga and that stump only partly healed, the sad-eyed, tall, leonine Kentuckian needed to be carried into St. Paul's on a litter. Jackson thought Sam, as Hood's intimates knew him, had the look of a man determined to not just endure, but to stubbornly enjoy himself.

Most would assume Hood's severe countenance reflected pain from his injuries, but Jackson thought knew the truth. Davis had told him that Hood had been courting a vivacious socialite by the name of Sally Preston for months, and had been having a hard time of it. Jackson was sure Hood would have invited her to the wedding, and since she was not on the guest list, it meant Hood's overture had been rejected.

Jackson's ponderings on Hood were interrupted by the arrival of Kate Corbin, led by her father. A beautiful young woman, Jackson thought. He knew her well from the previous winter, when his headquarters was encamped at Moss Neck, the Corbin family's estate. That war should bring these two together, Jackson thought, was just another facet of God's plan.

Anna whispered into his ear "Don't you dare fall asleep, Thomas J. Jackson. Don't you dare." Jackson grunted his assent, but the pew was far too comfortable for Jackson's taste, used as he was to bare wood, and he struggled through the entire wedding to stay awake. It was only with some discrete, firm elbowing from Anna that kept him from dozing off. So he watched dutifully, albeit drowsily.

After the couple was pronounced man and wife and the procession left the church, Jackson practically leapt from his seat and out onto the aisle. He could see Hood was still seated towards the front of the church, chatting with Alleghany Johnson. Probably waiting for the orderlies to come and help him back onto his litter, Jackson thought.

Jackson said quietly "Anna, there is a man I must speak to. I promise I won't be long. Go on out front, and I'll be along." He squeezed her hand, let it go, and strode off to see Hood.

The three generals exchanged salutes, and seeing Jackson wanted to speak with Hood, Johnson made his goodbyes.

"General Jackson, sir," Hood grinned. "Congratulations on your promotion! No man in our Confederacy deserves the honor more."

Jackson nodded and replied tersely "Yes, yes, thank you. Sam, we won't have long here before we are disturbed, so I must be brief. How are you coming along? Do you believe you will recover and return to duty?"

Hood's voice took on a more serious tone. "Yessir, I will. Don't mind this litter, sir. You know how it is. I am healing. Nature is taking her sweet time, but I am healing. The boys from my old Texas Brigade bought me a cork leg, and as soon as my stump quits being so tender, I'll be up and around."

"Good, good" replied Jackson. "I've had words with the President. As soon as you are mended, you are to be made Lieutenant General and posted to Georgia, serving under me and leading an army corps."

"General Jackson," Hood replied enthusiastically, "if you will permit me, that would be the crowning honor of my service in this war." He also thought the promotion might help his suit with the fickle Sally Preston, as it would make him the youngest of the Confederacy's top generals. Truly a man with prospects, fame, and a bright future.

Jackson nodded. Out of the corner of his eye, he saw Hood's orderlies approach, bearing Hood's litter. "Now Sam, later I shall need to call on you. You have some experience with the western army, and I should very much like to hear what you have to say about it."

Hood agreed, and then asked "General Jackson, do you remember a couple of years ago, when you asked me if I thought I'd survive the war?"

Jackson took on a grim countenance. "You said you expected to be badly shattered."

"And you said you would die before then. Well, it looks like we were only two-thirds right, wouldn't you say?" Hood said, dark, bitter humor in his voice, just before seeing a group of well-wishers coming up behind Jackson.

"No," Jackson replied flatly, as the man at the front of the group came up and asked to shake his hand. Ignoring him, Jackson met Hood's eyes, and said "This war is not yet finished with us."

Jackson said his goodbyes to Hood, and drew the group of gawking well-wishers to the front of the church with him for just a few minutes of idle chatter. He loathed it, but doing so gave the broken Hood some privacy for the unpleasant business of being placed onto his litter.

Finally free to go outside, Jackson joined his family to see off the newlyweds. As he watched the Pendletons depart by carriage for the train to their honeymoon with Sandie's family in Lexington, Virginia, he was gladdened the War Department had forced him to stay in Richmond for consultations until the day after Christmas, to have this precious time with his wife and daughter. For whatever time he had, he felt grateful, despite also feeling it was not nearly enough.

PART II
THE WINTER
DOLDRUMS

FEBRUARY TO EARLY MAY 1864

CHAPTER 4

February 13, 1864
Dawn
Sherman's Quarters, Army of the Tennessee, USA
Decatur Crossroads, Mississippi

Sherman awoke, blinking his eyes, pressing sleep from of his mind. That was shooting, he thought. Pistol shots.

By the time Sherman had his trousers on, he heard the telltale thump of a shotgun, fired from some distance away. Now he knew. Not a single man in a blue uniform on this side of the Mississippi carried a shotgun. Whatever was going on out there, it meant Rebels, most likely cavalry.

Sherman was pulling on his shoes by the time one of his aides burst into the bedroom of the rough-hewn, two-room cabin where he had spent the night. The aide, a fresh-faced young major, paused at the sight of William Tecumseh Sherman, almost fully dressed.

Sherman asked calmly "Report, Major Audenried? What the devil is going on out there?"

Saluting, Audenried said "Sir, Confederate cavalry are attacking a column of wagons at the crossroads. That train has an escort and is putting up a fight, trying to get the hell out of here, quick as they can."

Sherman ran his fingers through his red hair, stood up, and reached for his pistol belt. "What is the enemy strength? And what are the troops I had posted to guard that crossroads doing?"

"I believe the enemy strength is one regiment of cavalry, sir. It's quite a scrap out there, and I cannot make a precise count, but I have seen only the one stand of Confederate colors. I'm certain of that. As for the infantry you placed on guard, they seem to have gone, sir."

Sherman looked the major straight in the eye. "Gone? What on Earth do you mean, gone?"

The major nodded. "Just that, sir. They must have left during the night. I don't know why. I must say, General, we're in a top rail fix here."

"Let's go have a look, then," Sherman said, brushing past the man.

He spared a moment to thank the cabin's owner, Mrs. Elder, a middle-aged war widow who at that moment was seeking shelter in the nook formed by the cabin's thick log walls and stone chimney. Sherman then stepped outside.

Yes, the major's report seemed accurate enough, Sherman thought. Reb cavalry playing merry hell with a column of wagons on the road, about 200 yards away. The men detailed to guard the crossroads nowhere to be seen. The Rebs hadn't noticed the wagons by the cabin yet, but when they did, all that was on hand were a scant handful of aides, cooks, orderlies and teamsters.

His eyes still fixed on the fight taking place on the road, Sherman ordered "Major Audenried, take my horse. It's the fastest we have here by a wide margin. Take it and ride east until you find some support. That absent infantry regiment can't have gone far, and are probably on their way back right now, what with all the shooting. Go find them and get them back here, quick as you can."

Audenried snapped off a "Yessir" and a salute, and sprinted for Sherman's horse. Sherman called out to every man wearing a blue uniform around the cabin, ordered them to arm themselves and join him in the stout log corn crib that lay on a low rise a few dozen yards behind the cabin.

He continued to study the fight on the road for a minute, then walked to the corn crib at a measured pace. The troops assigned to guard those wagons were a damn sight better led than the regiment I put on the crossroads, he thought. They were fighting back hard, keeping the wagons moving, not making it easy for the raiders. Those infernal bandits had captured only just a few wagons thus far.

"Bully!" Sherman exclaimed. Then he turned his attention to the men in the corn crib. A couple of junior staff officers were the closest he had to real fighting men. A cook. A groom. A couple of teamsters. One of the latter had already pissed himself. Every man was armed, but this amounted only to revolvers and a pair of musketoons.

They needed bucking up, Sherman thought. "Don't worry, boys," he told them. "The wagon guards are putting up a capital fight. Those Reb dogs have their hands so full, I'll give odds on a month's wages they never come up here for a look." Sherman smacked the log walls. "And if they do, this corn crib is as stout as a blockhouse."

"Don't you worry, General Billy, sir," said the cook, priming his musketoon with some difficulty. "If them fellas come up here, all they'll get is a face full a lead for their troubles."

Sherman noted the cook was missing a couple of fingers off his right hand. That figures, he thought. A lot of fellows like him are maimed veterans, men who can't march or load a musket properly, but can perform other duties well enough.

"Where are you from?" Sherman asked.

The cook replied "Iowa, sir."

"An Iowa man is worth any three of these Mississippi bastards, up to and including old Jeff Davis," Sherman said back.

The Iowan grinned "I reckon I might be worth only two nowadays, General Billy."

Grinning, Sherman went back to watching the road. He thoroughly enjoyed in the informality of his western troops. They could never pass inspection in the paper collar, prim and proper east, something Sherman knew all too well from his experiences there early in the war. Even the eastern Rebs were often better turned out for a parade than his westerners, but his men could out-march and out-fight any outfit on Earth. As far as Sherman was concerned, you could take that fact to the bank and trade it on for gold.

Several minutes passed. A troop of Rebels rode off the road and into the fields separating the Willoughby farm from the crossroads and studied the wagons parked around it for a time. Then the firing from down the road picked up very rapidly. Within minutes, the grey cavalry absconded, along with a handful of wagons, trotting through the crossroads and off to the north. Skirmishers in blue were soon fanning out across the fields.

Sherman stepped out of the corn crib first. Turning to his aides, he said "Alright, gentlemen. Back to business. Get things organized. We push on to Meridian today."

February 13
Late afternoon
Headquarters, Army of Mississippi, CSA
Demopolis, Alabama

Leonidas Polk stepped up onto the rail platform, straightened out his pristine uniform coat, clasped his hands behind his back, and waited for the train rumbling its way up the line to come to a stop. An honor guard, splendidly turned out with bayonets glistening in the winter sun, and bearing the battle flags of the Army of Mississippi, fell into line behind him. Just off the platform, a band began playing "God Save the South."

Polk looked serene as he waited, assuming a pose that was the product of almost 40 years as a man of the cloth. He was 57, portly, and sported a beard meant to cover a double chin and make himself look more like a soldier and less like a priest. The ploy was only half-successful.

Polk had been to West Point a very long time ago, but had left the army shortly after graduation to pursue what he thought would be an easier route to power and influence, and that route led through the Episcopal clergy. He had been right, because whereas by the early 1840s Polk had risen to the Bishopric of Louisiana and considerable wealth as a planter, many of his fellow cadets were still lowly lieutenants. Appointed a general by his old comrade, Jefferson Davis, Polk had served extensively in the West, and was now the commander of the Department of Alabama and Mississippi, a semi-independent post under Stonewall Jackson.

The train slowed, practically crawling up to the station, and then screeched and rattled to a halt, showing every sign of three years of wartime neglect. After a short wait, Major General Benjamin F. Cheatham stepped off the train.

"Frank!" Polk cried, stepping forward to shake hands with the burly Tennessean.

Grinning, Cheatham took Polk's hand, gave it a firm shake, slapped him on the shoulder, and rejoined "Bishop. Good to see you again."

Like Polk, Frank Cheatham came from one of Tennessee's foremost families. He was a planter and horse breeder, had dabbled in politics, and he had the puffy features, pot belly and worn eyes of a hard drinker in middle age. A volunteer officer in the Mexican War, Cheatham ended it as a full colonel. The two men had served together since the earliest days of the current war.

Drawing back, Polk said "Frank, words simply cannot describe how happy I am to see you. And relieved, sir, relieved. With your mighty division of Tennesseans here, we shall smite Sherman and his heathens so terribly, they shall scurry all the way back to Vicksburg and never dare venture out again!"

The platform was starting to crowd with detraining soldiers. Polk dismissed the honor guard, and the two men went into the railway office for some privacy, sat down on plain wooden chairs, and talked.

Cheatham started. "Bishop, Stonewall hurried my boys onto the trains and sent us here before I'd heard even the first rumor that Sherman had left Vicksburg, and that's all I've heard ever since. Rumors. Everything from a little cavalry raid to Sherman leading 60,000 veterans right across Mississippi and Alabama, out to take Atlanta from the rear!"

You did indeed get here quickly, Polk thought. He had not even had a chance to submit a request for reinforcements to Jackson before he received word that reinforcements were already on the way. Part of the reason why was that Polk took his time in composing not one, but two requests, one for Jackson and one for Jefferson Davis, the latter to be sent out of channels. Polk had guessed wrongly that Jackson would be just like Bragg or Joe Johnston, and refuse to send him anything.

Of course, just one division wasn't enough, not for Polk, who thought he needed at least three. But he was pleasantly surprised by Cheatham's prompt dispatch nonetheless.

Polk said soothingly "Sherman has a strong host, but not that strong. He is advancing in two columns, each with one army corps, under McPherson and Hurlbut. The reports lead me to the conclusion he has about 25 to 30,000 infantry. That is still more than

I have."

"What do you have?" Cheatham asked.

"The divisions of Loring and French. Plus cavalry," Polk replied.

Doing the math in his head, Cheatham nodded. He had brought more than 6,000 battle-hardened Tennesseans with him. Polk probably had over 10,000 infantry of his own, give or take. Almost as much horse, all told, but that was spread all around the region.

Cheatham fished out his pipe from inside his coat. Pushing tobacco into the bowl, he asked "What do you intend?"

"Sherman will turn south soon, and press for Mobile. My spies in Vicksburg tell me as much, their navy is prowling around Mobile's waters, like the wolves that they are, and the Yankee newspapers report Mobile as his objective too. His corps were at Decatur and Newton this morning. When he turns south, and he must turn south soon, we will follow him, and smite at his rear." Polk smacked a clenched fist into the palm of his hand for emphasis.

"Yep, I see," Cheatham agreed. They might get a chance to hit one of the two Yankee corps, attack only part of their army, and whip them, just like they did at Perryville.

Polk pulled on his beard thoughtfully. "If I may be so bold, Frank, but pray tell, do you have an opinion of your new commanding general?"

"Old Jack?" Cheatham chortled, then continued matter-of-factly, "I do believe, Bishop, he is your commanding general too."

Polk smiled blandly, but said nothing.

The question caused Cheatham to recall his first real encounter with Jackson. Old Jack had ordered the army to hold big winter training marches, something that caused quite a lot of grumbling. On his first such march, Cheatham's guide had failed him, the division got lost, and then they stumbled into a wagon train. He was sorting the mess out when Jackson appeared, and then proceeded to upbraid him in public.

Cheatham managed to hold his temper in check, but he had suffered enough abuse under Braxton Bragg already, so he icily told Jackson that his resignation would be on his desk the next morning. He had finished the march and retired to his quarters to pen his resignation letter, when he was interrupted by two of his fellow generals, Patrick Cleburne and A.P. Stewart, together with Jackson's chief of staff, Sandie Pendleton.

They prevailed upon him to reconsider, go to Jackson, and patch things up now that tempers had cooled. Cheatham thought it was a waste of time, but went anyway, and was surprised to find Jackson amenable.

After reflecting so, Cheatham said "Well, he is a bigger bastard than even Bragg, if you can believe that. Trains the men, drives them. Officers. Harder than ever before. Works his generals like dogs too. We drill and march every day. Every day excepting Sunday, Bishop. Jackson is very religious. No work on the Sabbath, and always encouraging the men to attend services."

Polk brightened at that, but Cheatham didn't notice. Puffing on his pipe, he went on. "He dressed down a few brigadiers in public over the state of their latrines. Shoots deserters too. Even caught a colonel drunk on duty on Rocky Face Ridge, our defensive line north of Dalton. Cashiered the man, even though there weren't no fighting going on at the time. I suppose it was his own damn fault, poor sumbitch, but still seems a might bit harsh in this old fellow's eyes."

Polk sighed. Drinking was the curse of their army, a curse that extended to Old Frank himself. "That is sad to hear. Very discouraging. I had such fine hopes for the man."

"Well, it ain't all bad. I'll say this much for Stonewall Jackson. He is a stone bastard, but he gets his way. Let me tell you a story. Old Jack sent his chief of staff and his commissary man, Pendleton and Hawks, down to Atlanta. The first thing they found was that the War Department's commissary office in Atlanta was selling meat meant both for our army and Lee's army out the back door, if you catch my meaning, and making a pretty little fortune. Well, Jackson arrested the scoundrels, Davis sacked them, Jackson's people tightened a few other things up, and we started getting more and better food up in Dalton. Word has it some friends of Governor Joe Brown were involved, but nothing ever came of that."

Cheatham started laughing. "Old Jack also found and requisitioned a few thousand pairs of shoes away from one of Brown's militia warehouses while he was at it."

"Brown must have had conniption" Polk said, surprised. Brown was a populist, and as fierce a States Righter as they came, constantly at odds with Richmond. He ran Georgia as if it were his own little republic.

Shrugging, Cheatham continued "He was very upset. Jackson made an enemy of Brown, not that I think he cared. But the Atlanta papers made merry hell over the commissary scandal, so old Brown had to sweep the whole thing under the rug."

Polk changed the subject, telling Cheatham where he wanted his men to camp, and Cheatham stepped outside to pass the orders along to his staff. The two men then chatted for a while longer, but Polk, having what he wanted, turned his thoughts elsewhere. He looked past the conversation, past even dealing with Sherman, and onto what he hoped defeating Sherman might bring. Polk began to muse on succeeding Jefferson Davis, on becoming the Confederacy's second President.

Before the war, Polk had been satisfied with his place as a wealthy landowner and prominent clergymen, enjoying his wide influence, lording it over his slaves and preaching down to the flock. Yet becoming a general gave him an appetite for more. He had become accustomed to autocratic command, to real power, and now he wanted more of it. He had made the transition from bishop to general, so why not from general to president?

Already an influential and popular figure in the region, Polk had formed close, valuable connections during the war, connections with men just like Frank Cheatham. More to the point, he was a highly placed crony of Jefferson Davis, something that would matter when Davis's supporters began casting about for a successor. They would need a successor too, because without one they could never retain office, and the choice of the Davis party would be the man who would surely win. Not only would Davis's stature become unassailable after the war was won, but Davis's enemies were a fractious lot, united only in opposition and a mutual fondness for squabbling. None of those men would put his ambitions on hold for the sake of one of the others. They would quarrel and fall out amongst themselves, because quarreling was all most of them were good for in the first place.

Who else was more suitable than Polk? From what he understood, Lee had no interest in politics. Bragg was a cretin, as unelectable as he was inept at leading an army. Judah was a Jew. As far as Polk could see, he would be the only real choice, which meant the highest office in the land was his for the taking in 1867.

Only one thing was missing. As illustrious as Polk thought his war record was most of it had been spent in the background, saving the country from the failures of Braxton Bragg. Polk had never won a victory to call his own, but he felt that if he could win one, however small, it would cement his reputation. Do that, and the presidency would surely be his.

Polk dreamed big. Building a permanent presidential mansion in Richmond; lavish state dinners; fashioning a political dynasty like Jefferson's or Andrew Jackson's; perhaps even a little war all his own, such as seizing Cuba from Spain. If I can spank Sherman's bottom, Polk thought, the rest will fall into my lap like a ripe apple.

February 15
Midday
Sherman's Headquarters in the Field, Army of the Tennessee, USA
Meridian, Mississippi

When Sherman rode into Meridian at about 3:30 on the afternoon of the 14th, he soon discovered that he had arrived too late. While many warehouses were still stuffed to the rafters with foodstuffs, arms, and ammunition, the repair shops, the arsenal, and the hospital had been emptied of their precious machinery, tools, and equipments. For the Confederacy, such things were precious, almost irreplaceable, and according to the boasting local citizens, the guts of the Confederate war industry in Meridian had been put on trains and shipped away. The last of it slipped out mere minutes before the head of Sherman's column marched into town.

It was a blow to Sherman's plans, but not a severe one. Meridian was a railroad junction town, and Sherman's most important task was to smash that junction. That done, the Rebels would find it much harder to organize and supply any large scale foray to the Mississippi River, which in turn meant Sherman could reduce the size of his garrisons and send the freed-up troops to East Tennessee, where they would be needed for the spring campaign against Stonewall Jackson. To destroy Meridian's machinery and supplies would have been even better, but that was secondary to tearing up the railroads.

Well, the townspeople aren't gloating now, Sherman thought.

His troops were busy pulling up the railroad's tracks and ties, stacking and lighting the ties into bonfires, and using those fires to soften and bend the rails. They were also scouring the countryside and returning with herds of beeves, fat hams, sides of smoked bacon, baskets of sweet potatoes, sacks of corn meal and everything else the bounty of the Mississippi prairie could yield.

Sherman was satisfied that his main objective would be achieved, but the lost opportunity still rankled him. He paced back and forth on a now bare railroad embankment outside of town, shrouded in a haze of tobacco and bonfire smoke. Turning back towards Meridian again, he saw General McPherson ride up.

"Bill," McPherson said, saluting. He was a fit man in his middle 30s, with well-fed features and bright, lively eyes, and cut quite a figure in the saddle.

Leaning over his horse, McPherson extended his hand for a shake. "Your people told me I would find you out here. Is it wise, sir? To be out here alone? I know there are plenty of the men about, but this is still hostile country."

Sherman shook hands, and then took the cigar from his mouth. "Mac, I have a close call each and every campaign, and that scrape yesterday fills my quota for this one."

"If you say so," McPherson replied. "The scouts report all's quiet to the east. From what I can gather, word is Bishop Polk thinks we might turn south and march on Mobile."

Sherman nodded, replying "That's what the newspapers say we are about." He put the cigar back in his mouth and took several short, sharp pulls on it, billowing smoke. In Sherman's mind, newspaper men were little better than traitors and spies, so it was only fitting to use them to dispense false and misleading information.

Cigar still clenched in his teeth, Sherman asked "But knowing the Bishop, he's holed up in Demopolis, scared, and not sure what to do, despite Stonewall sending him Cheatham's Division. What about from the north?"

McPherson said "No word from General Smith."

That set Sherman back to pacing. When Sherman and McPherson set out from Vicksburg, General William Sooy Smith should have left Memphis at the head of more than 7,000 cavalry. It was one of several supporting movements Sherman had intended, meant to keep Bishop Polk from guessing what he was up to.

Unlike all the other diversions, however, Smith had been meant to meet him in Meridian. If Smith had gotten to Meridian on time, he would have caught at least the tail of the Rebel evacuation. Worse, without Smith it was too dangerous to press on and smash Polk's headquarters at Demopolis.

Sherman turned back to McPherson and shouted "Dammit! Where the hell is Smith and what has he done with my cavalry?"

McPherson looked away for a moment, then looked back at Sherman and said "I think we know what happened, Bill, and I can explain it with just three words: Nathan Bedford Forrest."

February 27
Late morning
Cheatham's Division, CSA
Meridian

Frank Cheatham rode into Meridian ahead of his column, followed by only a modest escort and a few of his staff. He was unconcerned about his personal safety, as he knew the Yankees had pulled out of Meridian a week ago.

He had a good idea what to expect, for the devastation began many miles east of town. The railroad ties were now heaping piles of ash, with rails stacked haphazardly on top, each one warped into a shallow V-shape. Every bridge and trestle lay demolished.

Even so, actually seeing what was left of the Mississippi rail town filled him with rage. He could see every single building in Meridian that was not a private home had been razed to the ground.

Cheatham took his hat off and ran his fingers through his hair. More than a week ago, he and General French had said Sherman was clearly not going to Mobile, that Polk's Army of Mississippi should march out and at least use the cavalry to put pressure on Sherman. Bishop Polk and that fool Loring insisted Sherman might still go to Mobile, and if he didn't, Sherman would march on Demopolis next, so the best thing was to sit tight and receive the Yankees on ground of their own choosing.

The result, Cheatham thought, was that Sherman had camped in Meridian for five days, five full days, all the while freely ravaging the countryside, tearing up the railroad for miles in all directions, and thumbing his nose at them while they sat on their fat old asses back in Demopolis. Polk finally marched for Meridian only after Sherman had absconded, and then they went forward so slowly that Sherman was probably all the way to Vicksburg by now.

A haggard-looking old woman shuffled up to Cheatham. "General, have you any food? The Yankees stripped us bare, left us with not a crumb, the vandals. Nothing!"

Cheatham noted her good clothes and realized this woman came from some substance. A proud woman, one who hasn't eaten in days. He told an aide to rustle up a few pounds of cornmeal and some bacon for the lady.

Cheatham nudged his horse forward and continued to survey what was left of the little Southern town. He saw the smoldering remains of warehouses and workshops. Even the post office was a charred ruin. A couple of houses were gone as well, probably burnt by spreading fires rather than by design.

Disgusted, Cheatham took a hefty pull from his whiskey flask, drowning the bitter taste in his mouth. The Yankees who did all of this were getting clean away, he thought, and there was no explaining it except that old Bishop Polk had just plain lost his nerve.

March 2
Early evening
Headquarters, Army of the Gulf, USA
New Orleans, Louisiana

Sherman stood on the deck of the steamer *Diana*, arms folded across his chest and wreathed in smoke, tapping his foot against the wooden planking so rapidly and loudly that it half-drowned out the churning of the paddlewheel. When the boat settled in alongside the jetty, he vaulted over the railing even before the boat could be lashed to the cleats. He strode off, leaving his aides scurrying behind him, and soon found the carriage that had been left waiting for his arrival.

Cigar still clenched in his teeth, Sherman snapped at his followers "Come on, come on. Let's get on with it. Can't keep General Banks waiting." All of them hadn't even sat down in the carriage when Sherman ordered the driver forward.

The carriage stopped in front of a fine house in the city, one of the few flying the Stars and Stripes from the front portico. Sherman dismounted, threw away his cigar butt, strode up to the open door and presented himself to a waiting orderly, who showed him to the parlor. A few minutes later, Nathaniel Banks walked in.

Sherman drew himself to attention and saluted. Although both men were major generals of volunteers, Banks held almost a full year of seniority over him at that rank. Technically, Banks was senior even to Grant, although not for long, since rumor had it Lincoln soon intended to reward Grant with a promotion to the revived rank of lieutenant general.

Banks saluted back, and then stepped forward to shake hands. Despite being a little short, he was a fit man in his late 30s, and cut a fine image in his resplendent dress uniform, adorned with gold-tasseled epaulettes, shining boots, buttons and buckles, and a magnificent sword.

Sherman inquired "General Banks, if I may ask, is there a special occasion?"

Banks replied "My wife and I are attending a party tonight, General Sherman. We would be delighted if you could attend, and I am sure an invitation can be arranged. My family was about to sit down for dinner, as well. Would you care to join us?"

"Why, I'd be honored to dine with your family this evening, and to accompany you afterward." Sherman hadn't bathed beyond a few splashes in the washbasin since setting out for Meridian a month before, and was now silently thankful he was at least wearing a clean field uniform. And that his heavy smoking smothered his body's backcountry odor.

Banks ushered Sherman into the elegantly appointed dining room, where he introduced Sherman to his wife Mary, his son, and his two daughters. They all sat down, and soon a first course of crabmeat ravigote was served. Sherman took to the dish with relish, having come to love Louisiana's cuisine during his brief tenure as superintendent of the Louisiana State Seminary and Military

Academy in 1859.

The small talk between Banks, his wife and Sherman continued as turtle soup, and then crawfish etouffee were brought out. Yet Sherman's fine feather over the food came to an abrupt halt when Mary Banks asked him "And where is home for you, General Sherman? And how is your own family?"

Sherman swallowed hard. His eldest son Willie, only nine years old, had passed away five months before. Typhoid fever. He blamed himself for the loss, since it was his idea to bring his family down to visit him in the pestilential late summer miasma of Vicksburg.

Glancing at the Banks children, Sherman smiled weakly and said "They are in Ohio, Madame. And they are well."

After the meal, the two generals retired for brandy and cigars before setting out for the rest of the evening.

Settling down, Sherman asked "Sir, I hope you don't mind if we have some of that talk I came down here for. I must be getting back no later than tomorrow afternoon."

"No, not at all." Banks took a pull on his cigar. "But first, could you tell me about your own recent adventure in Mississippi?"

Sherman glowed. "The short of it is I took 20,000 men, marched clear across Mississippi, sacked the state capital for the third time, destroyed Meridian township, and marched back again. The Bishop was so scared he never came out of his bolt hole. I inflicted $50 million worth of damage on the Confederacy, and no one so much as lifted a finger to stop me."

Banks replied affably "You know the newspapers tell a different story. They say Mobile was your target and call you a failure."

That soured Sherman's mood. "Yes. I know." It was the price paid, he thought, for deceiving Polk and Jackson. He spat "A newspaper man is nothing more than a whore, dressed up in ink instead of rouge."

Banks changed the subject. "As for the Red. The thick and the thin of it is that I am ready to start the campaign right now. I am lingering here in New Orleans only because I thought it prudent to be on hand for the inauguration of the new state government under the fine and loyal Governor-elect Michael Hahn. We'll take care of that on the 4th, and after that I see no significant impediments."

Banks went on to outline his plan for the Red River campaign, intended to extend Federal control into northwestern Louisiana and eastern Texas. It was a favorite of President Lincoln, who wanted blue troops on the ground in Texas to discourage the meddlesome ambitions of the French and their puppet in Mexico, Maximilian III. Grant scorned the idea, thought the best way to curb the French was to win the war, and thought the best way to do that was to seize Mobile, Alabama instead.

Sherman favored the Red River idea because it forced the Rebels farther back from the Mississippi, just as his Meridian campaign had. But what was more important to him was to get back the two divisions of 10,000 veteran infantry he was loaning Banks for this Red River business.

"It's a good plan, General, but you must bring the Rebels to book as soon as possible. I cannot stress this more strongly: A.J. Smith and his two divisions must be on their way back to Vicksburg in 30 days. Grant and I have Stonewall Jackson to contend with in northern Georgia. I must have those men back, and back on schedule."

Banks readily agreed, but Sherman noticed something, a suppressed grimace. A former Speaker of the House and Massachusetts governor, Banks was well-practiced in the art of concealing his thoughts and feelings, but that had slipped past his mask.

Sherman inquired "You can do me another service, sir. What can you tell me about Stonewall Jackson? We both had brigades at First Bull Run, Jackson and I, but we never danced. You fought him in the Shenandoah, though. I would highly value your opinions on the man."

"And at Cedar Mountain," Banks replied defensively. Sipping quietly on his brandy, he gave what sounded to Sherman like an honest description of his rout at Winchester and his tough, but ultimately lost fight at Cedar Mountain. Sherman thought the man's frankness did him credit, and it lent some credence to Banks's belief that he had come within a hair of whipping Jackson at Cedar Mountain. Banks was convinced he would have won if Rebel reinforcements had not arrived, or if he had been better supported. But Sherman noted he became more subdued as he went on, the buff confidence from earlier in the evening slowly evaporating as he told his story.

The two generals went on to the party, where Sherman was delighted to see some familiar faces, friends and acquaintances from his time in Louisiana before the war. During all the small talk and through the remainder of the evening, Sherman turned over his conversations with Banks in his mind.

It was very late and many drinks and toasts later by the time Sherman made it to bed, but by then he had made his mind up. Banks wasn't a bad man, but he lacked resolution and energy. Worse, he was unlucky, at least insofar as war was concerned. If there was a way to flub this Red River business, Sherman was convinced Banks would blunder into it.

Sherman forgot about bed, went to the desk in the bedroom provided for him, and began composing a letter to Grant. Red River, Shreveport and East Texas be damned, he was getting A.J. Smith and his 10,000 men back as promised.

March 2
Late evening
Headquarters, Army of Mississippi, CSA
Demopolis

Polk tore the telegraphed message in half, crumpled it up, and threw it across his office, his usually placid features contorted with bitter, petulant anger.

"How dare that man!" Polk screamed.

Upon returning to Demopolis yesterday, Polk found orders waiting from Stonewall Jackson that he should return Cheatham's Division as soon as practicable. Polk did not find the return of Cheatham practicable at all, and genially replied to Jackson that he needed to retain Cheatham's services to guard against future aggression from Sherman.

Jackson's response was swift and left no room for Polk's discretion or further discussion: send Cheatham back at once, and make the trains available if they were not already so.

Damn that man to hell! He was a Maury County Polk, cousin to James K. Polk, the eleventh president of the old Union! He had been ahead of Jackson on the lieutenant generals list! Now that Virginia school teacher was placed over him, lording high and mighty, issuing peremptory orders. Jackson the master, Polk the servant!

Polk briefly toyed with going around Jackson and taking his case straight to Davis, his old West Point roommate, sweetened with a hint that if he were allowed to retain Cheatham, he might be able to advance onto Jackson and Vicksburg. No, no, it wouldn't do, he thought. Even if Davis agreed, the price would be that he might actually be expected to make a genuine advance on Vicksburg, a course of action certain to kick over the Yankee hornet's nest.

"Cheatham must go back," Polk muttered bitterly. "He planned this, that jumped up bumpkin! He sent me just enough men to ensure my failure."

Sherman had absconded before he could be smote, and whatever Polk might claim in official reports and in the papers, the whole miserable affair was for naught. He knew it, and he knew it was all Jackson's fault. If Jackson had supported me with an entire corps, Polk thought, why, I could have boldly advanced, confident in the knowledge that Sherman was outnumbered.

"Who does that man think he is? I am Polk, by God! Polk!" he roared. Polk snatched up a chair and smashed it against the floor, over and over again, until the chair was kindling and he was left panting, hard out of breath.

He was alone in his office. Polk never condescended to such displays of temper outside of his intimates, and his aides knew to steer clear of him whenever a contrary message came over the telegraph wires.

While he caught his breath, Polk had an idea. Why can't I do what Sherman did? Polk thought. Yes, that will do! I will present my own plan for an offensive. Jackson will reinforce me with a corps. With two corps and my cavalry in hand, I could do a capital job of raiding Middle or West Tennessee, just as Sherman had raided Meridian.

The more Polk considered his idea, the more he liked it. His plan not only had a decidedly military ring to it, but also the demonstrable proof of what Sherman had accomplished behind it. What Sherman had done, Polk would also do, and ruin the Northrons' plans in the bargain.

Of course, such a plan had to be submitted to Jackson, and Polk surmised that Jackson would never approve it. To ensure his plan received a favorable hearing, he would submit a copy directly to President Davis as well.

Polk ran his fingers through his hair, wiped his face off with a handkerchief, straightened his uniform, opened his door, and called for his secretary. Blithely ignoring the pile of wooden debris, upholstery and stuffing from the smashed chair, he sat down behind his desk and began dictating his message to Davis.

CHAPTER 5

March 3
Early morning
Camp of the 41st Tennessee Infantry, Maney's Brigade, USA
Dalton, Georgia

Captain Robert L. Fletcher scowled as he stepped out of the cabin housing regimental command, carefully replacing the crude wooden latch on the door behind him. He was a stocky, fit man in his middle 20s, so broad that he looked short at first glance, despite his average height.

Despite his bulk, the chill of the dark, pre-dawn air bit at him, causing him to button up the last few buttons on his coat, adjust his scarf and hat, and turn up his collar for good measure. Thanks to the Grimes brothers, he would be out in the cold all morning and might as well prepare for it.

The morning had started the same way most mornings did since Old Jack took command, just before New Year's. As per the new general orders, every day except Sundays saw the roughly 260 men and officers of the 41st Tennessee rise from their cabins and tents at 5 a.m., and in the pre-dawn gloom shake life into their limbs in the icy winter chill of the north Georgia mountains, and those not responding to sick call would fall out for breakfast.

The unwelcome change in routine for Fletcher that morning started with word to report to Colonel Tillman, the regiment's commander, after reveille. Once there, Tillman gave him a stern talking to about two of his men, the Grimes brothers.

Sunrise wasn't for another hour or more yet. The air was full of the smell of corn meal frying in fatback. Captain Fletcher's stomach growled. He stopped by the officer's mess and took a tin cup of steaming spruce needle tea back to his company with him. Breakfast would have to wait.

"Private Nathan Grimes! Private William Grimes! Stand at attention!"

Fletcher's entire company numbered only little more than two dozen men, and they were grouped around a set of three campfires, cooking breakfast. He couldn't see who was who in the darkness, but two of the boys shot up at the campfire farthest from him. Fletcher walked over to them.

"Perhaps you boys would care to explain why you weren't on that firewood detail yesterday? Where were you?"

Nathan stood silent, staring straight ahead. He liked the Captain, but he didn't see that as cause to give in all at once. Standing next to him, Willie audibly gulped.

Fletcher asked again, impatient. "Come on. Out with it. Hardly the first time with y'all."

Nathan kept staring into the darkness, and flatly said "Just out foraging, sir."

Fletcher groaned. "Gah. You boys keep that up, you're liable to get yourselves shot. What if Old Jack gets wind of it? That man just loves shooting boys who wander off, more than Bragg ever did. I reckon the two of you will get yourselves bucked and gagged at the very least. Is that what you want?"

Both boys replied quietly "Nosir." Some of the chuckling in the company turned to laughter.

"Did you find any of what you were looking for?" Fletcher asked.

Nathan smirked. "Yessir!" Chuckles rose from rest of the company, still going about their business around their campfires.

Fletcher thought that a darkie would at least have more sense. "Well, this is what's going to happen. Since I got an earful from Colonel Tillman this morning on account of you boys, after adjutant's call, you will report to the sergeant major for duty, digging the new camp latrine. You still have to report for morning drill, target practice and the afternoon march. You dig that latrine on your own time, and it gets finished today, even if you go hungry, even if you have to work in the dark. Understood?"

The Grimes boys turned sullen. Digging the new latrine meant carving it out of the frozen ground. "Yessir."

"And whatever whiskey you found, Nathan, that goes to the supper ration for the rest of the company." Fletcher knew it was whiskey. When it came to food, the brothers had a generous nature, and there had been no extra food at the company mess last night. When it came to whiskey, Nathan kept it for himself.

Cheers and hoots erupted from the rest of the company. The Grimes boys glumly replied "Yessir."

"That isn't all. Tomorrow you boys are making up for the firewood you didn't cut yesterday, same drill. You meet your quota, even if you go hungry. And one other thing. You shirk this, and I am to buck and gag you. That comes straight from the Colonel. Dismissed."

The boys limped back to their places at the fire. Hope you fellas eat hardy this morning, Fletcher thought. You'll surely need it.

Fletcher made his way back to the officer's mess, musing on how he sometimes he wished he had never recruited the Grimes boys in the first place. They were almost more trouble than they were worth. Almost.

Robert Littleberry Fletcher, Jr. was a Marshall County man, his grandfather one of the county's first settlers. His father had been one of the men to lead the push for a new county, and when the Marshall County was carved out of the surrounding counties in 1836, it was the old man's proudest achievement.

Fletcher, Sr.'s other great ambition had been for his son to make his way in state politics, establish the Fletchers a proper, leading family in that corner of Tennessee. Fletcher, Jr. had trained as a lawyer, was good at it, and had made a fine practice which supplemented the earnings from the family land holdings and mill. Yet he had never gotten much traction in running for local office or the state legislature. Even so, Old Man Fletcher and his son were popular men in the region, so when the war came, Fletcher, Jr. was able to raise his own company of Marshall and Lincoln County men. The Grimes boys were among the latter.

Nathan was a skinny, underfed boy just barely 18 in the autumn of 1861, and Willie was just as thin and obviously underage. Life must have been terrible for them before the war, because both had somehow managed to fill out and grow up on army rations. Now the elder brother was a strong, compact young man with a worn face and weather-beaten look, and only his scraggly whiskers betrayed his youth. Willie was still skinny, but had grown tall and gangly.

Fletcher knew of their father, Nate Grimes, Sr., but only on account of his unsavory reputation. From what Fletcher had heard, Mrs. Grimes died giving birth to Willie, and after that Nate became a drunk, got into debt, and ended up a tenant on his own land. It made Grimes, Sr. a cruel, embittered man. The boys had volunteered into the company to get away from him.

Knowing that was part of the reason Fletcher tolerated their shirking, because he had never seen a lazier fellow than Nathan in his life. Another cause was that they were outstanding foragers. Fletcher had never seen anyone better than those boys at trapping a hare, stealing some local farmer's chicken, or finding a hidden quarter-cask of whiskey. He figured those skills were learned growing up under old Nate, what with the boys fending for themselves some of the time. Finally, while Willie was basically a good soldier, and Nathan was the real ne'er do well, it was also Nathan who was the fighter.

Fletcher arrived at the officer's mess and poured himself another cup of spruce tea, shaking his head. It never quite sat right with him that the laziest, most incorrigible man in his company had also always been its bravest. When a fight got started, Nathan was always up front. He never hollered or made a fuss about it. He just coolly and quietly went forward.

Getting the company moving was easy because of Nathan, Fletcher thought. As soon as I screw my courage up and step out, Nathan's right behind. Sometimes, that boy steps off even before I do.

Fletcher asked for his breakfast, sipped on his tea, and chuckled. After the Battle of Raymond, Colonel Tillman tried to recruit Nathan into the color guard, but the boy scoffed, saying the honor was "a waste of a fine musket man and the cheapest ticket there was to a pine box." Despite that rebuff, Nathan could have been a sergeant by now, were he not such a no account hard case off the battlefield.

March 5
Late evening
Headquarters, Army of Tennessee, CSA
Dalton

Sandie Pendleton proffered a bottle and asked "May I offer you fine fellows some brandy on this occasion?"

That brought grins all around. Sandie looked at his comrades as he poured each of them a cup: Captain James Power Smith, Jackson's chief aide-de-camp; Lieutenant Colonel John Harman, the chief quartermaster; Hunter McGuire, medical director. Wells Hawks was missing, away in Atlanta attending to commissary business. Together they had gone from running a tiny force in the Shenandoah Valley to running the country's second largest field army. Sandie was at least as proud of his colleagues as he was of himself.

Sandie raised his own cup and said "Gentlemen, to our third corps commander. To Lieutenant General Alexander Peter Stewart!"

The others raised their cups, and they all clanked them together to a low chorus of "Here, here." Each took a precious sip, and then sat down on camp chairs and stools, enjoying the warming effect of the liquor.

After Smith took a swallow from his cup, Harman leaned forward and said "Damn it all if I'm not surprised at you, Jimmy, with that brandy. Preacher's son and all."

Sandie smiled affably. Harman was the oldest of them at almost 40, but he loved ribbing people.

McGuire, a well-appointed man with a thick moustache and big, intense eyes, waved Harman off. "As his doctor, I told Captain Smith here that a modest intake of medicinal spirits is essential to a man living in this climate, to keep out the chill." Even though McGuire was only in his late 20s, he was the next oldest man in the tent.

McGuire continued. "Sandie, I know this must be a relief to you, getting the War Department to clear Stewart's promotion and your reorganization of the army."

Sandie said quietly "It was Old Jack's idea. The President approved it. I only drew up the papers."

But it was a relief for him, and he hoped maybe things would go a little more easily in the Army of Tennessee. If Old Jack was planning a campaign against the Union's armies, Sandie was already in the field, involved in a three-front struggle on the General's behalf over matters of organization, supply and training with Georgia Governor Joe Brown, the War Department in Richmond, and their own General William H. Hardee. Worse, Sandie felt he was winning the paper conflict only about half the time.

Hardee was the army's senior corps commander, and had been acting as head of the army before Jackson arrived. As a former West Point commandant and the author of the standard textbook on infantry tactics, Hardee enjoyed quite a reputation in the western army, and they called him "Old Reliable."

Yet Sandie and his people thought of Hardee as reliable only for pedantry and obstructionism. General Hardee objected to most everything that came out of army headquarters, replying to orders with long letters and reports, each of which was polite and proper, but each also lecturing at length on military protocol, regulations, training or tactics, and resoundingly negative in tone, outlook and intent.

That was where promoting A.P. Stewart came in. Jackson had wanted the Army of Tennessee reorganized from two into three corps. The reasons given to President Davis were three smaller corps would be more mobile and more flexible than the previous two corps arrangement, and that the freshly promoted John Bell Hood was untried in his new position. Jackson wanted to spread his eggs into more baskets.

The unstated reason was to reduce Hardee's contrary influence by shrinking the size of his corps and transferring some of the army's best divisions away from him. Davis was convinced of the plan, but for a time it looked like they wouldn't get Stewart, or "Old Straight" as everybody called him, for the new command.

Smith interrupted Sandie's wandering thoughts. "If ever there was a man better suited to Old Jack's way of doing things than Stewart, I reckon I have neither seen nor heard of him."

"Yeap," Harman replied. "Not Old Baldy, not Allegheny Johnson, not poor old departed Winder neither. Certainly not fucking Old Jube or His God Damned Highness, Little Powell."

Sandie said "Old Straight is a blessing. Our Jackson would call it

Providence, I'm sure, were he given to saying such things about people."

The others nodded. Old Jack was notoriously stingy when it came to compliments.

Sandie understood why so much of Jackson's favor fell upon Stewart. The two men had first met at West Point, when Stewart was a young artillery instructor and Jackson was a cadet, and this was important since Jackson went on to become a gunner. They hadn't seen each other for many years, but the two had separately become remarkably similar men. Both left the army to become professors, and both were devout Presbyterians.

As everyone in army headquarters knew, the latter characteristic was especially important to Jackson, but so were Stewart's qualities as a general. Old Straight had certainly earned his nickname, Sandie thought, as he was always thoroughly prepared, and most important of all, he did what he was told with nary a word of complaint.

Sandie continued, saying softly "I think Jackson decided upon two things after the first week here, if not sooner. He wanted to be rid of Hardee, and he wanted Stewart's elevation. Well, we got the latter."

The four men passed the bottle for another round, and continued to talk shop for a time, until they were interrupted by an orderly.

"Colonel Pendleton, sir. General Cleburne is here to see you."

What's he doing here? Sandie thought. "Well, gentleman, I can't keep the General waiting. You fellows have a good night." Sandie saw them out, offered a salute and welcomed Cleburne in, then motioned the General to a seat and offered him the last of his brandy, which Cleburne politely refused.

"What can I do for you, General?"

The man standing before him was widely regarded as the best division commander in the Army of Tennessee, and unlike Hardee, Cleburne deserved his reputation. He was an Irishman and doctor's son, who had been in the British military for a time, before immigrating to Arkansas in his early 20s. A lean man in his mid-30s now, Cleburne's prominent cheekbones and charming smile had a way of distracting one from his cold, dark eyes.

"Colonel," Cleburne said, his accent giving his words a musical lilt "General Hardee made a request on my behalf to convene a meeting of this army's high command, so as to discuss a proposal I wish to make on a matter of national military policy. A matter, I believe, of the highest importance. That was refused. I then made a written request of my own, which was also refused. I have come to press my case in person."

So that was it. Sandie had been worried that Cleburne might have come to complain about Stewart's elevation, since he was Stewart's senior in rank by several months.

"Yes, I remember," Sandie said. "I told General Hardee when he came to see me that the commanding general is not in the habit of holding councils of war for any purpose other than issuing orders, and was opposed to convening any formal council such as you requested on that basis. I further told Hardee, you are free to discuss any proposal informally and with whomsoever you choose, and Jackson would be pleased to meet with you to discuss any matter formally and privately. I also indicated both to him and to you that you are free to submit any proposal to General Jackson, who will then send it to the War Department if found proper. But given his views and preferred arrangements, those are your options. May I be frank, sir?"

Cleburne nodded.

"I've been with General Jackson from almost the very beginning. He isn't given to committees and all that fuss and jawboning. If it's as important a matter as you say, he will want to hear it. If you want it sent to Richmond, he'll likely do it without prejudice. He just doesn't want to bother with that in front of nine other generals, each wanting their own say. Respectfully, sir, if you want every general in the army to chew the matter over, you ought to do that on your own hook, and you can if you wish. I said as much to Hardee. Did not the General relate that?"

"He did," Cleburne said. Actually, Hardee had related so little of it and colored it so negatively as to make the response from army headquarters sound like a flat refusal. It all sounded much more reasonable, here and now, and straight from the source.

Cleburne slapped his hands together. "Very well, Colonel. I wish to discuss my proposal with General Jackson. May I have an appointment?"

"Monday evening? After the day's duties?"

Cleburne agreed. "6'o clock Monday, then."

March 7
Early evening
Headquarters, Army of Tennessee, CSA
Dalton

Cleburne arrived at army headquarters a little before the appointed time, and marveled again at how Stonewall Jackson, despite the harsh winter climate of the north Georgia mountains, was living in a tent. A wall tent with an iron stove, but a tent all the same. And not just him. His entire headquarters was operating out of tents!

Generals typically appropriated the local houses for their quarters, regardless of season. In winter, colonels often had cabins built for them by slave laborers, and junior officers shared similar cabins between them. Only the rankers lived in anything like tents, and even then it was usually a log and mud walled structure, with the canvas tent serving as a roof. Cleburne thought nothing of it, since it was common practice and in keeping with what he had come to expect from his own time as a ranker in the British 41st Foot, where men of rank and standing lived accordingly. When he first saw Jackson and staff living and working in tents, he thought it eccentric to say the least.

Then Cleburne observed its effect on the men. The entire rank and file was rife with discontent when Jackson cancelled Hardee's generous furlough plan shortly after his arrival, but when they heard Jackson was living in a tent, just like the rest of them, the grumbling quieted. When more food started coming in, with more blankets and more shoes right behind, the ill-will dissipated and they forgot all about it. The Irishman soon followed the example, and moved his quarters to out of doors too, from a nice, comfortable house and into something more like what his field officers were using.

Cleburne was admitted, and found Jackson busy at work at his camp desk, back turned to the tent door.

Jackson said "Sit down, General. Please. I will be with you shortly." Upon reaching a good stopping point, Jackson stood, picking up his chair with his one arm. He turned it around and sat down again. "You have a proposal for the War Department?"

"Yes, sir. I would be grateful if you would forward this letter. It has been signed by several other senior officers of this army, and perhaps you might wish to endorse it as well." Cleburne reached into a leather case and withdrew a memorandum of some two dozen pages.

Jackson spoke softly. "Would you describe the contents for me?"

"Of course, sir. If it is not too punctilious, may I begin by stating my view on the state of our war effort?"

Jackson nodded his assent, so Cleburne continued. "In a word, our position is dreadful. For three years we have fought hard and fought well, but at a human cost unimaginable when we began. Many of our best men are now maimed or dead, and we have lost a third of our territory in the bargain. I reckon what we have lost, spent or seen ruined in this war exceeds in value the sum of all the world's treasure."

"I believe this has taken its toll on our people, General Jackson, and on our soldiers. On the surface, spirits remain good around our campfires and hearths, but underneath I suspect most see our defeat as eventual and inevitable, and are weary of sacrifice and slaughter to no useful gain."

Jackson interjected "I do not think so many are convinced of our 'inevitable defeat,' as you say, although I concede that events have shaken the faith of many of our people. But please continue."

"Yes, sir. I propose to bolster our war efforts and strike several blows at those of the Yankee with one action: emancipate the slaves."

Cleburne waited for a response to what he knew would be a controversial statement. Jackson blinked, but said nothing, so he continued. "I first must say I believe the negro, above all else, wishes to be free, with his family, and in the place he calls home. By freeing them all, he receives that, and far from being a liberator, the Yankee becomes an invader. The loyalty of most or nearly all of the once enslaved transfers from the Federals to ourselves with a pen stroke, and with that loyalty, we can raise tens of thousands of new soldiers before the start of the spring campaign. Perhaps hundreds of thousands before the end of this year."

"At the same time, we will take away from Lincoln the crutch of emancipation. So much of his political support comes from abolitionism, and all of his support in Europe derives from it. Without slavery, Lincoln might not survive the next election.

Without victories, he might not survive the next election. With negro soldiers, we hit him on both points. And I know the British, General Jackson. If we emancipate the negro ourselves, it revives the possibility of recognition from the British crown."

Jackson had listened silently, sitting at perfect attention, betraying no sign of emotion. He considered Cleburne for a short time.

Jackson said "You believe things are as bad as that?"

Cleburne nodded. "Yes. I absolutely believe it. This time, now, is the crisis of the war, sir. I fear only that our leaders may not treat it as such, and when they do take decisive action, it will be too late to achieve useful purpose."

Jackson thought it over for a while longer, finally saying "Your proposal has much to it on the grounds of military merit. I do not see our future as darkly as you, but I see the merit in it. Although I believe we are in the rights and will ultimately prevail through the blessings of Providence, I must confess I would gladly welcome the addition of even a single division of soldiers to this army, even if they must be Negroes."

Cleburne brightened, asking "Then you agree? You will endorse my memorandum?"

Jackson responded with a question. "Have you ever been to Virginia, general?"

"No, sir, I have not," Cleburne responded.

"It's not like here, or from what I am told, like South Carolina or Mississippi. Many of our negroes in the Old Dominion are artisans, house servants, or hired out as laborers. Virginia doesn't have these plantations, with their many hundreds of farm hands toiling from sun-up to sundown each and every day, like the Israelites in the Books of Genesis and Exodus. Many of the older folks will tell you they thought slavery would wither away, and many more disdain the institution, or at least its inseparable and morally degrading aspects. General Lee does, as do I."

"Even so," Jackson continued "Virginia had Nat Turner. And John Brown. My home of Lexington has few slaves, General Cleburne, and some free negroes. Even there, your proposal to arm the negro would meet with little enthusiasm and much hostility. I know this. I had a church school for them in Lexington, to teach the negro to read the Bible, and even with something so small and benign, there were whispers among my neighbors that I was breaking the law, and that teaching a negro to read the would make him uppity, would come to no right."

Cleburne said patiently "Not all Southrons see it that way. Many of my colonels and brigadiers have signed this memorandum, and I know Generals Hardee and Cheatham agree with me in principle."

Jackson nodded "Yes, yes, that may be so. But many others will not. If you had presented this to all the lieutenant and major generals of this army, as you had intended, you would have found that out. Half would be outraged, maybe more. I imagine one of them might have tried provoking you into a duel."

Cleburne's mood darkened. "Such a man would be welcome to try."

Jackson ignored that and continued. "Furthermore, I believe the very same purpose that animates our nation and wills us to victory will see your intentions defeated. Our war is about liberty, not slavery, but part of that liberty is the freedom to live in this society that Providence willed for us, and that society includes slavery. If you put this proposal before the government, you will turn every man determined to keep his high place in life and his property against you."

Cleburne stiffened, saying "If that is the price I must pay to ensure we win this war, I will pay it gladly. You will not submit my proposal then?"

"I did not say that," Jackson snapped irritably. Relaxing, he said "If you wish, I will forward it to the War Department, but with no comment. I cannot endorse it, but nor will I condemn it."

Cleburne thought that was fair, and said so. Jackson bade him good night and dismissed him.

Once he was gone, Jackson muttered to himself "I'll send it, but in the strictest confidentiality. Not to the War Department, but directly to the President."

This had to be kept from becoming more widely known, Jackson thought. Cleburne is an excellent officer, one I can't allow to go out and ruin himself.

When Jackson first came west, he found that Cleburne's Division was maintaining standards of drill and camp hygiene that were, if anything, higher than his own. It took much to impress Jackson, but Cleburne had managed it.

Even so, Jackson disagreed with Cleburne on one important point: the negroes would not make good soldiers. Some might, but not enough to make much difference.

If I could find 10,000 negroes who could be trained as soldiers, Jackson thought, I would not give up until I had them. I would resign if I could not get them. But there aren't that 10,000 darkie fighting men, nothing like it, not in the whole Confederacy.

March 14
Late evening
Headquarters, Hardee's Corps, Army of Tennessee, CSA
Huff House
Dalton

Cheatham was greeted by one of Hardee's aides at the front door, and shown into the parlor to warm himself by the fireplace. He was the first of Hardee's supper guests to arrive, and helped himself to the decanter and three-fingers of Kentucky bourbon before plopping himself into a rocking chair.

He asked the aide, who was on his way out of the parlor, "So who all is coming tonight?"

The aide replied in a clipped tone "Generals Cleburne and Hindman, sir."

That settled it, Cheatham thought as he sipped his bourbon and watched the aide go. Those few members of the "down with Bragg" faction still with the army would be present. Old Reliable has decided to give Stonewall Jackson a dose of the same medicine as old Bragg.

He took a swallow of the sweet, spicy liquid, and felt warmer almost at once. Well, it won't wash, he thought. It won't wash. Not with me. Not this time.

Cheatham had guessed what Hardee was about as soon as he received the invitation for supper. Old Reliable was dissatisfied, and looking to make some trouble for the commanding general when President Davis came to visit in a few days.

Hardee had been incensed when Jackson had canceled his furlough plan. Mind you, Cheatham thought, Old Jack went ahead with all furloughs already on the docket, and he gave Hardee leave in February to go marry that girl in Mississippi. A filly half his age, the randy old goat.

Yet Cheatham reckoned what upset fussy old Bill Hardee the most was that Jackson never consulted him. Stonewall Jackson never consulted with anyone in the army about anything, as near as Cheatham could tell. He wanted facts and obedience, not opinions and jawboning.

As the Tennessean had heard Hardee say many times over the years, he was a former commandant of West Point, the man who had written the textbook upon which this war was being fought. Cheatham had lately heard Hardee add that he had been ahead of Jackson on the lieutenant generals' list, just for good measure. God forbid a man fail to ask William J. Hardee what he thought on military matters, the pompous old donkey.

Cheatham had already made his mind up that he would have none of it, not this time. Oh, he disliked Jackson, not so much as Bragg, but disliked him all the same. The endless flow of work and criticism from army headquarters had left more than a few officers disgruntled in its wake, Cheatham included. Every division commander in the army had been verbally censured by Old Jack by now, all except for Cleburne and Stewart's successor Clayton, that is. Even Hood had gotten an earful, shoddy administrator that Hood was.

But Jackson wasn't Bragg. For one thing, Cheatham thought, if I had ever extended the olive branch to Bragg, he would likely have snatched it up and broken it over his spindly knee. But that wasn't all that separated Jackson from Bragg, abrasive as they both were. It took Cheatham a while to put his finger on why the discontented were reluctant to storm into Jackson's office, cuss the man, and nail their resignations to Old Jack's desk with an Arkansas toothpick, but then he went to Meridian.

Watching the Bishop's scrotum shrivel up in Mississippi made him see the contrast, clear as day. Jackson wasn't going to take any horseshit, and everyone knew it, just by looking at him. Stonewall Jackson was a lot like Andrew Jackson that way. Both those men were winners because they stopped at nothing to get what they wanted, and destroyed whoever got in their way.

Give Jackson cause, and he'd drum you right out of the army. If he didn't get his way with Richmond, he would post his resignation. Hardee might think otherwise, but Cheatham believed there wasn't a man in the Army of Tennessee Davis wouldn't cashier to keep Jackson, and the country would cheer Davis for doing it. He was certain of it, absolutely certain.

Cheatham had just polished off his bourbon when Cleburne and Hindman arrived. No, he thought. I have no love for Old Jack, but only a damned, blinkered fool would get in that man's way.

He rose to shake hands with his newly arrived colleagues. They were the most contrasting pair he knew of, and they were a pair, close friends before the war. Dark, fit, coldly severe Patrick Cleburne and short, foppish, prissy, volatile Thomas Hindman. Cheatham treated himself to another bourbon. He didn't offer the bottle to his fellow generals, as he knew both of them were temperance men.

A short while later, Hardee appeared. A white- and grey-haired man of 49, resplendent in his immaculate dress uniform, Hardee looked the part of the storybook Southern general. After greeting his guests, he ushered them to the dining table.

Just because I'm not in for Hardee's intentions doesn't mean I can't have myself a little fun, thought Cheatham. He looked forward to the coming conversation with relish.

The first course was a fine, well-aged Georgia ham. With several slices on his plate and a half-full tumbler of bourbon, Cheatham asked, eyes twinkling, "How do you reckon they are getting on together, old bastard Bragg and Jeff Davis?" referring to Bragg's appointment as Davis's chief military adviser.

"Bragg was always an excellent administrator," Hardee said smoothly "but never a leader of men, nor a competent strategist. Sitting behind a desk will bring out the best in Bragg, I'm sure."

"Davis takes fine care of his cronies, fine care" Hindman declared, a hint of malice in his tone. "Bragg loses all of Tennessee, and he gets promoted to a place in the executive office. Crippled Hood can barely ride a horse, and he gets an army corps. All the while, deserving, capable officers are left to whither on the vine, or else left to rot in the wilderness. Jackson's cut from the same cloth, promoting his favorite, Stewart."

He was referring to himself, Cleburne knew. Hindman had been the acting corps commander until Hood came along. Seeing Stewart promoted over his head, able or no, left him doubly aggrieved.

"Stewart," Cleburne said quietly "runs a very tight ship."

"Yes!" Hindman raised his voice. "And that's why Jackson loves him. They both have the souls of petty, tyrannical little men."

Enjoying himself immensely, Cheatham weighed in with a jab at Hindman. "Now see here, Hindman, old fellow, you can hardly say our Stonewall plays favorites. He brought Old Pegleg out of Virginia with him, you are quite right about that, and right about General Hood's sad, shattered state. Feller needs to be strapped to his horse just to ride. But old Stonewall stood Hood up against it over how he ran his corps, though, now didn't he?"

Hindman shot back "That just proves my point. The man is a petty tyrant. Even a Yankee wouldn't lord it over a proper gentleman so."

"Is Hood a proper gentleman?" Hardee asked sarcastically. That brought laughter, from all save Cleburne.

The house servants, all slaves, entered with the main course: a quarter of boiled mutton, served with cornbread and dishes of winter greens, small potatoes and pickled vegetables.

As the food was served, Hardee interjected "I thought General Jackson was perhaps too severe in his choices this winter. Canceling the furloughs was bad for morale. And ordering training marches in the dead of winter was foolhardy, very foolhardy, especially in view of the fact that many of the men lack proper shoes."

Cleburne replied "I found Jackson's general orders on training, discipline and camp management far from tyrannical. For the most part, my division already worked on such lines. As for winter marches, I've always felt that exercise is better for a man's health than keeping idle and indoors."

Both while he spoke and after, Cleburne avoided eye contact with Hardee. Usually one to handle difficulties head on, his choice of sides in this issue left him feeling guilty enough to shrink from a direct confrontation. Cleburne might have learned soldiering from the British, but he learned how to be an officer and general from Hardee. Like Cheatham, Cleburne knew what Hardee was about in inviting them all to dinner, and despite Hardee being his mentor, he wanted no part of it. Unlike Cheatham, the Irishman's motivation was respect, because while Jackson was undeniably difficult to get along with, he was undeniably a soldier of accomplishment.

Hardee stared at Cleburne for just a few seconds after the Irishman finished speaking, before returning to his meal, saying nothing. He realized that Cleburne had flown the nest, right there, at that very moment. Jeff Davis had once called Cleburne the "Stonewall Jackson of the West." Now Cleburne had thrown in his lot with the original article.

For the rest of the meal, Cleburne and Hardee said little, and nothing at all to each other, while Cheatham enjoyed arguing with Hindman. Coffee, real Yankee coffee, was served. After each man had drunk his cup, Hardee called the evening to an end. Later that night, Cheatham went to bed warm and satisfied; Cleburne melancholic; Hardee bitterly disappointed; and Hindman frustrated and annoyed.

March 17
Army of Tennessee, CSA
Below Taylor's Ridge
Dalton

Davis sat atop the wooden platform, quite happy with his decision to accept General Jackson's invitation to come to Georgia for a grand review of the Army of Tennessee. Although the air had a cold, damp quality that played merry hell with his rheumatism, the parade and its fife and drum music gave him such a warm glow that his stiff, aching bones seemed a world away. The weariness of his stop in Atlanta, pressed as he was there by complaints from Governor Joe Brown and the other Georgia grandees, was completely forgotten.

Many units of the army were on duty, mostly facing the northern aggressors from their perch on Rocky Face Ridge, but every division was represented here. Hardee's Corps had just marched by, and now came Stewart's Corps. Henry Clayton, newly promoted to major general and leading Stewart's old division, saluted the President with his sword. Davis returned the salute. Behind him marched serried ranks of Louisianans, Georgians and Alabamans. Next were the soldiers of Carter Stevenson, who Davis knew slightly from the Old Army and the Mexican War. Davis put out of his mind that Stevenson and his men had surrendered at Vicksburg, in favor of the thought that this division truly represented the breadth of the nation, with men from Tennessee, North Carolina, Virginia, Georgia and Alabama.

Davis glanced at Jackson, seated next to him. How he envied him. If Davis had his druthers, this is what he would be doing: leading the South's western army against the hated, lowborn invaders. Jackson looked even more like a leader of men than at any of their previous meetings, with a fine, new uniform and a glittering sword, which he knew were gifts from Generals Lee and Stuart.

Though his heart swelled with pride over the army before him, Davis still noticed the deficiencies. Unlike their commanding general in his new, natty attire, these tatterdemalion legions could never be described as regulation, as the only uniform features of the troops were their broad-rimmed felt hats and the gum blankets slung over their shoulders. The men were clothed in butternut, grey, faded brown, soiled white and much else in between. Many still lacked shoes. They carried all manner of arms, but at least they were all armed. The same could barely be said of the artillery. Half the cannon that clattered by were puny six pounders, and the horses pulling them looked thin and ragged.

We have never enjoyed the material riches of the Yankee, Davis thought, but with these men, we will whip him all the same. We Southrons are the superior breed. We whupped the Britisher twice and the Mexican once, we and not the Northron, who are a race of mere pasty mechanics and weakling shop clerks.

The appearance of blue flags with silver moons heralded the arrival of Cleburne's Division, the only division in the Confederate Army allowed a battle flag all its own, the forefront of Hood's Corps. The Arkansans, Alabamans, Tennesseans, Texans and Mississippians of this division were the neatest marchers by far, the best at close-order drill. Behind them were the looser ranks of Cheatham's hard-brawling Tennesseans.

Thinking of Cleburne, Davis folded his arms across his chest. Jackson did the right thing in sending him that proposal to arm the slaves in confidence, he thought. As far as Davis knew, only Jackson, himself and Cleburne knew anything about it. The matter was incendiary, terrifically incendiary, the sort of thing only a foreigner or a damned fool would propose. Cleburne was no fool, but he was certainly not really a Southron either.

The band began playing "Stonewall Jackson's Way," producing a deafening cacophony of wild cheering from the ranks, the likes of which had never even been approached in Davis's experience. He noticed with some amusement that Jackson had turned bright red, and it was only with some reluctance that the man took off his hat and waved at his troops. By the time the din had subsided, Hood's Corps had passed, and Walker's cavalry rode in.

With the review over and the bulk of the Army of the Tennessee drawn up on the plain, Davis went to the podium to deliver the expected speech. Many in the army were too far away to hear him, but the speech had already been printed, and would be distributed around the camps by suppertime.

All gave the President their attention as he struck his points: that the Southern states had the inalienable right to secede from the Union; that the Yankees were responsible for this war and all its hardships, for it was they who invaded Southern homes, burned Southern crops and insulted Southern women; that the Confederacy wished only to go its own way and to be left in peace; that it was they, and not the Northron, who were the true heirs of the hallowed Revolution; that the war was being fought to secure the rights of that Revolution, not slavery; that the North had an immeasurably more difficult task, to subdue a free people and occupy a vast country; and that if the Southron only stood firm in defiance, the war would most certainly be won.

Jackson studied Davis closely, for this was the first time he had ever heard the President speak. In the past, he had assumed Davis was just another politician, and considered most politicians a gang of charlatans, parasites, scoundrels and harlots, attracted by a profession that gave great rewards to men who were willing to say or do anything, and say or do it loudly. There were exceptions, of course, such as Congressman Alexander Boetler and Virginia Governor John Letcher, or the past, great presidents like Washington, Jefferson and Madison. Yet these were few, and for much of the war Jackson had not counted Davis among them.

That began to change after taking this command. Following Lee's advice, Jackson scrupulously kept Davis informed of everything he did, flooding the wire with reports. Whenever time permitted, such as with his dearly desired promotion of Stewart, he asked for

Davis's opinion or presented him with options. And Jackson came to see that Davis was an honorable man who returned respect with respect, loyalty with loyalty, even when it cost him, as it undoubtedly had in Jackson's clashes with the Commissary Department and Joe Brown.

Jackson had heard many such speeches as the one Davis delivered, almost always coming from men who could be serving in the field and weren't; who had served, but left in a huff over some matter of rank and status; men who held their pride, lands and slaves dearer than their liberty. Davis was clearly not one of them. You only had to listen to the man to know he believed every single word, Jackson thought. Here was a man who would never surrender, never submit, never give in. Never.

Davis reached his peroration, and the Army of the Tennessee cheered him. Jackson clapped loudly, sprang to his feet and extended his hand to Davis. "Thank you, Mr. President. Thank you."

Seeing Old Jack and the President shaking hands only caused the troops to cheer louder. Visibly taken aback, Davis stammered "You're welcome, General. You are most welcome."

Riding back to Jackson's headquarters tent village, Davis thought he had much to be pleased with in Jackson. His reaction to Sherman's raid of a month ago was a model for how Davis had always wanted things handled in the West: prompt action combined with due deference to Richmond. If shaking the military administration of Georgia to the roots had caused Davis no end of political headaches, he at least felt consoled in the results produced. Even Lee's army in faraway Virginia was eating a little better because of it.

Davis was so pleased that he made a point of saying so when they reached Jackson's headquarters. "I commend you on the state of your army, General Jackson. To these old eyes, no army has exhibited such high morale since Caesar's Gallic legions. You have worked wonders here. The nation will have cause to thank you for it all soon, of that I am sure, as I thank you now."

Jackson said softly "You are welcome, Mr. President, but thanks for my part are unnecessary. Thanks should be paid to the Almighty. Any gratitude after that goes to the men themselves, and the staff I have been so greatly blessed with."

Davis dismounted, declaring "Well said, sir. Well said."

Jackson dismounted, and upon entering his tent, he offered the President hot lime water. "My staff was able to procure some honey, and the limes from the coastal regions. I fear no lemons were available."

Davis nodded his assent. "Of course," he said, thinking lime water was a strange idea, never mind hot lime water, but he was too polite to refuse.

Jackson poured Davis and himself a cup, and the two men sat down.

"Mr. President, now that we are face to face, allow me to express my sincere apologies on rejecting the offensive plan submitted to me by yourself and General Bragg," Jackson began. "But my study of the circumstances of this army, the enemy strength and the topography of this country led me to conclude it was not feasible."

Davis nodded. "Yes. Your memorandum was quite specific, and your subsequent reports buttressed your case quite clearly."

Davis and Bragg had proposed that Jackson, reinforced by a division from Polk's force in Alabama and a division from Beauregard in the Carolinas, join Longstreet's Corps in East Tennessee and with a combined army of over 70,000, invade Middle Tennessee and perhaps even Kentucky. Jackson had demurred, insisting that East Tennessee was a desert for an army, he could not live off the land there, and in winter it lacked even the sparsest vegetation for his animals. According to a report filed later by Jackson's quartermaster, Harman, the army would need an additional 900 wagons and 3,000 mules to carry all the necessary supplies for the effort. Even then, the necessity of having to take such a ponderous wagon train over the mountain roads would prevent the rapid movements necessary for success.

There had been two features of Jackson's rejection of the plan that had mollified Davis. First was the disclaimer that Jackson would see to it the wagons were built and the plan attempted anyway, but only if the 3,000 mules could be procured, hinting that he could find those necessary mules from the state of Georgia, were he given a free hand to requisition them. The other was that Jackson insisted that Lee would have need of Longstreet's Corps before long, so it should not factor into any offensive planning for the West. Davis could not recall even Robert E. Lee refusing the offer of a large body of reinforcements for the sake of a different department.

Davis might have been less mollified if he had known Jackson did not want Longstreet because he feared Old Peter's jealousy and resentment might make him impossible to work with. Jackson had kept that to himself, however.

"So, General Jackson, I take it you invited me out here to present a plan of your own devising? The plan you promised in December?"

Jackson nodded. "Yes, yes. If you will recall my reports on the Federal strength, you know that George Thomas has an army of three corps in and about Chattanooga; James B. McPherson has a strong corps in northeastern Alabama; and John Schofield has a corps, mostly of green recruits, in Knoxville. In aggregate, this force must number at least 110,000 strong, much more than double my own strength, but at this moment it is spread out over a distance of some 200 miles. It is my intention to take advantage of that dispersion by misdirecting the enemy, rapidly concentrate against one part of his host, smash it before they can launch their own offensive, and defeat them in detail."

"That was part of the plan laid by General Bragg and myself, to march against Knoxville."

Jackson nodded. "I recognize that, sir. As you know, we lack the transportation to move directly on East Tennessee, but my greatest concern is not the need to carry every biscuit and bale of hay. I am convinced that even were the transportation available, Schofield would retreat beyond our grasp before we could trap him. Celerity in those mountains, in this weather, and with a long wagon train is all but impossible, and without celerity we cannot achieve surprise. Without surprise, the endeavor must certainly fail."

"Then what do you propose instead?" Davis asked.

"To shift the corps of Hood and Stewart by rail to Selma, join with Polk, and invade Middle Tennessee directly. Once there, to destroy McPherson's Corps and get astride Sherman's supply lines into Chattanooga. To pry Thomas and perhaps Schofield out of East Tennessee, defeat them as well, and affect the liberation of Middle and East Tennessee."

Jackson's reply was so matter-of-fact, Davis was not sure he had heard it correctly. "I beg your pardon? How is removing more than half your army from before Atlanta more practicable than a direct invasion of East Tennessee?"

Assuming the patient, methodical tone he used many times in the classroom at VMI, Jackson said "The movement will rely on the railroad, at least as far as Selma. Based on the experience garnered from dispatching Cheatham's Division to Demopolis a month ago, my staff has drawn up a plan for shipping the two corps, plus the artillery, wagons and part of the necessary supplies. We can complete the move to Selma in three weeks."

Davis caught on. "You have known you wanted to do this for a month now!"

Jackson nodded. "Yessir. I wanted to study the matter thoroughly before submitting it to you."

"That is all very well and good, but I still cannot see how this is any better. If your intention is to attack McPherson, won't he retreat back on Thomas? And if surprise is so important, just how do you intend to keep the movement of two army corps a secret?

"Confusion and misdirection, Mr. President. And for that, I require your assistance."

Davis said cautiously "Go on."

"I forwarded to you a plan from General Polk, requesting that I reinforce him with one army corps for a raid on Middle Tennessee. I disapproved it."

Davis nodded. "Yes." He had also received the plan separately from General Polk, but there was no need for Jackson to know of that. Davis did not approve of Polk's campaign proposal either, and he knew Jackson was touchy on the matter of all communications with the War Department passing through his headquarters.

"I want you to give your blessing to Polk's plan, and more to the point, I want you to publicly announce your approval of it as soon as possible, and ensure the details of the plan appear in the Atlanta and Richmond papers."

"The enemy will receive all manner of reports from their spies," Jackson said, practically spitting on the last word. While Jackson had much use for spies himself, he detested any Southern man who spied for the enemy as the vilest, most cowardly form of traitor. "I will do everything in my power to obfuscate those reports, for I want the only clear reports reaching Yankee ears to be the ones coming from the halls of the Capitol. When the enemy hears from

Georgia that I have sent one division, two divisions, four divisions or my entire army to Polk, I want them reading about Polk's plan in the papers and from their spies."

Davis saw the virtues of it, because he could imagine how such a scheme might work on his own people. If Lincoln, Grant, Halleck, Sherman and the rest were expecting Jackson to send troops to Polk, and for Polk to mount a raid, they might discount those reports from Georgia that conflicted with that expectation. He knew from his own experience that intelligence reports rarely agreed on anything when it came to enemy intentions or troop numbers, and deducing what the enemy was up to and in what strength was all a matter of educated guesswork. As he thought it over, he wondered if such a bit of legerdemain might not fool him as well.

"So when you march from Selma, they will think you are Polk, and have only two army corps instead of three. And that is what will keep McPherson from falling back on Thomas?"

"If Providence wills it, sir. I expect they will send McPherson to intercept the raid, rather than allow it to advance into Middle Tennessee."

"And when do you propose to start?"

Jackson smiled. "As soon as you order me to send an army corps to Polk."

CHAPTER 6

March 24
Early morning
Headquarters, Army of Tennessee
Dalton, Georgia

Jackson set the papers down on his desk, and turned to face his officers. "Satisfactory, Sandie. Harman. Satisfactory. Three weeks to move Hood and Stewart to Selma. Put it into action. At once."

Harman and Sandie grinned. "Satisfactory" was high praise in Jackson's army. The two men were pale and bleary-eyed, having worked through the night to put the finishing touches on their plan, but excited nonetheless.

Rising from his seat slowly, Harman half-stretched his tired body as he came to attention. Shorn of sleep as he was, his eyes were clear. The first stage of the plan called for shipping the supplies, the wagons and the pontoon train. That was his department. He saluted with a "Yessir" and left.

Old Jack never shared his plans. He told you what to do, but never why. Yet for this campaign, Jackson had to share at least some of his intentions with his chief of staff and his quartermaster, because moving the men, mules, horses, guns, wagons, ambulances and supplies of two army corps was not something that could be improvised, and it was too complex for him to direct alone.

Now Sandie and Harman were the only men in the army who knew what their chief intended. The prospect of invading Tennessee was exciting as it was, but carrying and keeping such a secret was more so, lending them renewed vigor.

In hindsight, Sandie could see that Jackson had intended this change of base for many weeks, perhaps all along. In the first week after taking command, Jackson told him to put some railroad men onto the staff, who were then sent out to inspect every locomotive, every station, and nearly every rail car and section of track. Scouts had been dispatched investigate crossing points for the Tennessee River. Such work was typical under Jackson, who liked to plan for every contingency, so the staff never wondered about it, and outside Jackson's staff hardly anyone noticed.

Sandie was thankful he had brought with him the records from Richmond covering Braxton Bragg's 1862 change of base from Mississippi to Chattanooga. In Sandie's opinion, that movement was brilliantly conceived and executed, and it gave him a working model for his own plan.

"Now, sir, I have the telegraphy. General Polk has sent you his dispositions, as you requested." Polk was always prompt when he was getting what he wanted, Sandie smirked to himself.

Jackson took the papers from Sandie, and read through them. For his "raid," Polk intended to concentrate the infantry divisions of Samuel French and W.W. Loring.

"Loring" Jackson grumbled aloud. Man would bear watching, he thought.

Continuing, Jackson saw that Polk also meant to bring the cavalry divisions of Red Jackson and Nathan Bedford Forrest. Jackson had ordered Polk to supply his own cavalry from the outsized force of horsemen in his department, and Polk had complied. That was important, as it meant Jackson had no need to bring any of Wheeler's cavalry from Georgia with him, lightening his transportation burden. Finally, S.D. Lee would command the balance of the cavalry in Polk's department, shielding western Mississippi.

"Hurm. Forrest." There was that name again. In the East, Forrest had the reputation of being merely a talented cavalry raider, but the reports Jackson had read since his appointment as Army of Tennessee commander pointed to a man who was something more than that. There was no time to finish reviewing the mountain of paperwork, however, and there was a better way to get to the bottom of who the man was.

"Sandie, send over to General Wheeler. He is to report to me at his earliest convenience, but sometime before midday. And tell him

I want any brigadier or colonel who has served under General Forrest sent to me later this afternoon."

April 2
Early afternoon
Headquarters, Military Division of the Mississippi, USA
Nashville, Tennessee

Major Audenried found Sherman in high feather that morning, chewing on stewed chicken and going about his paperwork.

Sherman swallowed and said "Ah! Joseph. Come on in. Is that the latest from the telegraph office? Set it down here."

Audenried smiled an easy, pleasant smile. "Yessir. May I ask what has you in such a fair mood?"

Sherman wiped the grease from his fingers with a napkin, took up a piece of paper, shook it at Audenried, and then motioned for him to sit down. "This, my dear fellow, is my authorization from Secretary Stanton to take possession of all the railroads in the department. I've already told Colonel Anderson to seize every locomotive and car that comes into Nashville, and put them to work pushing supplies down to Chattanooga."

"That's marvelous news, sir."

Sherman was very nervous about matters of supply, given that his armies were at the end of a railroad line stretching back 300 miles, all the way back to Louisville, Kentucky. Half of that was hostile territory. Everyone knew that once the campaign started, Rebel raiders would play merry hell with that supply line wherever and whenever they could.

Part of Sherman's answer to this problem was to build up enough ammunition, food, forage, and sundries in Chattanooga to supply 100,000 men and 35,000 animals for 70 days. The difficulty wasn't collecting all that materiel, as Nashville was already a vast, bustling supply base, surely the largest in the world. Instead, the trouble was moving that materiel down to Chattanooga. With control of the railroads, Sherman could organize things as he saw fit.

"How long do you think it will take to push all the materiel down the line?" Audenried asked.

"30 days, give or take." Having delivered his news, Sherman returned reading the new reports and munching on his dinner.

Sherman had complete confidence in that figure. Although his quartermasters would need a day or two to sort out the new timetables, he had all the facts and figures memorized, and had already clicked away in his head at the sums. He knew it could be done if his people were efficient, and he had made sure a long time ago that they were quite efficient.

He read through half a dozen pages at a fast clip, absorbing every word faster than most men could merely glance things over. Then Sherman noticed something that made him remember his meeting with Banks the month before.

"Oh, Audenried. Send to General Corse. Smith and his boys ought to be leaving Banks in Louisiana and on his way back to us by now, but Banks is being evasive about it. Tell Corse he is to get down there and move things along."

"Yessir." Corse was Sherman's inspector general and chief troubleshooter.

Grant will send preemptory orders to Banks if need be, Sherman thought, and even halt the entire Red River business if that is what it takes. Still, I'm in Nashville and Grant is in Washington. It always helps to have a man on the spot if you want to get things done.

Sherman took up a new page, and his countenance suddenly darkened. General Thomas in Chattanooga had sent a report from his spies that infantry had departed from Dalton for Atlanta.

That settled it, Sherman thought. The War Department had been sending him reports these last few weeks that Richmond had approved a major raid under Bishop Polk, probably to try and cut his supply lines. Spies and newspapers were all indicating that Jackson would receive reinforcements from the Carolinas, and that Jackson, in turn, would reinforce Polk.

"Well, Major, I suppose we had to expect the Johnnies to make some kind of spoiling attack on us. Now we know. Bishop Polk is coming this way. Reckon he wants to serve me a taste of my own medicine."

That brought chuckles from Audenried, but the matter was serious enough. Sherman couldn't let Polk just stroll into Tennessee. The damage even the fumbling Bishop Polk could do with 25,000 infantry at his back would be bad enough, and the newspapers would go mad with exaggeration over the whole business. The only proper use for a newspaper is wiping your backside, Sherman thought, but people still read and believe that trash, God knows why.

He would have to send McPherson. McPherson was posted in northeastern Alabama, the closest to Polk's Tennessee River starting line. McPherson's Army of the Tennessee had five infantry divisions, and most of a sixth could be mustered up by pulling his Tennessee River garrisons back in, leaving behind just what handful of men were needed to hold Rebel banditry at bay. Sherman ran the figures in his head, and estimated McPherson would have 28,000 infantry and artillery, all of them Grant's hardened veterans, the best fighting men in the world.

Was he ready for the job? Sherman thought. He, Grant and many others beside thought of McPherson as the great, rising man of the war. More than once both he and Grant had agreed that if either of them were killed, it would be McPherson who would step into the gap and help finish the job. McPherson had done well at the head of a corps in Vicksburg, but as an army commander Sherman had always intended McPherson to operate under his loose supervision in Georgia.

Sherman looked at Audenried. "Major, you have writing materials? Good. Take this down."

He began dictating orders for McPherson to concentrate, collect supplies, and be ready to change his base and move to intercept Polk once that situation developed. As he spoke, he realized McPherson would need more cavalry. Kilpatrick was with McPherson, but with only a small force at hand. More than 4,000 horsemen were refitting in Franklin, only 20 miles down the road from Nashville. Some of those troopers must be made ready for action immediately.

He snatched up the draft once Audenried finished writing, reviewed it, made some changes and gave it back. "Take that to the chief of staff. And tell an orderly to have my horse saddled and an escort readied. I depart for Franklin directly."

April 7
Mid-morning
Headquarters, Army of Tennessee, CSA
Dalton, Georgia

Jackson's chief aide, James Power Smith, pulled back the flaps of the headquarters tent, and found Jackson busy at his desk. "General?"

Jackson half turned, pen still poised above the page. "Yes, Captain?"

"General Hardee is here to see you. His appointment, sir? He is a tad early."

Hardee was punctual, Jackson thought. By the book. At least that much could be said about him. "Fetch Sandie. Then bring him in."

Jackson put his papers away and composed his thoughts. The last of Stewart's Corps was departing today. The first of Hood's Corps would follow tomorrow. The time had come to tell Hardee he was being left behind to shield Atlanta. Hardee was an old soldier, and ought to obey orders. Yet too many old soldiers in this army obeyed only when and how they wished, and he didn't trust Hardee.

Besides, he was reluctant to share his intentions with anyone, even his most trusted. "If my hat knew my intentions" Jackson muttered, "I would snatch it from my head and shove it into the stove."

With his chief of staff and senior corps commander present, Jackson stood up and began. "General Hardee, tomorrow morning I have scheduled two important actions. First, a new division of infantry from the Carolinas will begin arriving in Atlanta, and Edward Walthall will assume command."

Hardee nodded with approval. He had been expecting the arrival of the new division, organized from brigades in the Carolinas. Walthall, a brigadier in Hindman's Division, was a good choice for the new command.

"Second, Hood's Corps will begin departing Dalton for Montgomery, and ultimately Selma, following Stewart's Corps. I shall accompany them. You will remain here, in command of four divisions of infantry and all of General Wheeler's cavalry. Your force, designated the Army of Georgia, is initially tasked with shielding Atlanta while I invade Middle Tennessee with the corps of Polk, Hood and Stewart."

Hardee blinked, and cried "What?"

"Invading Middle Tennessee." Jackson handed Hardee a sheaf of papers. "You shall command four divisions plus Wheeler during my absence. I have drawn up detailed written orders for you. In summary, your immediate tasks are to demonstrate before the enemy, so as to make your force appear larger and conceal the departure of Hood's Corps. Your orders contain several specific means for doing this, and you shall apply them all, along with any you see fit to add."

"Wheeler's cavalry is to patrol aggressively, as well as to block every pass into North Georgia, and take every step to inhibit spying and scouting. This is also described in detail in your written orders. Finally, you are to share this information with no one. If asked by one of your generals or a civilian authority where Hood or Stewart or myself have gone, you will deny they have left or answer with one of the stories provided."

"General Jackson, I must protest!" Hardee declared. "You leave me here with, what, 25,000 men? To oppose four times that number!"

Jackson replied patiently "Plus Wheeler, who has 9,000 cavalry. Intelligence indicates the enemy has no intention of advancing until May, and then in concert with their offensive in Virginia. The enemy army is not in close contact with our front on Rocky Face Ridge, and if you conduct your misdirection competently, they will not learn of our absence until after we have crossed the Tennessee River."

Hardee retorted "Only a third of Wheeler's men have horses, and most of the rest are off looking for new mounts. And this violates the laws of war! You are dividing our force instead of concentrating it, attempting two large projects at once, and all in the face of the enemy!"

Sandie grimaced. Jackson wouldn't care for being lectured so. Yet he held his tongue. He knew full well the only cause for his presence was to provide a witness, in the event that Hardee made an insubordinate threat of one kind or another.

"If the enemy advances upon you," Jackson continued icily, "either in whole or in part, my topographical department has prepared a detailed study of all the ground between here and Atlanta. Several lines of defense are suggested, where you can force the enemy to deploy, and perhaps even to attack you at your advantage."

Jackson could see that Hardee wasn't really listening to him, preferring to focus instead on complaining. He knew Hardee had already refused command of this army, and could tell he took pleasure in playing the role of the army's grand old sage, always ready with textbook answers and criticisms. Jackson had surmised that Hardee wanted no part of the ultimate responsibility of leading a field army, even the smaller field army Jackson was thrusting upon him.

"General Jackson" Hardee said, becoming visibly agitated, "I find your plans militarily unsound, and protest them on the gravest terms. I urge you to reconsider, sir. If you do not, I fear my lack of confidence in them compels me to request relief."

Jackson glared at him, shouting "General Hardee, if you truly wish to be relieved of your command, you are free to submit a formal request before I depart for Atlanta. I will endorse it. In the meantime, your orders stand. You will obey them to the letter, you will speak to no one of either this conversation or your orders except as specifically permitted, and you will continue to do so until such time the War Department sends a suitable replacement for you. Dismissed!"

Jackson watched him storm out. If he resigned, Jackson thought, good riddance to the man.

Sandie said quietly "If I may say so, sir, is it wise, leaving Hardee here?"

Jackson nodded. "Yes, yes." He wished he was as confident as he sounded. He would prefer to get rid of Hardee, and bring Richard Taylor in from Louisiana. But that would not happen, not unless Hardee consented to go, and like it or not the fussy, pedantic Georgian was among the best-qualified for the task of protecting Atlanta.

Sandie nodded. "Yessir. Do you think Hardee will go so far as to resign?" He worried that it was usually best to not have a man leading an enterprise if that man was convinced of its failure.

Jackson shrugged. "I do not know. If he does, Davis will try to persuade him otherwise for a time, then transfer him to some out of the way place. Hardee must know that. If he stays, he will follow his orders, if only to shield himself from blame."

If he does not follow his orders, Jackson thought, Hardee will bring down upon himself the selfsame disaster he dreads so.

April 12
Late afternoon
41st Tennessee Infantry, Maney's Brigade, CSA
Montgomery, Alabama

Fletcher was the first of his company to hop off the rail carriage, quickly stepping out to face the car from which his men were emerging. He had most of them collected when the bugle called for assembly, and the entire regiment fell into line.

Coming to attention, Fletcher sneaked a look over to the station platform. Old Straight was there, having a word with George Maney. Whatever it was, George didn't look happy.

Fletcher had never stopped thinking of his brigade commander as "George." He had known General Maney before the war, when Maney had split his time between a successful law practice in Franklin and serving in the state legislature. They had been on opposing sides of a couple of cases, and he had gone to Maney for advice a number of times as well. Maney was about a dozen years older, and enjoyed the measure of success Fletcher wanted for himself.

General Maney stepped to the edge of the platform, before the center of his brigade. "Boys, I'm afraid I have some bad news. Last time we came by here, it was by river to Selma. Well, General Stewart tells me that there aren't enough boats. Some steamers broke their engines, some barges have burst their seams. Laid up for repairs. Can't wait here for our turn, so we're walking."

A year ago, that would have produced groans, Fletcher thought. Not now, though. Things were much tighter in Jackson's army.

Maney paused, and Fletcher thought Maney might be waiting for groans himself. When there were none, he continued. "Now here's the good news. We're due in Selma in four days, boys. That's about 16 miles a day, give or take, and we'll have the road all to ourselves. Some other boys went ahead of us, but they left yesterday. And General Stewart's seen to it that commissary wagons are waiting for us all down the road, so no need for you boys to carry rations."

There wasn't even a murmur, and Fletcher could feel the men brightening all around him. No soldier would ever complain of being relieved of the burden of carrying rations for a four-day route march.

"Now, I feel the need to remind you boys, since we're taking to the road. According to our special orders, we keep our flags rolled up. If you meet a civilian or an officer or a soldier who is unknown to you, you are not to tell him where you are from, what unit you are with, where you are going or what officers you serve under. In fact, the less you tell that fellow, the better. Disobedience to this order will meet with the severest penalties, understood?"

A deep, loud "Yessir!" rose from the ranks.

"Alright then. We camp outside of town tonight. One more piece of good news. General Stewart asked the fine citizens of Montgomery to furnish us with a hot supper. So there's plenty of Brunswick stew and buttermilk cornbread waiting for us."

That brought a chorus of enthusiastic cheering. The brigade marched out of the rail yard and through Montgomery, but unlike their last visit in February, they avoided the center of town.

Another thing that's different, Fletcher thought. All the secrecy. Fletcher wasn't sure how much of Cheatham's Division was even going to Selma, just as he didn't know for sure they had been going to Selma until just now.

The next day, in high spirits from a fine breakfast of leftovers from previous night's fare, Maney's Brigade set out on the Selma Road, marching according to Jackson's rule: march for 50 minutes, rest for 10 minutes, and march again. The roads were muddy, but hardly the worst Fletcher had seen. That night the brigade camped near Magnolia Crest House. The next day, they resumed the road march and reached White Hall Plantation.

The regiment fell out. Most of the men lined up at the commissary wagons to receive their ration of corn meal for that night and the next day. Looking over to White Hall, Fletcher had an idea. After asking Colonel Tillman for permission, he went over to the house, and returned about 20 minutes later with a bundle of old bailing wire in one hand, and a piece of paper in the other.

Fletcher carried his wares straight over to the Grimes brothers. "Evening, boys."

The boys had their shoes off, airing out their feet. "Evening, sir" they replied in unison, both sounding a bit suspicious. Fletcher was being casual, so they didn't bother to get up or salute.

"I have a use for your talents, boys." He tossed the bailing wire down by where Nathan was laying. "Over yonder is a bend in the river. I reckon if you boys set some snares, we'll have fresh meat for breakfast."

The brothers relaxed. They had been trapping since they could walk, filling out what little their father put on the table, and they enjoyed doing it.

"Get your shoes on, and get out there while there's still some daylight. This pass will see you through." He proffered the paper to Willie, who sat up and took it. "Just so long as you steer clear of the big house, there. The duty officer will wake you before reveille, so you can check your traps and be back before breakfast."

The boys set out, walking the stiffness out of their backs and limbs, and carrying their muskets should they run into bigger game. They stopped only long enough to ask the darkies what the easiest way down to the river was. The slaves pointed them to a place they called Enconochaca, warning that it was haunted from a fight with the Creeks that took place there many years before.

"Good" Nathan said, as they walked away. "I reckon either the darkies ain't trapping there because they scared, or the trapping's so good they don't want us going down there."

The boys went looking for animal tracks, laying rabbit snares and squirrel poles until the setting sun turned the light red. Not sure where they were exactly, they turned south and trudged toward where they knew the road would be.

Emerging from the woods and onto the road, the brothers found themselves face to face with a mounted captain wearing a fine, clean uniform, who called them to attention. Behind the captain was a small party, all mounted. A one-armed colonel in a shabby coat and cap rode forward.

"You men, what are you doing here?" he demanded.

Nathan replied "We's on a detail, sir." He looked up at the colonel, but couldn't really see his face in the shadows.

"Do you have any papers?" the colonel asked sharply. The colonel had a funny way of holding the reins, the boys thought. His thumb was sticking up for no reason.

"Yessir." There was a pause, and Nathan realized nothing was happening. He nudged Willie with his elbow. "Give it to him."

Willie shook his head.

The colonel grew impatient. "Do you have the pass or don't you?"

"Colonel, sir," Willie said quietly, "Our paper says our regiment, our colonel and our captain. We's under orders, sir, not to tell none of that to anyone strange, including officers. I reckon I can't give it to you. Sir." Willie saluted again, to emphasize his obedience.

Willie's words were met with silence, and then the shabby colonel laughed, slapping his hand on his thigh. "Good, good. That's good."

April 15
Mid-morning
The Lee House
Headquarters, Army of Mississippi, CSA
Selma

Polk had come to Selma to meet the reinforcements for his raid, and had chosen the Lee House for his quarters. He liked the fine Greek Revival house for its stately appearance; for its location, only five blocks from the Selma Ordnance and Naval Foundry, where his reinforcements were arriving; and because he appreciated the serendipity that it was built by cousin of the famed Robert E. Lee.

After a leisurely breakfast, Polk strode down to the riverfront arsenal, where he had occupied some offices and set up headquarters. A.P Stewart himself had yet to arrive, but the last of his troops had already begun to offload from the river boats and barges ferrying them down from Montgomery.

Polk was in an expansive mood as he sat down at his desk. Stonewall Jackson had thoughtfully sent a large quantity of supplies before Stewart, so he needn't worry about the grimy business of keeping his Army of Mississippi in biscuits and bullets. Since the

Yankees had abandoned Corinth in January, and the railroads around Meridian and Corinth had both been repaired, those supplies could be sent by train to Florence. It was a rickety, roundabout ride to be sure, but quicker than mule-drawn wagons over central Alabama. The rest he would forage from Tennessee itself.

A few days to rest the men and organize them, and he would push on. Polk expected that by the time he was over the Tennessee line, Jackson would be busy with the drudgery of fending off Sherman, while he basked in the glory of marching on Nashville.

He had just begun composing a report for Richmond when an aide knocked at his door.

"General Polk, there is a Colonel Milner just arrived. He says he is from General Stewart's staff and has important business with you."

Polk replied "Yes, please show him in, son." He watched as a colonel in a disgracefully seedy coat, muddy trousers and boots entered his office.

The colonel said "Thank you, lieutenant," and closed the door himself. He doffed the crumpled cap from his head.

Haltingly, Polk said "General... Jackson? Stonewall Jackson?" Polk had never met the man before, and knew him only from newspaper sketches and other such things.

"Yes, yes. Pleased to make your acquaintance General Polk."

Jackson stood waiting. Flabbergasted, Polk realized that he was waiting for a salute. Polk stood to attention and gave him one. Jackson returned it.

Taking a seat, Jackson said "I must apologize for this deception, but it is very necessary. Very necessary. No one is to know of my presence here. You are to remain in titular command of this expedition, with private orders emanating from me through General Stewart's headquarters."

Polk hid his growing sense of alarm. "Titular command, sir? But, this is my raid. The Army of Mississippi is to strike Middle Tennessee. I have orders from Richmond."

"That is part of my deception. You still are invading Middle Tennessee. Only you are going with your men, Stewart, and Hood. I have here a letter from President Davis. He asked me to give it to you. And it goes without saying, General Polk, that your department is legally part of my command."

Polk took the letter, replying weakly "Yes, of course."

"What are your dispositions?"

"Red Jackson's cavalry is here in Selma" Polk said mechanically. "My infantry is in Demopolis. Forrest's cavalry is in Tuscaloosa."

"Good, good" Jackson nodded. "Hood's Corps will be here in Selma by day's end tomorrow. The 17th is the Sabbath, so the army will rest then. On Monday, we march. You rejoin your Army of Mississippi in Demopolis, now a corps in the Army of Tennessee, and we will advance north on parallel roads. Draw up orders for Forrest to remain far in advance of our columns, with the mission of advanced reconnaissance and driving off any enemy cavalry he should encounter. Red Jackson's cavalry will provide close security and serve as Forrest's support."

"The Sabbath, yes. I shall draw up the orders for Forrest, as you say."

Jackson stood up. "Good day, General Polk."

Polk sat immobile for a time. Then he picked up the letter from Jefferson Davis. Silently, he crumpled its ends in both hands, and tore it apart.

CHAPTER 7

April 19
After dawn
Kilpatrick's Division, Army of the Tennessee, USA
Southwest of Jasper, Alabama

The Confederate outriders came down the road at a trot, a motley party of a few dozen. Behind them followed the rest of their regiment. They came through lightly forested country into an open field, passing a pasture marked by a low stone wall, to climb a gentle slope up to the farm cabin at the top. Upon reaching the crest, the outriders were greeted by a hail of bullets.

With the sound of gunfire, the blue horse troopers hiding behind the stone wall sprang up, leveled their carbines, and raked the main body of the Rebels. Many fell in that first volley, and many more were cut down in the confusion and awkward turning about that followed. A bugler tried to sound "Come About," but he too was shot. In less than two minutes, the ground was strewn with felled men and horses.

From behind the low hill, a bugle call tooted out "Charge," and a mass of blue troopers raced over the crest. They roared a deep-throated shout as they thundered down the hill, building up speed. Sabers gleamed in the sun as the cavalry charge smashed into the disordered butternut horsemen. The Rebel cavalry broke, sending the survivors galloping back down the road, trailed by a handful of riderless horses.

A few minutes after the shooting stopped, Judson Kilpatrick emerged from the cabin where he had watched the ambush from behind the protection of log walls. "Bully, bully!" he cried, exultant over such an excellent start to his expedition.

Kilpatrick swung up onto his horse, and rode down to survey the aftermath. Men in grey and butternut jackets groaned and sobbed, and horses whinnied. From what he observed, Kilpatrick reckoned his own casualties as light, very light indeed.

He called to Colonel Eli Murray, commander of his division's Kentucky cavalry brigade. "Well done, Murray! Well done. You really put the twist on them. Shot the secessesh bastards right down, cut them up!"

Murray saluted and said "Thank you, sir." He was polite, but unenthusiastic. Murray had opposed making this glory-chasing expedition in the first place.

Ignoring the Kentuckian's flat tone, Kilpatrick went on. "Now we pull back, join the rest of the division, and lure Forrest into battle on our own terms. We lick him, push farther south, and see what General Polk has planned for us."

"If you say so," Murray replied, once again very proper, but very flat.

Damn the man, Kilpatrick thought. What, does he think this war is going to win itself? To beat the Rebels, we need to hunt down and kill men like Nathan Bedford Forrest, or at least give them a good licking. All the better that I get to do it, and win all the fame for whipping this so-called "Wizard of the Saddle" myself. As good as beating Jeb Stuart, that would be.

Now he could hear some of Murray's troopers muttering "Kil-cavalry" under their breaths. Well damn them too, Kilpatrick thought. Unreliable, unpatriotic Kentuckians. These Kentucks are all secessionists at heart anyway, and they have no appreciation for my vision. If we pull this off, we'll all be famous.

He could see it now. Beat Forrest at the start of Sherman's campaign, earning promotion to the head of Sherman's cavalry. Play a big role in beating Stonewall Jackson, maybe seize Atlanta all by himself in a bold, lightning quick cavalry drive. Ride that glory to election as governor of New Jersey after the war, and then onto the White House itself.

That was what he wanted, and that was what he was going to get. The idea came to him shortly after receiving his orders from McPherson, orders to cross the Tennessee River at Decatur and patrol the south bank of the river. Those orders gave him discretion to probe into central Alabama if that proved necessary to develop the strength and intentions of Bishop Polk's Army of Mississippi. That was all the discretion he needed to go chasing after Forrest, rumored to be about Tuscaloosa.

He came south, stopping in Jasper along the way, but only long enough to put the town's courthouse and other public buildings to the torch. Kilpatrick's Division then moved on, looking to pick a fight.

Or rather, Kilpatrick went looking for a fight. His senior officers, such as Murray, were well aware of Kilpatrick's twisting of their orders, and considered the expedition a dangerous folly. Their lack of enthusiasm filtered down through the ranks, and that along with Kilpatrick's "Kil-Cavalry" reputation for ambitious, self-serving recklessness, soured morale.

Kilpatrick ordered "Get your men organized, colonel." And damn if you or any of your half-Reb sonsobitches are going to stop me from getting Forrest, either.

Murray soon had his brigade moving north toward a rendezvous with the rest of Kilpatrick's cavalry division. They rode at a moderate pace, for that was part of Kilpatrick's plan as well, as he wanted Forrest to catch up, so as to reel the man into battle on ground of his own choosing.

Kilpatrick had a pretty position selected at Holly Grove Crossroads, with breastworks thrown up and artillery in place. Just thinking about Forrest battering himself to pieces against his line, defended by men armed with quick-firing breechloaders and repeaters, gave him a wide Cheshire grin.

Murray's Kentuckians and Kilpatrick had only been riding north for an hour when the Confederates struck back. For several minutes, butternut outriders dogged the tail of Murray's column, exchanging potshots at extreme distance with the column's rearguard.

"Sir, the Rebels are gaining on us," said Murray, sounding worried. "We need to step up the pace."

Kilpatrick replied cheerfully "No, Colonel. We need to draw those Rebs onto the rest of the division. If they are nipping at our heels, that is exactly what I want."

Murray scowled. "They won't be nipping on our heels for long. They'll be jumping on our backs!"

Kilpatrick said nothing in response, choosing to ignore rather than argue with Murray. He was serene and confident, right up to the moment he heard a distant bugle sound "Charge," followed by an eruption of battle noise from his rear guard.

Kilpatrick turned his horse about, wondering aloud "What the devil?"

Murray ordered his bugler to sound first "Come About," and then "Trot," and his two regiments came quickly back on their rear guard to find it being overwhelmed by hundreds of butternut horsemen, brandishing six-shooters, musketoons and shotguns. Murray ordered a charge, and the Kentuckians surged forward, pistols and sabers drawn.

Studying the scene from a distance, Kilpatrick noted the flags, revealing the Rebs as Mississippians. He was amazed the bastards had brought up so much force so quickly, and decided Forrest's main body was not far behind.

The Kentucky cavalry soon pushed the Mississippi horsemen back. However, Murray had only just started reorganizing his troopers when the Rebels were back on the road, just close enough to draw a bead on the fringe of his brigade.

"Colonel Murray" Kilpatrick shouted. "I believe it is time to pick up the pace. Put some distance between us and the enemy, if you please."

Murray complied. The Federal horsemen drove hard for the next ten miles, a growing number of Southern troopers snapping at their hooves. Kilpatrick became anxious, wondering how the Rebels could be bearing so hard down on his rear. Murray's horses were spent. How could they do it?

Kilpatrick sighed with relief when the entrenchments manned by Klein's and Smith's Brigades came into view. Just below the crest of this low ridge, the blue horsemen had dug out a shallow trench and piled the dirt in front of it. They had cut down every tree and shifted every rock within reach to reinforce that pile of dirt, although the largest trees had been cut down so the tops pointed outwards, turning the branches into barriers. There had not been time to cut away the foliage and sharpen the branches into stakes, but Kilpatrick paid that no mind.

The men had been at it for half the night. While not as expert at fashioning earthworks as the coffee boilers, Kilpatrick felt his troopers had made a workable job of it. Above were the guns of

Kilpatrick's sole battery of artillery. On the reverse slope, one man in every four stood by with the horses.

Reaching the top of the ridge, Kilpatrick swung off his horse and withdrew his field glasses from his case. Murray took his cavalry behind the lines and into reserve, where he could rest his tired horses.

The shooting hadn't stopped. Kilpatrick could see that as soon as his pursuers had laid eyes on what waited for them, they had come about, dismounted, and taken up positions facing the right of his line.

Kilpatrick became excited. It's working, he thought. Walking over to his battery, he ordered it to open fire on the Rebels.

"Are you sure, general?" asked Captain Beebe, his chief gunner. "That's only three regiments of dismounted cavalry out there, that I can see, and they are spread out in a skirmish line. It's not a good target, and Confederate artillery ain't even up yet. I've only got so much ammunition in the caissons. The wagons are back in Jasper."

"Put fire down on those bastards. That's an order!" snapped Kilpatrick. Within moments, his six guns were pelting the Rebels with solid shot and bursting shell.

The two lines sniped at each other for the better part of two hours, the Federal troopers from behind their entrenchments, and the Confederate horsemen from behind trees, rocks and whatever cover they could find. Kilpatrick observed that the Confederate line was gradually thickening and reaching out to his left, and estimated the butternut numbers on the firing line had doubled by noon.

Kilpatrick was still studying the skirmishing, satisfied and congratulating himself, when Colonel Murray and his other two brigade commanders, Lt. Colonels Smith and Klein, confronted him.

"General Kilpatrick, sir, this is madness," Murray pleaded. "If that is Forrest out there, we have no knowledge of his strength. What we see here before us is at least the equal to our own, and we can be pretty sure that's not all that's coming."

The other colonels concurred. Klein said "We bushwhacked Forrest, sir. General McPherson's orders said nothing about bringing on a general engagement with the Confederate cavalry. We're out on a limb here, and if we wait too long, Forrest is going to cut it right off."

Kilpatrick was disgusted. Run? The Johnnies hadn't even pushed them that hard yet. This is what comes from having brigade commanders who weren't trained, West Point professionals.

"I don't want to hear any more talk of the Rebels outnumbering us. Not one fucking word. I've heard you westerners go on about what big fighters you all are, and here you are. You should be ashamed of yourselves, clucking like toothless old women. I heard plenty such talk back in Virginia. Now get back ..."

Kilpatrick was interrupted by the boom of new artillery, coming from across the valley and on the opposite ridge. Snatching up his field glasses, Kilpatrick saw a dozen Confederate cannon had been unlimbered on his front, pushed up all in one go.

The artillery fire signaled the dismounted butternut troopers before his line to attack. They came on in the Indian rush style, with squadrons laying down fire so their comrades could advance to the next patch of cover. Advancing in this manner, the attackers turned the Federal's leafy obstacles against them, using the felled trees as protection.

Kilpatrick's commanders rushed back to their units, just as one of the cannon to Kilpatrick's left was smashed to bits, struck by solid shot. A third grey brigade emerged from the valley woods below, on the extreme left of Smith's mixed bag of Hoosiers, Buckeyes and Kentuckians. Dismounted as well, these troopers advanced up the slope.

Kilpatrick mounted his horse, spurred to a gallop and caught Murray. "Colonel Murray, a new brigade is menacing our left. Lead your men against them. Charge them, give them the saber and roll them back downhill."

Murray blinked. "You want me to charge massed, dismounted cavalry?"

Kilpatrick screamed "Damn your eyes! This isn't a fucking debating society! Get your ass up there!"

Murray instructed his bugler to sound "Forward," and then shot back at Kilpatrick "If we survive this, sir, afterward you can expect me to call on you to account for your manners." Murray rode to the front of his men, waving his saber and pointing it forward as he led them at the walk up to the front line.

Just before reaching the crest, the brigade was ordered up to a trot. As they crested the hill the pace was increased to a gallop, and then for the second time that day, Murray's Brigade charged downhill.

The advancing grey troopers halted and opened fired on the thundering blue cavalry, shredding the front ranks of Murray's pair of Kentucky cavalry regiments. Their comrades in the main Rebel line savaged the charge's right with fire. A section of Rebel cannon that was primed and ready to fire sent two balls slicing through the massed ranks of horsemen, creating still more bloody carnage. And still Murray went on, his horsemen cutting right through the porous skirmish line, slashing and shooting as they went.

The dismounted Rebel troopers were soon put to flight, but not soon enough for Murray. Gunners everywhere thought cavalry made for marvelous targets, and by that time all the Rebel cannon had shifted from counter-battery fire to shooting up his brigade. He was bringing the tattered remnants of his outfit about when a fresh brigade of dismounted troopers emerged from the woods, bearing Kentucky banners.

"Lyon's Brigade," Murray said, choking back a sob. Not this way, he thought. Kentuckians in grey. Please, God, not this way.

The Kentucky Confederates leveled their motley assortment of carbines, muskets and musketoons, and rattled off a volley into Murray's troopers. What was left of the blue brigade broke, fleeing back to the relative safety of Smith's lines. More were gunned down as they ran up the slope.

Kilpatrick was horrified, not over the rout and slaughter he had just sent Murray and his troopers to, so much as at the presence of that fourth brigade. On top of the 12 guns, it was clear that Forrest, if indeed Forrest it was, really did have him outnumbered.

It's time to skedaddle, Kilpatrick decided.

He rode over to his artillery. "Captain, I want you to shift your guns over to the left, to meet this new threat. Give them a faceful of double canister, make them back off. Then limber up and put your guns on the Jasper Road."

Beebe looked to his four remaining guns and shook his head. "General Kilpatrick, I barely have any canister left. I've been firing on them Rebel troopers, just like you said. I'm almost used up."

"Dammit!" Kilpatrick screamed. He couldn't count on anyone, he thought. Why didn't this fool keep a reserve? Did he have to think of everything himself?

"Alright," snapped Kilpatrick. "Limber your guns up and get on the Jasper Road." He then went over to his left, to examine the situation there more closely. He arrived just in time to see the fresh Rebel brigade, formed in loose order, lap up and over Smith's rapidly retiring lines.

Kilpatrick had just decided it was time to pull himself and his staff back when he felt a hard impact to his left leg, followed by a fiery, piercing lance of pain. Simultaneously, he felt his horse shudder and heard it scream. He instantly realized both he and his mount had been shot, and now the horse was falling over. His left leg was useless, so he could do nothing. Kilpatrick screamed as the horse slammed down on his wounded leg, crushing and grinding his mangled bones and pinning him to the ground. Mercifully, he passed out.

He awoke to the bitter odor of smelling salts and found himself laid out on a rough-hewn table in a log cabin. Kilpatrick realized it was late afternoon from the light. His left trouser leg was cut open, and he had to suppress gagging when he saw the frightful state of his lower leg, bones jutting out from his torn flesh. A tourniquet was in place, the only thing preventing him from bleeding to death. A young Rebel surgeon in a blood-stained smock was there, as was an even younger lieutenant in a tattered tan uniform.

The surgeon spoke. "Ah, General Kilpatrick. You are awake, sir. Lieutenant, go fetch General Forrest."

Kilpatrick pushed down his tears of pain and despair. His leg lost, and he was Forrest's prisoner. That it had come to this, and all because of blundering Murray. Stupid Beebe, not holding back enough ammunition. Cowardly Smith and Klein, who left him on the field to be captured.

The surgeon laid out the grim tools of his trade on a nearby chest. "I'm glad you responded to the salts, sir. I prefer my patients to be awake. No waking up in the middle of the operation, the worst possible time, thrashing about and taking us all by surprise. Also, unconscious patients have a propensity to heart failure, or so it is my experience."

"Now, take this" he said, proffering a bottle. "It's all I have, but it's strong stuff."

Kilpatrick often preached to his men against drinking, but was certainly no stranger to it himself, and at that moment he would have swallowed a barrel of whiskey if it would dull the agony of his leg. He propped himself up, took the bottle, and swallowed several large gulps. His stomach was empty, and the strong liquor went straight to work. Kilpatrick watched as the room began tilting slowly to the right.

As soon as the surgeon left to summon some orderlies to help hold Kilpatrick down, Nathan Bedford Forrest swept into the cabin, followed closely by the youthful lieutenant. He was a tall, strongly built man, but moved gracefully, and in his movements and appearance resembled nothing so much as a cougar. He seemed to fill what space remained in the cabin's cramped confines.

Removing his hat, he said "I was sorry to hear of your misfortune, General Kilpatrick. If there is any…"

"Oh, you've done enough, you secessesh son of a darkie whore!" Kilpatrick spat, half drunk. He was a stupid, mean drunk. It was the reason he abstained from intoxicating liquors, insofar as he actually did abstain. "I don't want any charity from the likes of you. A fucking bastard who sends his cowards out wearing enemy uniforms. When this war is over, I'll see you all hanged!"

That last insult was a lie, and everyone in the cabin knew it, Kilpatrick included. Forrest had employed many ruses against his enemies, but never an attack by men dressed in full Federal uniform. He glared at Kilpatrick with undisguised, murderous contempt.

Forrest slowly pulled off his left gauntlet, one finger at a time. When the gauntlet was off, he took it into his right hand very deliberately, and then suddenly lunged forward to smack Kilpatrick across the face with his open left hand. He put most of his shoulder and hip behind the blow, snapping Kilpatrick's head around.

Stepping back, he asked his aide for writing materials. As Forrest dictated a brief note, the alcohol-induced color drained from Kilpatrick's face. Forrest fixed his signature to the note, handed it to the cowed Kilpatrick, then put his gauntlet back on, turned smartly on his heels, and left without saying another word.

The note bore more flourish than Forrest's actual dictation, this added by his more literate aide, and it read:

April 19, 1864
Holly Grove Crossroads, Alabama

Dear Sir,

The man bearing this letter, Brigadier Gen'l Judson Kilpatrick, USA, was wounded on the field of Holly Grove Crossroads. He is to be accorded every possible courtesy, given the best treatment, and I request every effort be exerted to speed his recovery.

Gen'l Kilpatrick has unfortunately made insulting and intemperate remarks, provoking my person in a way no gentleman's dignity could tolerate. Naturally, I have challenged him to fight. When he is well and fit enough to travel, I must further request you award his release, if that lies within your power, without waiting for exchange and on the sole condition that he seek me out for satisfaction at the earliest possible time. If this is not within your power, I request you notify me, so that I might press for Gen'l Kilpatrick's parole under the described conditions.

Sincerely and respectfully,

NB Forrest
Major Gen'l of Cavalry, CSA

Once outside, Forrest's mouth curdled in anger. He swung about on his heels, and punched the log wall of the cabin, skinning his knuckles badly.

Forrest had already been chafing at the bit before he paid his courtesy call to Kilpatrick. His blood was up from the battle, and he longed hungrily to pursue the fleeing Yankee cavalry. Then that damn, arrogant, ungrateful fool of a Yankee, Irish half-bred dog had the gall to say such things to him! It would serve Kilpatrick right, Forrest thought, to put him back where I found him, pinned underneath his dead horse.

Forrest thought it had been the easiest victory of his career, this battle. Scouts had kept him informed of Kilpatrick's movements, and locals described the lay of the ground to him. He knew if Kilpatrick tried to defend that position at Holly Grove, he could easily work around his left, so he hoped that the fool would stay put.

What was more, the odds were probably even for once, Forrest having four smallish brigades to Kilpatrick's three. On top of that, Forrest did away with the textbook practice of having one man in four hold the horses, and put every man into the assault, and he had more guns as well.

Even so, two-thirds of the Yankee cavalry got away. Most of his command was exhausted and low on ammunition, but Lyon's boys were in good shape, and rode some fine Bluegrass horseflesh to boot. They could lead a pursuit. All things being fair, he ought to be chasing the enemy down, pushing them hard, shaking them to pieces.

But Forrest's orders from Bishop Polk were very detailed, very specific, and very contrary to a pursuit. That bothered Forrest, and not just because he resented the tight leash or the lost opportunity. It was strange. The Bishop was usually more careless. It wasn't like Polk, not at all.

Forrest shrugged. If Polk wanted a tighter rein, Forrest could deal with that later. For now, he would not mar his victory with blatant insubordination. Instead, he limited Lyon's orders to sprinting for Jasper, where a hundred Yankee wagons were rumored to be waiting.

April 20
Late afternoon
Headquarters, XV Army Corps, Army of the Tennessee, USA
Watkins House
Huntsville

McPherson hurried up the walk to the Watkins House. A big Georgian-style town mansion endowed with a tower, the house served as the headquarters of the largest corps in his army, the XV Corps. He was met on the front steps by a pack of junior staff officers.

"I want to see Black Jack," he demanded.

McPherson was quickly ushered into the office of John A. Logan, who rose from behind his desk. A dark, swarthy bull of a man,

Logan welcomed his chief with the big smile, iron handshake, and firm slap on the shoulder of a career politician.

Before either of them had a chance to sit down, McPherson declared "Do you know what that damn fool Kilpatrick went and did with my cavalry? He rode down to Jasper, picked a fight with the Rebs and got himself a thorough drubbing, that's what! Captured to boot! I just got the wire from Decatur not 15 minutes ago."

Logan pulled up a chair instead of returning to his desk. "Go on."

McPherson sighed and plopped down. "According to Colonels Klein and Smith, after he crossed the Tennessee he rode straight down the Jasper, raised some hell, and then went looking to pick a fight with the Rebs. Klein and Smith reckon they ran into Forrest, who hit them with four brigades and 12 guns. Got whipped, Murray's Brigade is cut to pieces and Murray missing. The only good news is that Kilpatrick got himself captured, and spared me the trouble of a court martial."

Logan sighed. "Kil-Cavalry. Glory seeking, scheming little man, in some ways worse than McClernand ever was. Why does Washington insist on sending us these no account failures from the eastern army?"

"The man had been to West Point. One would think that would drill some sense into him," McPherson said, shaking his head.

"If you ask me, Mac, West Point is overrated."

"You would say that, John, you would," McPherson replied, smirking. Logan was in his late 30s, and had been an Illinois Congressman at the start of the war. A civilian at First Bull Run, he had snatched up a musket and shot back at the Rebels. Sherman in particular loved telling that story. Shortly thereafter, Logan raised his own infantry regiment, showed real talent for fighting and leadership, and rose accordingly.

"So, what will you do?"

"Well, thank God I didn't send Kilpatrick off with all my cavalry. I still have Minty."

Logan nodded slowly. Robert H.G. Minty was one of the Army of the Cumberland's best cavalry officers, leader of the crack Saber Brigade. Despite the name, every man was armed with not just sabers, but also revolvers and Sharps breechloaders. Moreover, the outfit was made up of a mix of volunteer and regular cavalry, all veterans now.

McPherson spoke with the firmness of a man who had already made up his mind. "Smith and Klein are shaky, but intact. I'll form a new cavalry division around Minty, and give him acting command. I will likely have to break up poor Murray's survivors, fold them into Smith's 2nd Kentucky."

"Don't let Sherman saddle you with Edward McCook. Man's not as bad as Kilpatrick, but still not very good," Logan replied.

McPherson got up, walked around a little bit. "I won't. I want Minty, unless Sherman offers me someone better." After a pause, he continued. "If nothing else, this disaster tells us that something is indeed simmering down in central Alabama. We need to get back out there, see what direction it's headed, where the Bishop will try to cross the Tennessee."

"What do you want from the XV Corps?"

McPherson pointed to the map pinned to Logan's wall. "Minty is on his way to Decatur now, and has tomorrow to refit his new command. Then I want him out patrolling an arc, running along Mt. Hope, Basham's Gap, and Day's Gap. But, after what happened to them at Holly Grove, I want you to send an infantry division to support them."

Logan agreed. "Done."

May 1
Noon
Army of Tennessee, CSA
Tuscumbia

Jackson stood on a high bluff overlooking the south bank of the Tennessee River. It was the Sabbath, most of his men were resting, and, he hoped, enjoying Sunday services. His engineers, however, were hard at work putting the finishing touches on the pontoon bridge. Red Jackson's cavalry and Polk would begin crossing before dawn tomorrow.

He was confident that the enemy knew his position, but not his true strength. Forrest defeated the enemy's reckless foray at Holly

Grove, and was now holding their cavalry back about 25 miles to the east. The Yankees still slumbered in Chattanooga and Knoxville, leaving Hardee in peace. His presence with the army remained a relative secret, as did the presence of Hood's Corps. It was camped half a dozen miles south of town, and Jackson had thrown a curtain of provosts around Hood's camp, keeping soldiers in and civilians out.

The army had advanced at a moderate pace until now, collecting supplies as it went, applying an especially heavy hand to places like Winston County, which harbored a strongly disloyal and Unionist sentiment. Once across the river, Jackson intended to move more quickly, forcing a foot race for Nashville, so he could come over and catch McPherson strung out on the march.

"Gen.. um, Colonel Milner?" Polk called, interrupting Jackson's reverie.

Jackson turned away from the river. "Mmmm. Yes?"

Polk bore a basket. "Well, sir, I had heard that you bear a considerable appetite for fruits. These came through my supply chain, and I thought of you."

Jackson took the basket and removed the covering cloth. "Fresh strawberries!" he cried joyfully. "Why, General Polk, I cannot thank you enough!"

Putting on his serene, clerical smile, Polk mused on how easy it was to please some people. He hadn't given up his grievances, not at all, but he had realized that one didn't deal with a man like Stonewall Jackson in the same way as one might a Braxton Bragg. Oh no. More subtlety was called for here.

And Jackson makes it so easy, Polk thought. Like so many Southrons, the man has a predilection for religious figures.

That brought Polk to his next chore. "There is something else. I have been approached by John Hood, about his being baptized and brought into the flock. I know you are not of the Episcopal Church, and Hood struck me as hesitant... one might say a might bit shy about inviting you, but I was hoping you would join us and attend the service this very evening."

"Of course. I would be delighted. Delighted and honored, sir, delighted and honored."

Bully, Polk thought. Two birds in my clutch, all with the same shot.

Later that night, Jackson, Polk and a small escort rode to Hood's camp. John Bell Hood was baptized that night in a barn, by lantern light and using a horse bucket as a baptismal font. Unable to kneel due to his wooden leg, Hood bowed his head, and insisted upon standing rather than sitting for the ceremony.

May 2
Morning
41st Tennessee, Maney's Brigade, CSA
Outskirts of Tuscumbia

Sitting at a mess fire, Nathan Grimes remarked "I'll bet any fellow a month's wages them orders to drill this morning came from Old Jack. Hood ain't that fussy about such things. Cheatham and Maney neither. Old Jack, though, he ain't one to miss a chance to sweat us. Won't give us a morning off, no sir, no how."

"You ought not be gambling," Willie said quietly. "Ain't right, ain't that what the good book says?"

Nathan rolled his eyes. He hadn't even been serious, but Willie had caught the revival in the winter camps, and ever since it had been all the Bible this and the Lord that, drinking ain't no good and gambling's a sin, and always trying to drag him off to church on Stonewall's Sabbath day.

"Willie, ain't too many pleasures allowed a common soldier. I reckon how a private in this man's army spends his pay, that's his own business. His right. Ain't that what we fighting for? Our rights? No preacher, no officer, no sheriff, and no Yankee from Washington ought come by and tell a man how to spend his time or his money. Let alone come by and put some damn darkie above a white man." That brought some low, throaty chuckling and "here, here's" from the other men around the fire.

Nathan muttered "Anyhow, ain't like we'uns get paid so much."

Fletcher walked over to the mess and squatted by the fire, saying "At ease, men. At ease," knowing no one would stand to attention anyway. His company could tell when he meant fuss and business, and when he did not.

One of the men proffered a tin cup. "Captain, care for some

yaupon coffee? Last of the Selma issue."

Fletcher shook his head, chuckling. "Fellas, yaupon gives me the Tennessee Trot worse than corn meal with the cob ground in." That produced a round of knowing grins and laughter.

He looked to the Grimes brothers. "Nathan, Willie, there is a story going about that you both had words with Stonewall. I'd like to hear it myself, from the source."

Nathan looked to Willie. It was more Willie's story than his.

"Well, Captain, you recollect how Nathan and me, you sent us trapping? We come back out of them old Indian woods, and were fixing to walk back to White Hall camp, when we was stopped by some officers. One was the shabbiest colonel you ever saw, with one arm and a big beard. He wanted to see our pass, and I wouldn't give it to him, on account our orders not to, which he liked very much. Sent us on our way."

Nathan spoke up. "Weren't 'til later that we knew who that colonel was. Almost dark and all."

Fletcher nodded. "Well, thank you." He got up and left. It was clear the men believed it, and the Grimes Brothers weren't much for tall tales, whatever their other failings might be. It was an open secret that Jackson was with the army, but word didn't get around until after Selma.

After breakfast, Fletcher and the other officers drilled the regiment, some odd 260 men. The boys would obviously have preferred to spend the morning at leisure, knowing the orders for later that day were marching orders. Spirits were high, even so.

They ought to be, Fletcher thought. My company isn't 75 miles from home.

The regiment struck its camp, and at the appointed time marched for the road, taking its place with Maney's Brigade. This, in turn, took its place with Cheatham's Division, and it with Hood's Corps. They had been on the road for less than an hour when the column came to a halt. The men stood in their ranks for half an hour, marched forward a short distance, and then halted again. Finally, the order came to fall out. The march was stalled.

Farther up the road, Jackson rode with a few staff officers into Tuscumbia. As he passed the men of Stewart's Corp, the boys grinned and silently waved their hats. They were flattered that Old Jack had chosen to travel with them, and enjoyed playing into his game.

Arriving at the road junction just before the Tennessee River, Jackson found Loring's Division tied up with the wagon train of French's Division, coming from opposite directions and both insisting on the right of way. Loring was there, in the thick of it, arguing with a major.

Approaching the squabbling pair, Jackson yelled "What happens here? What is the meaning of this?"

Loring was a balding, middle-aged man with dull, black eyes. Like Jackson, he wore his left sleeve empty, having lost that arm in the Mexican War.

He shouted "How dare you! Of all the impertinent... Jackson? By God, Jackson? What the devil are you doing here?"

"I asked you the same question," Jackson snapped. "Report! Without the blasphemy, and with your salute, General."

Astride his horse behind Jackson, Sandie smiled, enjoying Loring's discomfiture. Leave it to the Scared Turkey, he thought, to remain ignorant of what every man jack of the army already knew.

Flustered, Loring saluted. "I am on the march, General Jackson. Under orders and on schedule. This jack-n-ape refuses to yield the road. He is behind schedule and refuses to turn it over, that which is mine by rights. What is more, he refused a direct order from his superior officer, me, to do just that. I demand his arrest!"

Jackson ignored Loring and looked to the major. "You are French's quartermaster? What have you to say? Out with it!"

The major saluted smartly. "Yessir, that's right. We were delayed this morning on account of a bridge over yonder, needing repair. Got that done quick as we could, got here an hour behind schedule. Marching orders say delays don't change a thing, when we get here, we go. So I reckoned I should keep my wagons rolling. General Loring here insisted, and when I wouldn't give him the road, he seized the road and stopped the wagons."

Sandie nodded. He knew what the marching orders called for. He and Harman had written them. But where is Polk, he wondered? Should not Polk be sorting this mess out?

"General Loring," Jackson snarled, "this man is correct. You are in the wrong. Worse, you have compounded this delay by almost an hour. I will not tolerate any further deviation from orders, is that understood?"

"But.." Loring sputtered.

Jackson shouted him down. "Do you understand?!"

Loring assented sourly. "Yessir."

Jackson barked orders for Loring's men to clear the road, which were smartly obeyed. He then quietly told Sandie "Send to French today. Admonish him about that bridge. He had almost two full days to send an engineer to inspect it."

"One of those days was the Sabbath" Sandie replied.

"Yes, and I was building a bridge. French could have been at least inspecting one."

May 2
Early afternoon
McPherson's Headquarters in the Field, Army of the Tennessee, USA
South of the Tennessee Line

McPherson and his immediate staff had just made their planned stop when the first courier of the day galloped up. Already almost twenty miles from Huntsville, his desire was not so much for the luxury of a hot meal, but to allow couriers from Huntsville, such as this one, to catch up with him. The muddy rider handed his dispatch to one of McPherson's aides, who brought it to the General.

Reading its contents, McPherson exclaimed "Capital! Capital!"

McPherson heard cheers of "Black Jack! Black Jack!" and looked up. Logan was pounding down the road at the gallop. Not bothering to dismount, he slowed his mount and walked him over to McPherson.

"Mac," he said, tipping his hat. "So, we're certain it's Tuscumbia?"

"Indeed I am. It's the logical place. With the shoals there, the Rebels can protect their pontoon bridge from the Navy's gunboats. If they want to run their supply line through there, the pillars from the old bridge are still standing. Those can be turned to a more permanent span easily enough."

"What is more," McPherson said, waving the dispatch, "Minty says he poked his head into Anderson this morning, about 15 miles west of Athens. There was no sign of the Rebels there. My guess is that they have yet to cross the river. Why, I do believe we've stolen a march on them!"

Logan understood. Dodge's XVI Corps started from Athens this morning. His own corps was about as far along. Without the need to cross a major river, that put their army a full day's march ahead of Polk's, and to Grant's veterans a full day of hard marching meant at least 25 miles.

McPherson had planned his first campaign as an army commander carefully and cautiously, weighing all the variables. He had elected not to intercept Polk's Army of Mississippi in central Alabama, because of the dense forest that lay between him and Jasper. That was no place to have an army. Instead, he preferred to catch Polk in open ground and without a river to his back, and that meant meeting the Bishop somewhere in southern Tennessee.

"What does Sherman have to say about it?" Logan asked.

"He approves. I imagine he will be pleased when I tell him I think we've bagged a march on the Johnnies."

Sherman had been clucking like a mother hen, burning the wire with messages. Even so, Sherman had limited himself entirely to asking questions, and offered no advice or instruction unless McPherson asked for it. It was quite a contrast to the prodding from pedantic old Halleck back at the War Department, who had been prodding him to attack Polk for weeks.

Sherman's largely hands off approach pleased McPherson, because against his expectations, he found he needed no reassurance or support from headquarters. Far from being an extra burden, he found the challenge and responsibility of an independent command exhilarating. Sherman just needs more to do, McPherson thought. Bill always became fidgety when he wasn't kept busy.

Logan said "Well, the boys are a little tender in the feet after spending the winter in camp, but they are making time. I reckon I'll make Pulaski tomorrow."

McPherson nodded. "Good. You take care, John."

May 2
After dark
Army of Tennessee, CSA
Florence

Jackson required most of the day to put the bulk of his army across the Tennessee River, as the bottleneck of the single span reduced progress to a trickle. Left behind to screen the army from prying eyes, Forrest's cavalry crossed the river the next day.

Before dawn on Tuesday morning, May 3rd, Red Jackson's cavalry rode north and east, spreading out through Anderson and up to the Tennessee line. Stewart's Corps followed, taking the Loretto Road through Masonville, Green Hill, and ultimately Lexington. Polk and Hood used Andrew Jackson's Military Road, screened by a brigade detached from Forrest. By the end of the day, both infantry columns were astride the Tennessee line.

PART III
LAWRENCEBURG

MAY 1864

CHAPTER 8

May 4
Dawn
Minty's Division, Army of the Tennessee, USA
Lawrenceburg, Tennessee

Newly installed in command of McPherson's sole cavalry division, Robert Minty's orders were to occupy Lawrenceburg, the county seat and crossroads town, and to develop more information on the whereabouts and movements of Polk's Army of Mississippi. His Federal cavalry had begun encountering advance parties of Rebel horsemen, never more than a squadron in size, starting late the previous afternoon.

An Irish immigrant in his middle 30s with five years' experience as a junior officer in the British Army before coming to America, Minty had wise eyes. Those eyes balanced his flamboyant style, and distracted from his energetic and a pugnacious nature. He responded to the Rebel presence with a plan to concentrate his horsemen that night, punch through to Lawrenceburg, and have a look around. He put his division on the Pulaski Road well before dawn, and they met the first Rebel pickets at sun-up, four miles west of the town.

Those butternut troopers were mostly asleep, so the Federal advance guard captured many and scattered the rest with almost no resistance, and with only a few shots fired to raise the alarm. Minty had seen this sort of ill-preparedness from the Rebels before, and he was not the sort to let such an opportunity pass. He sent his old command, the Saber Brigade, lunging into town.

The Sabers caught the Rebel horsemen only just mounting up in their camp, on the southern outskirts of Lawrenceburg. The Federal cavalry softened up their disorganized foes with a short, terrific fire from their rapid-loading Sharps carbines, drew their pistols and sabers, and charged through the Rebel camp. The butternut cavalry reeled and ran to the south, down the Military Road or across the open fields.

Minty looked on with satisfaction. It was his opinion that most Confederate cavalry, while undeniably fierce in a fight and gifted with a natural talent for raiding, were an ill-disciplined lot and otherwise of little use in the more routine tasks of screening an army and gathering intelligence.

If the job lacked dash, Minty thought, the Rebels aren't much for it. And catching them with their trousers down in the early morning was first rate sport.

Leaving one brigade to secure the town, and the important junction of the Pulaski and Military Roads along with it, Minty led his other brigades south in search of more trouble. As soon as the Federal cavalry was back on the road, the sky opened up with the dregs of the spring rains. The Military Road was not macadamized, but it remained relatively firm. Five miles south of town, at a junction with a local road, Minty encountered more Rebel cavalry.

He instantly recognized that these weren't the butternuts the Sabers had chased out of Lawrenceburg, and they were in brigade strength at least. As his first priority was to hold the town and its crossroads, Minty elected to retire on Lawrenceburg, and throw out a defensive line on some defensible ground south of town. He also sent word of the morning's developments to Dodge's XVI Corps, then marching west on the Pulaski Road.

9 a.m.
Polk's Corps, Army of Tennessee, CSA
Redding Ridge
South of Lawrenceburg

Upon receiving word that his advanced cavalry had been chased out of Lawrenceburg, Polk left the bulk of his corps behind to go forward and have a look for himself, not bothering to notify anyone else in the army of the early morning scrape just yet. About three miles south of Lawrenceburg, he found his advance cavalry, Johnson's Brigade, who looked to be in low spirits. Stopping just long enough to spare the Alabamans some kind words and inquire where the front was, Polk rode on and found William Hicks "Red" Jackson already there.

"Red, I didn't expect to find you here," Polk inquired. "You are supposed to be out by Pulaski way, yes?"

Red's whiskers and serious expression gave him a terrier-like appearance, complementing as much as clashing with his barrel chest and bulky limbs. "Yeap, but I had to come this way first. Roads and such. It's all in my marching orders, sir. I shouldn't worry too much about me being in your way. The Yankees are just over there, opposite this ridge."

"Show me, if you please" Polk ordered.

Polk found Red had thrown out a line of dismounted troopers on a rise called Redding Ridge. On the left was Shoal Creek and some very rough, thickly wooded ground. The ridge extended a few miles east, ending at an elevation, Haynie Hill, located right in front of a little stream, Haynie Branch. Beyond that, all was rolling plains and farm country. The Military Road ran north, through the left-center.

Red said "Yankees have a dismounted brigade deployed over yonder," pointing to a low ridge about three-quarters of a mile away, "and more blue bellies are prowling in the farms to the east, screening the Pulaski Road I reckon. Johnson said they came in from there, so I reckon more Billies must be coming up that way, but I have yet to have a look myself."

They rode to the top of Haynie Hill for a better vantage point, where the cavalryman continued with a more detailed explanation the ground. Polk pretended to listen, but preferred to study the ground for himself and to draw his own conclusions, peering through his field glasses and applying his God-given talent. After all, Polk was not only a scion of one of the South's leading families, and thus born for military command, but had been to West Point too.

The Bishop soon deduced that the left of Redding Ridge was an unattractive place for launching an attack, and that the right would be much more profitable. On the right, the troops could move quickly over the open ground, and Haynie Hill afforded a magnificent gun platform. Fixated on the ground around Haynie Hill, Polk ignored what Red had said about another hill his scouts had found beyond Shoal Creek, a hill that dominated the town and the enemy position, and as of yet, had no blue troopers on it.

After a time, Red asked "Do you want me to push the Yankees out of Lawrenceburg, sir? Or have a gander at the Pulaski Road?"

Polk pondered that. His orders from Jackson required him to march to the Maury County line today, but said nothing of him fighting to reach it.

"No, Red. I do not. We have no orders to force an engagement. We must refer this matter back to the commanding general." Polk then remembered that Red was attached to Stewart, and Jackson was traveling with Stewart, so both generals would soon know what was transpiring here. He had to send his own message forthwith.

Polk's also realized that, as the vanguard of the army, he would be required to deploy to confront the Federals. That would put him around the road, on the left and left-center and far from Haynie Hill, the place he expected any major Confederate assault would spring from. Polk silently cursed his luck.

"What about those heights past the creek, General Polk?" Red Jackson asked eagerly. "I could detach some troopers..."

"No, no, no!" Polk snapped, his mood souring rapidly. After pausing to compose himself, he continued more graciously. "Your cavalry is all we have to face the faithless invader for now. We can't have you dividing your strength at a time like this. Go on back to your men, and see if you cannot discern what the Yankee is doing on the Pulaski Road. Dismissed, General."

10 a.m.
Headquarters in the Field, Army of the Tennessee, USA
Lawrenceburg

McPherson was in Pulaski when he received Minty's report about his rout of the Rebel cavalry in Lawrenceburg. He instantly set out down the Pulaski Road, overtaking the head of Dodge's XVI

Corps just two miles west of town. Riding into Lawrenceburg, he was met in the town center by Minty and Grenville Dodge.

Dodge, an engineer and railroad man before the war, had a stooped posture and piercing eyes, traits that combined to make him look like some mean-spirited old man, well ahead of his 33 years. Shaking hands with McPherson, he asked "How goes, Mac?"

"Well enough. Report, please."

Dodge glanced at Minty, who crouched, picked up a stick, and started drawing on a patch of soft, muddy dirt. "General, I put the Sabers out in a dismounted line on a ridge two miles south of here, off the Military Road. Their right is anchored on a double horseshoe bend of Shoal Creek. That bend is wide open, and overlooked on our side by Raven's Bluffs, a steep set of cliffs. A man would need to be stupid or blind drunk to try and force that place. The ridge extends about three miles, sloping down onto the flatter country due east. We've taken to calling it Oak Ridge, after that a wooded hollow down behind the east end. White Oak Hollow, the locals call it."

Minty then went on to describe the Rebel position on the opposite ridge. To McPherson, it looked as if things were working out just as he had planned it. In little more than an hour, Dodge would start deploying on Oak Ridge, blocking the road. Logan's much larger corps was right behind. If Polk attacked, McPherson would smash him. If Polk tried to get around him, he'd strike him on the march and cut him to pieces. Finally, if Polk retreated, he would hound him back to the river, and crush him there.

But first, he had to look at the ground and see for himself if this was the place to fight. "May I have a tour, Colonel Minty?"

"Yessir, but there is one more thing. Not ten minutes ago, my scouts informed me of a hill, Wildcat Ridge, just beyond the creek. It dominates out right flank, sir. I just sent my reserve over to secure it."

"Then let's start there," McPherson replied.

Arriving at the hill, he could see what Minty meant. Dodge whistled and muttered "Damn." The hill towered above the surrounding country, and from it they could look directly upon the top and rear of Oak Ridge. If the Rebels got artillery up on Wildcat Ridge, McPherson knew it would unhinge his entire defense. He had to keep this hill or else leave and find some other ground to fight on.

"Dodge, Veatch's Division is at the front of your column, is it not?" McPherson asked. "I want you to send Yates's Sharpshooters up here, quick as you can, and some artillery."

XVI Corps had only two divisions, Veatch and Sweeney, while Logan's XV Corps had four. When Logan gets here, McPherson thought, I can post a whole brigade on this hill, but in the meantime the sharpshooters and their Henry repeaters are the best I can do.

10:30 a.m.
Headquarters in the Field, Army of Tennessee, CSA
Military Road
South of Lawrenceburg

When Jackson received word that his cavalry had been driven out of Lawrenceburg, he left Stewart's Corps and rode for the front. As he gave Polk instructions on where to deploy his corps, he was told by Red Jackson about a dominating hill, Wildcat Ridge, lying northwest of the Federal line.

"Show me!" Jackson demanded.

Supplied with a guide, a few aides, and a small escort, Jackson departed. Once on the Military Road, the small party soon encountered the marching ranks of French's Division. Riding down alongside the column, Jackson's party was met with waves of hearty cheering. He ignored the rolling fanfare, too busy to reprimand French and his officers for the disobedience to his orders regarding secrecy and that he was not to be cheered.

After a few miles, the guide turned off the road and led the way across a ford in Shoal Creek. The party then turned north, and rode parallel to Shoal Creek until they came within sight of the big hill. Jackson withdrew his field glasses from their case, and set about surveying the hill with a gunner's studied eye.

Yes, yes, he thought. That hill commands the enemy right flank and center. With artillery up there, I can make their defense untenable, drive them back through the town, catch them in a disorderly withdrawal and cut them to ribbons. A few hundred blue troops are already there, so the enemy knows the importance of this place...

Jackson returned his glasses to their case, and without saying a word to anyone, turned his horse around and started back for the ford. By the time they were back on Military Road, the head of Loring's Division was coming up. Having made up his mind, Jackson dispatched an aide to summon Loring.

"How may I be of service, General?" Loring asked, without enthusiasm. He offered a lazy salute.

"General Loring," Jackson said, "You are to take your division off this road, across this ford behind us here, and advance on a prominent hill dominating the enemy's position. Attack and occupy that hill."

"My entire division?" Loring asked, his voice betraying a slight incredulity.

"Yes, yes," Jackson, replied impatiently. "Once there, you are not to wait to deploy all your men. We cannot afford the time. Hit them as soon as you can with your lead brigade, then put the rest of your men in after, quick as you can. This man," he said, pointing to the guide "will show you."

Loring said nothing, but instead sent an aide to halt the head of his column, with orders that it should turn around and rejoin at the rear. Jackson watched as Loring then went to turn the second brigade in the column off the road first, as it was closest to the ford.

Jackson looked on with grudging approval of Loring's basic efficiency, and while he watched he reviewed his thinking. He knew that the enemy would reinforce the hill, probably before Loring could start the attack. By committing Loring's entire division, Jackson believed he could ensure winning the battle of reinforcements, as the enemy would send support more sporadically. Loring would soon have the upper hand, and push the enemy off that hill. It was so clear in Jackson's imagining, he thought he could see the hand of Providence in it.

He shared his reasoning with no one. Instead, Jackson's only further words on the subject were to send a courier to Polk, informing him of Loring's orders. He then rode south for Stewart's Corps.

Noon
Maney's Brigade, Cheatham's Division, CSA
The Alabama-Tennessee border

A band was playing up ahead, and to Fletcher that was a sure sign they must be coming up on the state line.

General Maney galloped up and down the length of his brigade's marching column, shouting "Three cheers boys! Three for Tennessee! Next stop, Mother Earth and Nashville, and then onto the Ohio!"

The ranks hurrahed lustily. Colonel Tillman pulled out of the column, came alongside his regiment, and called out "Three cheers for Maney and Old Frank Cheatham, men! Tennessee volunteers, one and all!"

The regiment cheered again. Fletcher smirked. Tillman had been kissing Maney's backside ever since the 41st Tennessee Infantry had been assigned to his brigade.

The moment passed, and Fletcher went back to smoking his cigar, and to his gloomy, worried thoughts. Going back to Tennessee meant picking a fight, sure as sunshine. Battle was waiting for them somewhere up north. A bloody, pointless homecoming, now that it was so obviously all for nothing. The war was lost, any fool ought to see it now, and it was the wrong damned war to start with.

The Fletchers were Whigs who had been for John Bell and Union in 1860, just as most Tennesseans had been for preserving the Union in some way or another. Fletcher had never believed in secession over the election of Lincoln, not in the war, and especially not Tennessee's place in any of it. Governor Isham Harris had dragged them all into the Confederacy under a shroud of dubiousness and illegality, and because of it the Yankees now owned almost every molehill and dunghill in the state.

It wasn't secession per se Fletcher opposed. In theory, he believed the states were sovereign and retained the right to depart from the Union. Nor was it slavery. He wasn't some black-tongued abolitionist. Fletcher owned some three dozen slaves, or did before Lincoln's emancipation. In his view, the South could have easily defended slavery from within the old Constitution, and gone on doing so for decades to come. Fletcher had volunteered for the army solely to repel what he regarded as an illegal invasion of his state by the Federal government.

Fletcher had tried to explain his cooperationist views once, in the Ohio prison his regiment was confined to after the surrender of Fort Donelson. As a lawyer, he felt that if you lost the argument, there were all kinds of ways you continued the fight. What you did not do was burn down the courthouse, tar and feather the judge, and run him out of the county.

But that's what the South did. They lost an election, so they burned the old Constitution, and ran the old Union out of town.

Fletcher had badly misjudged his audience. Men who were moderates before the war were hardened, bitterly intolerant secessionists now. The memory of that prison mess conversation made him feel foolish and bitter. His words were received with dismay and icy stares by the other officers, and one captain even accused him of defeatism and disloyalty.

He felt lucky to have avoided a challenge to fight that day. Not that he feared dueling, but he knew that even if he won, the consequences would blacken his name. He kept his sentiments to himself after that. In this war over our rights and liberty, he thought sardonically, a man wasn't free to speak his mind without fear of being called out and shot for it.

As the regiment marched past the band, it began playing "Bonnie Blue Flag." Fletcher chose that moment to hock up and spit.

No, as far as he was concerned the war was over, but for the fuss and the dying. All he wanted now was to go home with some dignity and take as many of his men back as he could, in particular his precious volunteers.

2:30 p.m.
Loring's Division, Polk's Corps, CSA
South of Wildcat Ridge
West of Lawrenceburg

The guide stopped his horse. "I reckon here's as far as we get, General, not without being seen."

Loring motioned for his chief aide while telling his staff "The rest of you men stay here. I want to have a look for myself."

He cared very little for what he saw. The guide's assessment was sound. The division could advance no farther without being observed, and it still had a mile of difficult ground to negotiate before reaching the foot of that hill. The prominence, Wildcat Ridge, was a strong position, held by a battery of artillery and what looked like at least a thousand men.

Loring said to his aide "I dislike this entire business. By the time we get up there, the Federals will have had plenty of time to sound the alarm. And it's a strong position, mighty strong. I will need most of my division to carry it. This is a fool's errand, a bloody fool's errand."

The aide agreed diplomatically. "It's quite a hill, sir, and I believe you are correct about the enemy's strength. What are your orders?"

Silently cursing Jackson, Loring thought about that. It was bad enough that crackbrained fool had gotten him exiled to the west, to thankless tasks, while the great Stonewall Jackson stole all the chances to achieve real glory where real glory was being won. No, it was even worse. Having stolen that glory, Jackson now came west himself, and by all appearances was determined to ruin him still further with persecution and bloody, forlorn assignments like this one.

Loring wrote out a message and said "Send to General Polk. With my compliments. I have arrived at the hill, as ordered by General Jackson, but find it reinforced, and therefore request confirmation of Jackson's orders to attack."

Taking the proffered message, the aide spurred his horse and galloped away. Loring returned to his division, and issued orders for the men to fall out where they stood, fill their canteens, and cook rations.

3:30 p.m.
Headquarters, Polk's Corps, CSA
Redding Ridge
South of Lawrenceburg

Loring's aide didn't dawdle, but he didn't hurry either, and took more than an hour to make his way to Redding Ridge and find Polk's headquarters, located in a small log cabin at the end of a track off the main road. He found General Polk there, sitting in a camp chair and under a shady tree, reading a newspaper.

Polk, whose feathers were already ruffled by the detachment of Loring, an action taken with neither his counsel nor consent, set his paper aside and read Loring's message. He instantly recognized Loring's intention: to thwart Jackson's orders by dragging things out. Polk found himself nodding with approval over that intent, both out of pique and because he had made up his mind that he could win no glory here, so he had best save his men for another day, a day where accolades could be won.

Loring played an old game, Polk thought, the old game with John C. Pemberton and Braxton Bragg. Oh, but this Jackson is not Bragg. Dear Jeff Davis will spare me the wrath of Jackson, but no one else. I cannot be seen opposing him openly.

Polk went to his improvised desk inside the cabin, and wrote out a message:

May 4, half past 3 o'clock
Headquarters
Andrew Jackson's Road, Lawrenceburg

William W. Loring, Major General of Infantry, CSA

My dearest general,

I regret to learn of your concerns regarding the hill beyond our left, and of the Federal strength upon it. I cannot offer you the confirmation you request, but I promise to approach the general commanding with your concerns. Continue making your preparations, and instructions will reach you shortly.

Sincerely and respectfully,

Lieutenant General L. Polk
Commander, Army of Mississippi, CSA

Polk gave the message to the waiting aide. "Take this back to

General Loring, and give him my blessings, my son."

He then returned to his shade tree and his newspaper. Twenty minutes later, Polk finally got up, called for his horse, and rode off to where he knew Jackson would be on Redding Ridge, where he was instructing A.P. Stewart as to where to place his corps. Polk handed Loring's message over as he related its contents to his fellow generals.

Overhearing what Polk said, Sandie and James Power Smith cast knowing glances at each other, like they both had the same thought. Loring, that Scared Turkey, was chirping again.

Jackson was aghast. "What does he mean by this? Even if the enemy is a thousand strong, Loring has them outnumbered almost six to one!"

"From the message," Polk said soothingly "I can only assume that General Loring's intention is to prepare for the ordered attack, while inquiring as to whether it should continue under changed circumstances. That is surely within a division commander's prerogative."

"That man's orders were not discretionary," Jackson snapped. He called for writing materials, and scribbled out a brief note from the saddle, which he gave to Captain Smith.

Jackson ordered "Take that to Loring. He is to attack at once, no more delays, with whatever he has ready. See what is going on over there, and report back to me. Be quick about it."

Smith tore off, riding hard. After he left, Polk took his leave and returned to his headquarters.

Once they were alone, Stewart, a man with handsome, sharp features and haunting eyes, leaned forward and said quietly "Tom, perhaps you ought to go there yourself. Loring sounds unsteady. If you wish that attack made promptly, you might as need to push it on with your own hands."

Jackson considered this advice briefly and discarded it, saying nothing. His place was with the larger portion of the army, and that was on Redding Ridge. Loring had his orders and he would obey, as a God-fearing soldier ought to. If he did not, he would reap the whirlwind for it.

Stewart said nothing more, and returned to the business of supervising his deployment. He was not in the practice of arguing with his superiors, nor was it his custom to volunteer in maligning a fellow officer, however justified that maligning might be.

5:15 p.m.
Loring's Division, Polk's Corps, CSA
South of Wildcat Ridge
West of Lawrenceburg

Loring was sitting on a fallen tree trunk, surrounded by his staff. When Smith rode up to him, he dismounted from his foaming, mud-spattered horse and delivered his message. Loring's expression darkened as he read it:

May 4, half past four o'clock

W. W. Loring, Major Gen'l of Infantry, CSA

Your original orders stand, and in the first instance were not open to interpretation. Attack at once.

T. J. Jackson
Gen'l, CSA

Loring pulled out his pocket watch. *Quarter past five,* he thought. *There are only two hours of good daylight left, and it would take almost all of it, if I were I to deploy my entire division...*

He ordered his staff "Gentlemen, we have our orders. I will lead General Adams's brigade forward and place his men myself. You see to Featherston and Scott coming up on Adams's left. Quarles will form our reserve."

"General Loring, begging your pardon, sir" Smith said with alarm. "General Jackson's orders call for you to attack immediately, not to deploy three-quarters of your division first. If you do the latter, you won't be in action until nightfall, and General Jackson wants you engaged as soon as possible."

"My written orders say 'attack at once,' but nothing about advancing my brigades in a ridiculous, piecemeal style."

"I was there, sir. The commanding general's intent..."

Chest puffed out like a strutting turkey, Loring snapped "Captain, I am not in the habit of allowing junior officers to lecture me about the interpretation of my orders!"

Smith suppressed a smirk. "Yessir. My apologies, sir."

"Wait here. I'll have a message for you to carry back to Jackson shortly."

Loring sat down, laid a saddle bag across his lap, and began scribbling his message. He folded it up and handed it to Smith. "Take that back to your general, and be quick about it."

Smith rode back to Redding Ridge quick as he could, driving his horse to utter exhaustion. Even so, it was 6 o'clock by the time he found Jackson's headquarters tent, pitched next to A.P. Stewart's headquarters, behind the Confederate right-center.

Handing Jackson the message, Smith said "General Loring intends to deploy three brigades into line of battle before attacking, sir."

Jackson's eyes narrowed. "Captain Smith, do you mean to tell me that Loring had not already deployed his men? He is only about that now?"

Smith nodded. Jackson exploded, his voice filled with hill country twang. "What has that man been doing all afternoon?"

He opened the message and read it, then carefully folded the message back up, went into his tent and put it away. He then strode over to Stewart's tent, accompanied by Smith and Sandie Pendleton.

After Stewart dismissed his staff, Jackson ordered "Sandie, arrest Loring on charges of disobedience and dereliction. He is to report to Florence to await specification of charges and trial by court martial."

Jackson's words shocked Stewart, but Sandie and Smith appeared unmoved, as if they had been expecting it for some time now. Jackson had ordered the arrest of generals in the past, including even A.P. Hill, and for far less. Loring, the old Scared Turkey, had ambled his way right up to the chopping block.

Sandie asked "What if Loring protests?"

Jackson's mouth curled, and he said spitefully "I want that man off my field. If he refuses his orders, put him in irons."

Turning to Stewart, Jackson said "General Stewart, I require you to go to Loring's front. Determine if that hill can be carried successfully before nightfall. If so, order Loring's replacement..."

"Featherston is the senior brigadier, sir," Sandie interjected.

"... order General Featherston to make the attack. If not, recall the division. I give you full discretion."

Now it was Sandie and Smith's turn to look surprised. Old Jack rarely gave discretionary orders, and never about combat. Yet here he was, sending Stewart out with just that very thing.

Stewart spoke quietly. "Loring's Division is from Polk's Corps. General Polk is..."

Jackson cut him off. "General Polk is not here. I need this done as quickly as possible. And..." Jackson paused for a moment "... I know your judgment is sound. About your business, all of you."

As the trio left the tent, Smith asked Sandie with a grin "Would you care for some company?"

"No, he would not!" Stewart snapped. Mounting his horse, he glared at the youthful pair of staff officers, both more than twenty years his junior. "This is not some theatrical for your amusement, Captain Smith, and you would do well to remember that."

They left for the circuitous ride out to Wildcat Ridge. The sky was darkening as they neared Loring's front, and Stewart had already decided that the attack would probably need to be called off.

Sandie presented himself to Loring, saluted, and said flatly "General Loring, you are under arrest. You are to report to Florence immediately, and there await formal specification of charges."

"What? The blizzards you say?" Loring sputtered. Adopting a military pose, he sneered back at Sandie "General Jackson does not have the authority to relieve a general of division, Colonel Pendleton. But if either you or he were professional soldiers, you would know that."

Stewart quietly asked one of Loring's stunned aides where Featherston might be found. Finding the scene unpleasant, he went off on his own to collect the division's new acting commander and inspect Federal position.

Sandie smiled mockingly. "I may not have your eighteen years of military service to my credit, sir, but I understand plain English well enough. You are not relieved. You are arrested. If you wish to add to the charges at your court martial by refusing to leave this field, I must tell you now I have the authority to have you put in restraints and carried off. General Jackson's orders. Sir."

Loring paled. His lips trembled with a mixture of fear and rage. A long, quiet moment passed. Then Loring turned, walked away, and mounted his horse.

Looking down at Sandie, Loring said icily "Colonel, I shall send a formal demand for the specification of charges in the morning. And the War Department shall hear of this outrage!"

Sandie said nothing, but felt relieved. He had intended more diplomacy, lost his temper, and regretted his words as soon as he uttered them. While Sandie didn't think Scared Turkey had the moral courage or the wits to force upon Old Jack the outrageous blunder of clapping a Confederate major general in irons, like some uppity negro, he wasn't absolutely certain. You never could tell what a vain, angry bird like Loring might do.

Yet Jackson never joked about such things. Sandie knew he had meant every word, and had Loring gone to confront him or refused to leave the field, he would have trussed Loring up and locked him away.

8 p.m.
Headquarters, Army of the Tennessee, USA
Oak Ridge
South of Lawrenceburg

McPherson had taken a tavern between Lawrenceburg and Oak Ridge as his headquarters, just off the Military Road and overlooking White Oak Hollow. The tavern was a two-room affair, built as a pair of log cabins with a corridor between them, and then sheathed in clapboard, so it was more rustic than its outward appearance might have suggested.

Exhausted, McPherson sagged in his rocking chair. He had spent most of the day in the saddle, personally inspecting every aspect of the Army of the Tennessee's deployment. He trusted most of his officers, but knew even the best men made mistakes or misunderstood their orders, and just as he knew things had a way of going askew if given half a chance.

Dodge and Logan were both there, along with most of the Army of the Tennessee's division commanders. From the XVI Corps came tall, skinny James Veatch, a Hoosier lawyer turned solid soldier, as well as Thomas Sweeney, a salty old regular, and widely regarded as the fieriest, most combative, and hardest swearing Irishman in an army that had a hefty share of such characters.

Logan had brought three of his division commanders with him: William Harrow, a Lincoln crony and hard drinker; professional and reliable Morgan Smith; and Peter Osterhaus, a German émigré and product of the Prussian officer corps. The XV Corps' remaining division, under John Smith, was far to the rear, having started its march from Decatur and the south bank of the Tennessee River, and not expected to arrive until well after midnight.

McPherson listened as each division commander gave a report on his position and status. Veatch, Sweeney, Harrow and Smith were posted on Oak Ridge, a line of 10 brigades covering a frontage of just under three miles. Veatch was tied into Shoal Creek, and deployed on the thickly forested, hilly and broken ground on the right. Sweeney was next, astride the Military Road. Harrow and Smith followed, facing thinly wooded bottom country and extending down to where the ridge met the plains.

Yates's Sharpshooters had since returned from Wildcat Ridge, replaced by a brigade from Harrow's Division and 12 guns, including the army's sole battery of 20-pounder Parrot rifled cannon. Osterhaus's troops were hidden in White Oak Hollow, shrouded by the thick woods and the surrounding hills. Minty's cavalry was now on the extreme left, covering the Pulaski Road. The army's wagon train, only recently arrived, was parked in the town.

After Osterhaus finished, McPherson stood up. "Gentlemen, today while we've been busy entrenching, the enemy advanced pickets to within 200 yards of our line. I have two orders for the morning. Sweeney, Veatch, Harrow and Smith are to throw out a skirmish line just before dawn, drive the enemy pickets, take prisoners for questioning, and provide protection for my second order. That is to send out work details, fell trees and construct abatis."

"What about John Smith's division?" Logan asked.

"I want them to bivouac in Lawrenceburg. From there, they can guard the trains, quickly reinforce either Wildcat Ridge or Minty on the Pulaski Road, and if need be, they aren't two miles from the front line."

"And the left, sir?" Logan continued. "They've got a hell of an artillery platform in Haynie Hill. If they try to get around my flank…"

"They can't approach you unobserved," McPherson said. "If they try to turn your flank, there will be plenty of time, and you have Osterhaus close by."

Some smaller details were discussed, and the meeting broke up. As they walked back to their horses, Dodge had a word with his commanders.

"Sweeney, you've got the Western Sharpshooters. Veatch, you have Yates's Sharpshooters. Both those regiments are armed with Henry rifles. When you push out your skirmishers, I want them front and center. Those repeaters are hungry, so give each man a double issue of ammunition. Burn those Rebs back. Drown them with lead."

10 p.m.
Hood's Corps, Army of Tennessee, CSA
North of the Military Road and Loretto Road Junction
Six Miles South of Redding Ridge

Hood rode into his headquarters camp with the relief of a sick man finally at the end of a wearisome day. He returned the greetings of Cheatham and Cleburne, both sitting on a fallen tree trunk and waiting for him, and then rode around to the other side of his tent to endure the day's last ordeal.

Sagging in the saddle, Hood waited for his orderlies to loosen the straps that held him in place. They then gently pushed his cork leg over the saddle, and gingerly lowered him to the ground. While one man helped him stand, another brought his crutches. Hood shooed the orderlies back, and straightened out his uniform coat with his one good hand. Making an effort to put some spring into his step, he loped forward on his crutches.

Hood found his camp chair already set out. "Evening gentlemen" he said, carefully positioning himself and settling down. "I trust you did not wait for me before pitching in."

Cleburne chuckled. "Sam, I had to hold Frank here back from

eating the last of your bean soup and cornbread."

Cheatham shrugged. "Ain't my fault I was born with God-given, red-blooded, healthy appetites." He stepped up and proffered a small bottle. "Sam, before your supper, would you care for some? It's the last of my family's own special spirits. Brought it out for this grand occasion, of being back here in Tennessee."

Hood extended his tin cup. "Mighty thankful, Frank." He then waved away the offer of food, too tired and sore to eat.

"What did Old Jack have to say?" Cleburne asked. Even the corps' lowest drummer boy knew the Yankees were waiting for them in Lawrenceburg, and the camps burned with talk about what the next day held for them all.

Hood grunted. He resented having to ride all the way to army headquarters to receive humdrum orders that could have easily been sent by courier. If he wasn't shattered before making the twelve-mile round-trip, he certainly was now.

"Reveille at the usual time, make sure the men fill their canteens, get a good breakfast and 60 rounds of ammunition, and march them up to the front at the regulation pace. The usual thing about driving stragglers like cattle."

Cheatham smirked. "Serving in this army makes a man into an old woman, reading tea leaves all God damned day." He paused for a time, then continued. "You know about Loring, I reckon?"

Hood replied "Ever hear of Richard Brooke Garnett? No? Well, Garnett had the Stonewall Brigade after Jackson, and one day found himself outnumbered, out of ammunition, and attacked on three sides. He retreated, and if I can say so, did a damn fine job of it to get out of a fix like that. But he did it without orders, and Old Jack didn't care for it, not one little bit. He charged Garnett with dereliction, accused him of cowardice. A court martial was started, but never finished. Garnett died at Gettysburg."

No one spoke for a while after that. Hood finally said "It was much worse for Garnett, because he had the Stonewall Brigade, you see. Old Jack used to be very touchy about his old brigade."

Cheatham said nothing. He had sized up Stonewall Jackson as one tough, mean bastard early on, and was determined not to cross him if it could be helped. If Loring couldn't see that, he was a plain fool, and would eventually reap a fool's reward. Jeff Davis might save Loring yet, Cheatham thought, but only by sending him to the

Trans-Mississippi, to exile in Kirby Smithdom. Or bringing him to Richmond and putting him behind a desk, like Davis had done with Bragg.

Deciding to change the subject, Cheatham asked "What do you think's waiting for us, up Old Hickory's road?"

Hood flinched from a spasm in his back. Shifting in his chair, he said "I know exactly who is waiting for us up tomorrow. Mac's waiting for us."

Seeing that confused them, Hood continued. "McPherson. I went to West Point with him. He graduated first in our class. I know that might not mean much for you two, but Mac was as much a protégé of Robert E. Lee as I was. More even."

"So he's one to be wary of?" Cleburne asked.

Hood stared into the fire, sad eyes growing sadder. "Hands down, money on the barrel, James Birdseye McPherson is the best man in their army. He won't run, he won't make mistakes, and he will make things very hard on us tomorrow."

CHAPTER 9

May 5
Shortly after midnight
Headquarters, Army of Tennessee, CSA
Redding Ridge

"I failed in my duty after Romney," Jackson said quietly. "That much is perfectly clear now. Loring was insubordinate three years ago, and has been insubordinate ever since. I should have pressed the case against that man more forcefully then, made sure he was cashiered. Instead, I took the easier path. I allowed the War Department to sweep the ugly thing under the rug. They sent Loring here. We had a chance to win easily here today, Loring's sins ruined it, and at the bottom it's all because I relaxed in my duty, and let him off the hook."

Stewart replied "I doubt you will get your court martial, you know. Some generals have done as bad or worse, and nothing ever came of it. Sometimes Richmond prefers to shove them farther from sight, instead of getting rid of them. So, they go to some less important, less visible place. Maybe they do better, maybe they do more harm. Gideon Pillow comes to mind, in that respect. He's now a conscription officer, I'm told. Loring has friends in Florida, and I think cashiering him might be an expense Richmond wants to avoid."

Jackson soured. His western Virginia twang crept into his speech. "I won't let them. Not this time. He must be punished, and the failure to punish corrected. We cannot have a dutiful, disciplined army if we do not have dutiful, disciplined officers."

Stewart nodded, but said nothing.

"This business with Loring is, in miniature, the story of our country in this war. It is as I told you before. When I think on this war, with its half-victories, its quarrelsome generals, squabbling and ineffectual politicians, the cost in blood and treasure, and all of its lost opportunities… I cannot help but think God's purpose is to correct our ways. That we will win and have our own country, but only after we have become a better people, only after we earn it."

"And I've told you before, Tom. Providence wills all momentous events, but I would be careful about thinking the will of the Divine can be so discerned. We cannot look back upon even the events of antiquity and read His will with any certainty."

Jackson shrugged. "Yes, yes. But Providence has a purpose. There is no harm in wondering at it, I suppose, only in presuming upon it. A man must endeavor to always be humble before God."

Stewart smiled. They had discussed theology many times before, and he imaged Jackson was much like the Crusader of old. The more costly the task, the more it called for devotion.

Jackson stood up. "Well, Pete, I don't want to keep you any longer."

Stewart rose. "Do you have any orders for tomorrow?"

"No, no. Expect written battle orders shortly, but not yet."

Stewart saluted and left. Jackson took to his knees and prayed for a time. Then he sat down and thought things over. He didn't bother with his map. Every detail was already fixed in his mind, as he had studied every square yard of ground through the day.

I have 46,000 of all arms, Jackson thought, while the enemy cannot have above 35,000. If he is still there tomorrow, it's because McPherson does not yet know he is outnumbered. My obfuscation won't last long, perhaps not past tomorrow morning. I must strike him now, despite this mediocre ground, while I still have the advantage, else he falls back to Huntsville or Nashville. I cannot allow the enemy to gain the safety of their fortresses. If that happens, all will be for naught. If my strategy is to bear any fruit, I must strike McPherson here and now.

Jackson's conclusion was to attack, but to attack where, and in what manner? A wide flanking movement, out between Lawrenceburg and Pulaski, would take too long. A shorter movement to flank and assail the enemy's left would surely be observed, would reveal the size of his army, and could be easily countered. Worse, success would only push the enemy back on Lawrenceburg and the Military Road, leaving open their line of retreat. Finally, the enemy would surely expect an attack of some kind on their left. General Polk had been urging just such a maneuver all day.

Jackson settled on his plan. He had Sandie woken up to prepare the initial written orders. At dawn, Polk's and Stewart's Corps were to put out a double skirmish line, deploying two companies instead of the more usual one, to seize control of the valley between the two armies. It offered a partially covered approach for an attack, and that at least had some potential. He granted permission in advance to strengthen the skirmishers and bombard enemy work parties with artillery if necessary.

Jackson checked his watch. It was just past two in the morning. With his staff busy writing orders for Polk and Stewart, he sat down and penned a new, separate set of orders himself.

Stepping out of his tent, Jackson handed the folded paper to a courier. "Send that to General Forrest. Wake him if necessary. He is to report to me immediately."

Forrest was asleep when the message reached him, bivouacked with his men in an open field southeast of Haynie Hill. He rubbed his eyes, got up, and took the message over to a nearby campfire for better reading light.

May 5, Army Headquarters

Maj. General Nathan B. Forrest, CSA

Upon receipt of this message, turn command of your brigades over to Brigadier General Abraham Buford, and report to me for further orders. Instruct General Buford to have his command ready for action at first light.

Respectfully and sincerely,

T.J. Jackson, General Commanding

He blinked. "Does this mean what I think it means?" he mumbled aloud, and read the message again. Forrest decided it did.

Twice before, Braxton Bragg had ordered him to hand over the cavalry he had personally raised, trained and armed to the command of another. The second time he responded by verbally abusing Bragg in his headquarters tent, cussing him down like a dog and challenging him to fight.

Now here Forrest was again, his command taken away from him by Stonewall Jackson, a West Pointer and one who had not even bothered to call on him yet, and given to another West Pointer, Abe Buford. That Forrest liked Buford didn't assuage his anger. This was one outrage too many, and Forrest made up his mind then and there he would suffer no more injustices from the West Point clique that ran the army, even if they hanged him for it.

Although he was filled with baleful anger, Forrest remained outwardly calm, and quietly ordered his horse saddled. Getting onto his mount, he told his aides in clipped tones to remain in camp, and that he would be going to headquarters alone. Whatever happened, it was best if none of them were involved.

Arriving at Jackson's tent village, Forrest dismounted, and strode from his horse straight through the busy throng of staffers.

James Power Smith stepped forward. "Begging your pardon, General Forrest…"

"Get out of my way" Forrest said, deliberate menace on each word, as he effortlessly shoved Smith aside and almost off his feet.

Bursting into Jackson's tent, Forrest shook the message in his hand and shouted in a thick West Tennessee drawl "What do you mean by this? Shitfire! To rob me and give my men to one of your dandy eastern favorites? You ain't going get it. I ain't going tolerate this here insult, not from you, not from any other West Point scoundrels. You can all go on back to Richmond and to Hell, far as I care. You may as well tear up these here orders, because I ain't obeying them, and I dare you to make me try."

Jackson stood flabbergasted, but only for a moment. Taking a step forward, he met Forrest's glare and snarled "You sit down, General, and be silent. Silent, silent, I say! Or I will give you cause to regret it."

Forrest had gone into that tent fully determined to challenge Jackson to fight him with pistols, right then and there, rather than give up his cavalry for a third time. He expected to be shot or hung for it, not that it mattered, for he could tolerate the indignities heaped upon him no longer. Yet now that he saw how Jackson's eyes were lit up, he paused. Instead of smacking Jackson in the jaw, he took a step backward.

Smith sprang into the tent, armed with a cocked revolver. Jackson instantly cried "Out Smith! Get out!" the hill country twang tearing through his speech. Then he bellowed at Forrest "And you! I thought I told you to sit down!"

Forrest stood motionless, eyes moving like those of a pensive cat. Smith snapped off a flustered salute and withdrew. Jackson glared at Forrest. Staring straight back at Jackson, Forrest sat down.

"I do not know what you are on about, and nor do I care" Jackson snapped at Forrest, his accent returning to normal. "I want you to assume temporary command over all the cavalry with this army. Your division and Red Jackson's."

Forrest's eyes widened. His anger dissipated instantly, replaced by the shameful sensation of having acted like a fool, a damnable, hot-tempered fool.

He was about to speak, but Jackson cut him off. "At first light, I want you to amuse the enemy left flank with one division. Give them a good theatrical, make it look like there is an army corps deploying there. With the other division, you are to cut the Pulaski Road, attack the enemy cavalry there, and drive it as far back onto the town as possible. Understood?"

"Yessir! General, I want to..."

"There is no time for that!" Jackson snapped. "It will take the rest of the night for you to get ready. You have your orders. Now get out!"

Forrest stood to attention. "Yes! Sir!" he said, deliberately emphasizing each word.

As Forrest turned to leave, Jackson said "General Forrest, if you ever so mutinously abuse any officer under my command again, I'll have you stood up against a wall and shot. If it costs a thousand lives, I'll do it."

Forrest looked back. "You won't need to worry about that, General Jackson. You have my word."

Forrest passed the tent flap. Smith was standing there, pistol lowered, but still cocked.

"Your name is Smith?" Forrest asked.

"Captain James P. Smith."

"Captain James P. Smith, I declare my temper got away from me, and I ought never to have laid hands on you like that. I hope you will accept my sincerest apologies."

Forrest extended his hand. Smith eyed the cavalryman briefly, and then took his hand. "Gladly, general. Gladly."

Jackson lingered by the tent flap until Forrest rode away. Once the cavalryman was gone, Jackson slumped onto his cot, weary and embarrassed. He had worked a lifetime to shed the accent of the western Virginia hills, to sound more like the genteel member of the Shenandoah's professional class that he had worked so hard to join. His hill speech sometimes slipped out when he became agitated, but never as badly as that before, and never as often as it had several times through that day.

He had clashed with subordinates many times before, and had been anticipating a violent confrontation with some rough-hewn western general long before now. With Frank Cheatham, perhaps. He hadn't expected anything like this. Exhausted, he blew out the lantern and fell instantly to sleep.

5 a.m.
Army of Tennessee, CSA
Oak Ridge

Just before dawn, blue soldiers quietly crawled out of their trenches and into the early morning gloom. They went over their embankments and across their shallow ditches to muster before their lines, one company from each regiment on the front line. In front of the XVI Corps, the entire strength of Yates's Sharpshooters and the Western Sharpshooters filtered out as well, taking up a position in front of the regular, musket-armed skirmishers. They formed into a loose, open formation of small groups, and began carefully walking down the slope and into the valley below.

The more alert butternut pickets heard the oncoming Billies, even if they could not see them. The jumpiest fired from their shallow rifle pits, producing random stabs of flame in the inky dark.

In the center, the Western Sharpshooters divided into three groups and rushed into action. The group in the middle advanced right up to the tree line, marking the start of the thin woods on the valley floor, and began to fire as quickly as their 16-shot repeating rifles allowed. Confronted by a shocking flood of bullets, the Rebels clung to the dirt of their shallow rifle pits, while the blue sharpshooters on the left and right charged right through the picket line, firing rapidly as they went. Within minutes, dozens of Johnnies were surrounded. Called upon to surrender, the Rebels rose from their rifle pits in their groups of two and four, threw down their muskets, and raised their hands.

On the eastern end of the valley, the skirmishing was more evenly matched, both sides carrying similar arms and turned out in similar numbers. Still, the job of the Rebel pickets was to give a warning, not to stand up and resist a serious attack. Stewart's men returned fire for a few minutes, and then fell back through the wood lots and across the valley floor.

Yates's Sharpshooters and the other blue skirmishers advanced into very different terrain on the Federal right. They moved into a thickly overgrown and wooded ravine bottomed by Coon Creek, and found the Rebel pickets waiting for them on the other side. The Billies took cover behind trees, rocks and under bluffs, and kept up a steady fire. They inched their way forward, and when they got close enough, the butternuts shrank away from the sharpshooters and their deadly repeaters.

Veatch's skirmishers advanced up and out of the ravine, and over the low hill that separated Veatch's line from Featherston's Confederates. Finding another ravine on the other side, they stopped, found cover, and sniped at the Confederate main line, a little less than 200 yards distant.

The musketry in the valley wound down to random cracks, but only for a short time. At first light, a doubled line of skirmishers from Stewart's Corps advanced into the valley to resume the struggle. Polk's skirmishers, somewhat tardy, went forward a little later.

6 a.m.
Stewart's Corps, Army of Tennessee, CSA
Haynie Hill

Stewart watched the Federal lines closely through his telescope. There was little light to see by, but he could tell the Yankees had gotten the jump on his men. Now his skirmishers would have to fight their way forward if they were to control the woods between the armies. He could also see those work gangs emerging from the Federal entrenchments, setting out to cut timber for obstacles and to strengthen their works.

Turning to his chief of artillery, Stewart said "Colonel, you have a clear line of fire along that slope all the way to the Military Road. I want case shot put down on any man swinging an axe. Don't worry about counter-battery fire. Keep it hot on those work details, and whoever else you can see and hit.

The guns on Haynie Hill and Stewart's portion of the Redding Ridge line fired off one by one. These were Stewart's rifled cannons and 12-pounder Napoleons, since his 6-pounder field guns and his howitzers were too puny to hit targets at this range.

Enough to harass, Stewart thought. But not enough to stop the work.

"Send to General Polk" he said to his aides. "Give my compliments, and request that he open fire with his artillery, targeting the Federal work gangs. Then send to General Jackson, requesting that some of Hood's heavy guns be passed forward and posted to Haynie Hill. And send word down to the brigade commanders: reinforce the skirmish line to the strength of three companies."

8 a.m.
XV Corps, Army of the Tennessee, USA
Oak Ridge

McPherson found Logan observing from the extreme left of the Oak Ridge line, just above where the ridge came down to the farming country beyond. Dismounting, McPherson went over and shook hands.

"Good morning, Jack" McPherson said. "I heard you have some activity on the left. I came to have a look for myself." He pulled out his field glasses.

"Yeap. It's cavalry out there, thick as flies in a hog's waller. You can see infantry marching around behind them, between the farms and wood lots. Two batteries have unlimbered out there too, and I see more rattling around."

"I see them," McPherson said quietly, calmly. "It's busy, but thin out there. No sign of a concentration yet."

Logan nodded. "I know. I'm not worried. If they mass for an attack, we'll see it for two miles off. That is plenty of time to bring up Osterhaus."

McPherson smiled. If he had a man who won't holler for reinforcements until he absolutely needed them, that was John Logan.

"There is one other thing, Mac. Confederate batteries are playing merry hell with my work details. Sharpshooters too, what with those long-ranged, British-made rifles they have. My axe men are taking heavier casualties than my skirmishers."

Sweeney's having similar troubles, McPherson thought. Only Veatch is making real progress with fashioning his abatis. There is quite a brisk engagement going on down there in the valley. The Rebels have thrown forward a heavy skirmish line. And this artillery. Lots of smoke, but nothing heavy yet. Maybe the Bishop can't decide what to do?

"Keep your skirmishers out, but pull your work details in," McPherson ordered. "Send that to Sweeney too. No sense in paying for work we aren't going to finish."

9 a.m.
Red Jackson's Division, Army of Tennessee, CSA
The Pulaski Road

Upon assuming command of all of the army's cavalry, Forrest detached one brigade from his old command, now under Abe Buford, added them to Red Jackson's Division, making that into his striking force. He then instructed Buford to demonstrate against the left of the Federal line, as Forrest regarded his old troopers as the more experienced in his particular style of military theater.

Setting out before dawn with four brigades, Forrest followed a circuitous route that took them several miles east of Lawrenceburg, before heading back toward town. Coming up from due east, the scouts reported sighting Federal cavalry in the fields south of the Pulaski Road, about four miles from town.

Forrest set out to have a look for himself, and grinned maliciously at the sight of the 3rd Indiana, a regiment that had gotten away from him at Holly Grove.

Forrest hissed "Bring up the lead brigade. And do it quietly!"

Ross's Texas Brigade came up at the trot and formed behind the stand of woods sheltering Forrest and his scouts. Forrest hurriedly gave Ross his orders and launched him straight into a mounted charge at the passing blue cavalry.

The Texans thundered out from behind and through the woods in three converging columns. Instantly recognizing their predicament, the Hoosiers turned tail and ran for the road. Ross's troopers tore after them, only to charge headlong into a concealed roadblock.

As soon as the Hoosiers galloped past, dismounted blue troopers rose from swales on either side of the road and laid down a terrific fire with their mix of muzzle-loading carbines, Spencer repeaters, and Sharps breech-loaders. Dozens of men and horses at the front of the charge fell in a matter of seconds, the charge stumbled to a halt, and the Texans turned their horses about in disarray.

Watching from a short distance to the rear, Minty ordered "Signal the charge."

The bugles sounded, and a pair of fresh, mounted regiments sprang out from concealed positions at an outlying farm. Pounding down rapidly over the fields, they were upon the disorganized Texans within minutes.

Forrest found himself in the midst of a confused melee. A Yankee came up beside him and swung with his saber. Forrest ducked forward, the saber removing only his hat, instead of the top of his skull. He quickly seized the trooper by the sword arm before it could be pulled back for another blow, and yanked him forward. Snatching the musketoon from his saddle holster, Forrest stuck the gun into the man's chest and pulled the trigger. The Yankee was knocked from the saddle in a blast of buck and ball.

After holstering the musketoon, Forrest drew both of his pistols, spurred his horse forward, and shot his way out of the battle. The Texans were already withdrawing from the Yankee ambush. A few hundred yards back down the road, the Rebel cavalry reorganized.

Riding up to Ross, Forrest drawled "Don't you worry now, General Ross. My oldest rule about being in a fight is if you can't win, skedaddle."

Ross, a veteran Indian fighter from the Texas Rangers, nodded. "Can't say I disagree. What are your orders, sir?"

Forrest smiled "That's where we get to my second oldest rule. After you skedaddle, hit them back hard as you can, soon as you can. Don't let that other fellow get no airs." Forrest commanded an aide to bring up the rest of the division.

A few hundred yards to the west, Minty ordered his men back to their mounts. They were fine feather, having started the day by getting a good, clean twist on their rivals.

Minty sent them back to a more defensible position. "When the Rebs come back, let them hit empty air, and then lunge forward to find us, putting them off-balance again. Then we'll try hitting them again."

10:30 a.m.
Hood's Corps, Army of Tennessee, CSA
Redding Ridge

The head of Hood's column reached the area behind Redding Ridge with suitable fanfare, a fife and drum band leading the way and playing "The Campbells Are Coming." Hood soon spied the seedy, familiar form of Jackson, sitting on a tree stump and sucking on a lemon.

The bugles sounded "Halt." Fletcher watched as Hood, Cheatham, and Maney all rode over to greet the scruffy, one-armed man in the colonel's coat and crumpled, threadbare kepi.

Fletcher glanced over his shoulder. "Willie, is that him?"

Willie was grinning, "Yessir!" Nathan stood next to him,

chuckling.

Fletcher turned his attention back to the generals. Jackson stood over some bald ground, sketching something in the dirt with his sword. Cheatham and Maney were on their feet, but Hood remained mounted. Probably because of Old Pegleg's straps, Fletcher thought. Too much fuss and bother to get him down, not for mere decorum.

Minutes later, Maney returned, calling in his staff and the regimental colonels. After a brief discussion, the brigade was led off the road and into the woods neighboring it. Fletcher turned out his company as the regiment formed a double line of battle, two rows of two ranks each. The rest of the brigade formed on the regiment's right. Then orders came to fall out, but stay in formation.

No sooner had the Tennesseans sat down and begun rummaging through their haversacks when Old Jack himself rode up, in company with Old Frank and Old Pegleg, plus staff. Most of the regiment was instantly on its feet, waving their hats and pumping their muskets in the air, but remaining completely quiet as per their orders not to cheer.

Jackson smiled and tipped his kepi. He said to Cheatham "I want these lines spaced a further 60 paces apart. And when your other brigades form on Maney's rear, General Cheatham, space them accordingly. I don't want these men crowded together, so put plenty of room between them all. Sam, the same dispositions for Cleburne when he gets here. Understood?"

Both generals nodded. "Good. General Hood, would you accompany me to your artillery?"

The generals went their separate ways. The Grimes brothers plopped back down. A few minutes later, Colonel Tillman ordered the regiment's second line to retire 60 paces, leaving Fletcher's company and the front line in peace.

Nathan rooted through his haversack. Willie leaned forward hungrily. "What you got in there, Nathan?"

Nathan raised an eyebrow. "Boy, I thought I told you not to eat all your hoecake this morning. You know I ain't got so much." The regiment had been issued three days rations and told to cook them up after crossing the Tennessee, and that was three days ago.

"I know, I know, but that ain't stopped a good boy from being hungry yet, ain't it?"

Willie was always like that, Nathan thought. Give him three days rations and they were gone in two, if not one. He took out his last hunk of half-stale, pan-fried cornbread, broke it in half, and gave it over to his brother.

Standing nearby, Fletcher's own belly was cold and devoid of appetite as he stared up the wooded slope before them. He couldn't relax, and wondered how anyone could. They could all hear the ringing of the cannon in the distance, and they all knew they were sitting in an attack formation. More tense than actually nervous, he fidgeted by rubbing his hands, sipping from his canteen, and fussing with his sword.

How can any of them eat and joke, Fletcher thought, knowing the elephant was just past that ridge there, waiting to trample them.

11a.m.
Army of the Tennessee, USA
Oak Ridge

As he stood behind the lines watching the artillery duel, oblivious to the odd bursting shell or bounding solid, McPherson marveled at the industry of his men. Though the effort to cover the front and left flank of his entire position with abatis had been abandoned, details of troops took their axes and saws into White Oak Hollow, in the army's rear, and began felling trees there. Osterhaus's men, standing in reserve there, joined the effort. A steady stream of timber for head logs and braces, improvements for the entrenchments, had been trickling up to the front ever since, and all of it without orders.

The Confederate artillery worried him, however. He watched through his field glasses as another Rebel battery limbered up and retired off Haynie Hill, just to be replaced by a fresh battery minutes later.

It's all too damn efficient, McPherson thought. Rumor had it that A.P. Stewart was over on the Confederate right, which coincided with intelligence from before the campaign started. He could credit those rumors. The cannon over there were handled very smoothly, and matching his artillery gun for gun. It had all the hallmarks of a former gunner turned mathematics professor.

Another problem was the loss of the battle of skirmishers that had been going on all morning, a point that annoyed McPherson. Unwilling to feed any more men into the firefight that had smoldered and sparked all morning on the valley floor, he had pulled his skirmishers back to the main line under mounting Confederate pressure. Now the butternuts were sniping at his main line, but at least his boys could shoot back from the protection of solid earthworks.

McPherson was about to return to his headquarters when a dusty courier on a foaming, sweaty horse arrived, bearing a message from Minty:

Morning of May 5, 10:00

To: Maj. Gen'l James B. McPherson
Cmnd'ing, Army of the Tennessee

As previously reported, Rebel cavalry now block the Pulaski Road to the east, and assault my front with dismounted troopers, supported by 12 guns. They are working around both my flanks. I am compelled to withdraw two miles to a new line closer to Lawrenceburg.

I urgently request infantry support. Without reinforcements, I am uncertain of my ability to hold my new position or keep Rebels out of the wagon park for more than two hours.

Your Obedient Servant,

Robert H.G. Minty
Colonel, US Cavalry

"Forrest," McPherson thought aloud. "It has to be Forrest." He knew Forrest was out there, and such a determined attack by mounted infantry and dismounted cavalry could only mean him. He also knew how highly Sherman rated the Memphis cavalryman, considering him at least as much of a threat as Stonewall Jackson.

McPherson rode back to his headquarters, and swiftly wrote out orders for General John E. Smith, the middle-aged Swiss immigrant, Galena, Illinois jeweler, and Grant crony who had surprisingly turned out to be quite a good soldier. Smith was to march to Minty's relief and take overall command, leaving behind adequate guards for the wagon park.

That will bring the force west of Lawrenceburg to about 7,000, McPherson thought. Smith and Minty ought to be able to stop Forrest's advance cold with that much.

11 a.m.
Headquarters, Army of Tennessee, CSA
Jackson's Headquarters

Polk rode to army headquarters at the head of an entourage of staff officers, all nattily turned out in clean uniforms with sparkling gold braid and trim.

Standing off to one side, Sandie chuckled and whispered to Dr. McGuire "One wonders why he left the marching band at home." The doctor nodded, grinning. Polk had the most spit and polish staff either man had ever seen in any army, east or west, north or south.

Dismounting from his horse, Polk prepared his emotions for the meeting with Jackson, carefully tucking away the foul temper aroused by the commanding general's arrogant and overbearing conduct. Not only had Jackson sent Loring to attack Wildcat Ridge and then sacked him without even so much as a "by your leave," but then that man had sent Stewart and not Polk to decide whether that attack should go forward. It was as bad as any of the slights perpetrated by Braxton Bragg, but Polk knew he had to proceed carefully and remain the good cleric in his chief's eyes. For now.

Sandie greeted Polk, and led him into Jackson's tent. After some brief pleasantries and questions about Featherston's status on the left, Jackson began issuing orders.

"General Polk, you will commence the attack in one hour, at 12 o'clock, by advancing Featherston's Division en echelon, by brigade and to the right."

Polk understood. He was to commence a rolling attack down the line, one brigade after the other.

"Sir, begging your pardon, but Featherston's three frontline brigades have been in a vicious little fight all morning with Yankee skirmishers. It ended only a short while ago, and they have shot off half their ammunition. The men must replenish their cartridge boxes before making a major attack. If I could have but an additional hour to do that…?"

Sandie expected Jackson to tell Polk to redistribute ammunition from his reserve brigade, bringing everyone up to an acceptable level, or even that Featherston should charge with pikes if he had to. Instead, Jackson quietly nodded, giving his assent.

Behind his serene smile, Polk was satisfied, if only slightly. He didn't actually know how much ammunition Featherston's men had used or how much they needed, let alone how much time would be required to top up their cartridge boxes. What mattered was that he had gotten his say in, and it stuck. That was a start.

Jackson continued. "When Featherston's last brigade goes forward, General French is not to move. Instead, he is to remain where he is and wait for a passage of the lines."

"And just who will be passing through French's line, General?"

Jackson ignored the question. "Featherston is to keep the pressure on. He is not to break contact with the enemy, not without direct orders from me. I want you to keep a close eye on him, General Polk. He is new to division command."

Polk realized the interview was over. He stood and saluted. "Yessir." Sandie handed him a set of written orders, one for himself, one for Featherston and one for French, and sent him on his way.

1 p.m.
Headquarters, Army of the Tennessee, USA

McPherson was reading the latest report from John Smith, indicating the situation east of town had stabilized, when he was approached by his chief of staff, Colonel William T. Clark.

"Mac, I have the initial reports from those prisoners we took earlier this morning. They confirm the identity of the four secessionist divisions posted opposite. I think the presence of

Stevenson, Clayton and French are beyond doubt. It's definitely Polk's Army of Mississippi infantry, plus Stewart's Corps."

McPherson nodded. Clark was an eastern-educated lawyer, and was very good at sorting through papers and reports. It was why McPherson had brought him up to his present post.

"There is something else, sir."

The fretful tone in Clark's voice caused McPherson to give him his full attention. "Yes? There is a problem?"

"Many of the prisoners boast that Stonewall Jackson is over there, and he has Hood's Corps with him. Now it could just be loud, no account talk. You know how the Rebs are. But the other fellows cussed and hushed the braggarts up quick."

"But that isn't all, is it?"

"No, General. The prisoners from what we think is Loring's Division. They say it's now Featherston's Division, on account of Jackson putting Loring under arrest."

That aroused McPherson's curiosity. Rebel prisoners were often full of bluster and balderdash, and sending out false deserters with orders to spread equally false information was an old Confederate ploy. Even so, that last detail was a little too elaborate. It had the whiff of truth to it.

McPherson stood up and said "I want to see these men, and hear that story myself."

"I thought you might, sir."

CHAPTER 10

1 p.m.
Featherston's Division, Army of Tennessee, CSA
The Confederate Left

Winfield Featherston was a trim, handsome man in early middle age, armed with the genial smile of a Mississippi lawyer and politician. His men called him "Old Swet," and he didn't lack for personal courage. Yet he knew the more senior generals whispered he was unfit for higher command, so he was eager to prove himself. He was keeping a close eye on his watch, and when the minute hand struck one, he nodded to his bugler. The call rang out, and the advance was begun.

The skirmishers crossed a thickly wooded gully with a muddy, rocky watercourse at the bottom, and climbed up onto the tableland beyond. Featherston's three lead brigades followed, marching in columns by division so as to pass more quickly over the rough terrain. Even so, it took almost an hour to cross the half-mile distance and form a new line on the other side. Featherston's fourth brigade brought up the rear, following a few hundred yards behind and in reserve.

As his main line formed up and dressed their ranks out of sight of the enemy, Featherston dismounted and went forward, to the edge of the ravine with the skirmishers. Taking up a position behind a tree, he surveyed the ground before him, and what he beheld left him appalled.

All the forest and undergrowth in the ravine had been felled and turned into a maze of abatis, a tangle of sharpened tree branches. At the bottom of the ravine was a stream, Coon Creek, and the Yankee line stood on the other side. The ground the Federal position stood on was too gnarled with tree roots to dig up, so instead the Yankees had built log barricades, fronted by a palisade of sharpened stakes.

Featherston sent back for his superior, and showed him the Yankee fortifications. "I can't attack this, General Polk," he whispered, so as to keep the men from overhearing him. "Sending the division to assail that line isn't war, it's murder!"

"You have no choice, General Featherston," Polk replied quietly, standing in the open and unfazed by the bullets cracking against the nearby tree trunks. "The commanding general has ordered it, and must be obeyed. You saw what happened to poor Loring when he protested too much."

Featherston imagined himself sent back to brigade command with his hopes dashed, or perhaps meeting an even worse fate. Robert E. Lee had already sent him packing from the Army of Northern Virginia more than a year ago. He knew Old Jack was a harsh taskmaster, and the thought of what he might do...

"Very well, although I want my protest noted. For the record, General Polk."

"So noted, General Featherston." Polk smiled, seeing himself as nursing the grievances of men like Featherston, laying bricks of support. Polk was isolated now, his resentment unshared, but that would change, given time. The anti-Bragg faction wasn't built in a day, after all.

The Mississippians of Featherston's own former brigade advanced out of the trees and onto the slope of the ravine, and were met instantly by blasts of canister. They rushed forward through the spray of iron balls, pouring down the ravine through the gaps in the abatis. Bunched up and disordered, the butternuts splashed through the stream to find their way around the next layer of obstacles, when the Yankees rose from behind their log walls, pointed their muskets down, and unleashed heavy, rolling volleys of fire.

The advance quickly stumbled to a gory halt, the Rebel infantry throwing themselves behind the abatis, the odd boulder, or onto the slope before the Yankee line, anywhere that offered even the slightest hope of escaping the avalanche of bullets and canister balls pouring down onto Coon Creek. They were joined by Scott's Alabamans, and then Adams's Mississippians. With all three brigades in the ravine, the Federal fire spread noticeably thinner, and Featherston saw a chance.

"Sound the charge," he ordered his bugler.

After a few minutes' pause, men all along the creek began the crawl up the slope in small groups, returning fire as best they could. Featherston saw General John Adams, the sole Old Army man among his brigadiers, stand up, brandishing his sword and calling on his colors to follow him. His whole brigade came on slowly behind him. They had advanced not more than a dozen yards before Adams fell, mortally wounded. The advance on the right halted, men throwing themselves back down onto the ground.

"Retreat! Sound the retreat!" Featherston cried. The division was soon scrambling back up their own slope and to the cover of the tree line, the Federals shooting at their backs the entire way. Scott's Brigade fell into positions behind the trees and rocks around Featherston, returning fire. He watched as a trio of men hauled a gum blanket bearing Thomas Scott into the woods.

"Scott! Sweet Jesus, Scott! Are you alright?!"

Scott was oddly cheerful. "Never fear, Winnie. I took a ball in the foot. Can't walk, but I reckon I'll live. Can't say the same for poor old Adams. You saw?"

Featherston nodded, stifling tears. He suddenly realized Scott was putting on a show for his men, and that he was spoiling it with his outburst. "Yes. Yes, I did. General Scott, turn command of your brigade over to your next man…"

Scott interrupted "That'd be Snodgrass, sir. Will do."

"… and I'll send word to Quarles. He'll bring his boys up and replace yours on the firing line." After that catastrophe, I need a fresh brigade on the firing line, Featherston thought. Quarles is that brigade.

Featherston saluted and saw Scott off before returning his attention to supervising his line. His orders were to stay in contact with the enemy, and for that a long range firefight would do. He wouldn't put his men back into Coon Creek's seething cauldron, whatever god damned Stonewall Jackson might do to him.

2:45 p.m.
Hood's Corps, Army of Tennessee, CSA
The Confederate Center

Jackson closely watched the Federal line from the place where the Military Road crossed Redding Ridge, paying no heed to the odd cannonball or exploding shell. The roar of muskets and guns coming from the enemy right, over by the Horseshoe Bend, told him all he needed to know.

No need to wait for Polk's confirmation. He knew Featherston was engaged. Forrest had reported strong infantry on his front hours ago, so the enemy had committed at least some of his reserves to a place that was miles away from the critical point, where his main blow would fall. Stewart had most of the army's heavy guns, and was bombarding the enemy's left. Hood's Corps was formed up behind the center. It was time.

Jackson's eyes lit up brightly, but otherwise he appeared calm. He said flatly "Order the artillery pressed forward, Captain Smith," and then rode away to join Hood.

From late morning and into the afternoon, Hood's light, six pounder batteries had been infiltrated from behind Redding Ridge, through the thin woods. Now these batteries were unleashed. Several of these guns clattered out onto the Military Road and went forward, stopping to unlimber some 300 yards from the Federal line. The muzzles of several more field guns emerged from the woods, 200 yards before the Federal left-center. These guns opened on the surprised blue troops, blasting selected points of their earthworks with solid shot and canister.

Union artillery reacted quickly, smoothly diverting counter-battery fire from Stewart's heavy guns on Haynie Hill to this new threat. Within minutes, the first Rebel gun on the Military Road was silenced, soon followed by another. Covered by Stewart's guns and under some cover, the Rebel cannons in the valley fared better, and these soon had the Yankee infantry and gunners in front of them keeping their heads down.

Cheatham, Cleburne and Hood were in the rear, sitting mounted along with their staffs amid a stout lance of a column, eight brigades strong, aimed squarely at the Union center. Hood and Cheatham were chatting and in high spirits, while Cleburne was barely mindful of the conversation, his thoughts focused on the attack to come.

Having taken full advantage of the time afforded him, Cleburne had ordered all his division's muskets to remain unloaded, putting his staff and even himself to work with spot inspections to ensure the division's weapons stayed that way, all the while painstakingly briefing his officers on what why he wanted it that way and of what was expected of them. There would be no temptation for his men to stop and fire, not with the added necessity of having to load from scratch. What was more, his men had started the day on full bellies and with full canteens, were well-rested, well-armed, and well-trained.

In Cleburne's experience, such preparation and attention to detail was the key to battlefield success, starting in the training camp, and running right up to the very moment the orders were given and the men committed. Burdened with this attitude, Cleburne always fretted before an attack, worrying whether there was anything more he could do. But he always kept that anxiety tucked away behind a practiced mask of grim severity. Doubt was infectious, and he took care not to send the wrong message to his soldiers.

A courier came for Hood. He thanked the man graciously, and read the message. Hood said "It's time. Gentlemen, I'll see you at the top."

Cleburne and Cheatham rode back to their divisions. Reaching the front of his Tennesseans, Cheatham pulled his flask from under his coat and guzzled the dregs. Turning to his chief of staff, he said "Major, reload me" and traded his empty flask for a fresh one.

Thus fortified, Cheatham trotted between the double lines of Maney's and Strahl's Brigade. Fletcher and his company were standing in Maney's first line, a front row seat for Cheatham's brief speech.

"Boys," Cheatham called out, "I have a confession to make. I pine for my homeplace, for my family. I admit it, I'm homesick! The thought of it makes Old Frank here weepy as hell!"

After the laughter from the ranks died down, Cheatham continued. "I want to go home, boys. And I know I'm not alone. Ten minutes of shitfire and lead, and then it's on to Nashville. Who will come with me?"

Fletcher looked to the ground as men all around him gave Cheatham three hearty hurrahs. He was past cheering about anything to do with fighting, even for Old Frank.

The order to advance was shouted out, and Fletcher stepped off, the Grimes brothers alongside him. Maney and Strahl's brigades walked over the top of Redding Ridge, where they found French's Division, the men lying down behind their earthworks. Shouts of "Prepare for passage of lines!" were heard up and down the line. French's soldiers lay prone, doing their best to stay out of the way of the passing Tennesseans, and shouting encouragement as they went by.

From French's main line, they walked down into the light woods in the valley bottom. The odd shell or case shot exploded in the tree tops, but these did little harm unless they struck just so, adding wooden splinters to the shower of iron. After a few minutes, the advancing Johnnies passed another line, this time composed of French's retreating skirmishers, and repeated the passage. This was even easier than before, as the skirmishers were in loose order and there was no earthen embankment to cross.

Coming up to their own artillery, the forefront of Cheatham's advance, Maney and Strahl, halted their brigades briefly, sidling to the left and into proper alignment. Marching a little more slowly, but with somewhat greater care to precision, the first line of Cleburne's lead brigades, Granbury's Texans and Lowery's Alabamans, arrived on Maney's left and paused for a few minutes to dress their ranks just as Cheatham's troops stepped off.

Maney's Brigade was the first to step out of the cover of the undulating forest and into the afternoon sun. Fletcher squinted and saw what looked like 200 yards of open ground leading up to the Yankee position. Up and down the line, officers drew their swords, and waved them above their heads or jabbed them at the earthworks ahead, shouting "Forward! Onward!"

Fletcher merely gritted his teeth, made a conscious, deliberate effort to put his foot forward, and stepped out with a shout of "Come on!"

Nathan smirked. The Captain was never much for show, even less so over the last year. Brave, but not flashy. It was one of the things Nathan liked about him. Then he heard the boom, hunched his shoulders and put his head down in an involuntary spasm, but continued to press forward. He looked up and suddenly realized he was alone, no one standing to either side of him.

Nathan spun around and found Willie lying two steps behind him, already trying to sit up, part of his face thick with blood. He threw himself down to his brother with a cry.

Willie mumbled "I'm alright. Alright!" feeling at his face with one hand and trying to shoo Nathan away with the other. Nathan batted Willie's hands out of the way, pulled his brother's jacket open and felt down the right side of his chest, where the coat had been perforated. He pulled out a shredded Bible, full of bits of metal and wood, and then threw it away.

"Nathan!" Willie cried, confused, but outraged at the loss of his Bible. Nathan saw Willie's musket, lying nearby and smashed to bits. A splinter from the stock had sliced his brother's face open, and was still stuck halfway up his cheek. His eye was still there, clear and fine. Nathan had seen wounds before, terrible wounds, and almost laughed with relief at the sight of this one.

"Reckon your musket were hit by a bolt or something like that." Canister rounds were packed with one-inch iron balls in the main, but also with whatever leftovers happened to be on the foundry floor.

Willie cried "Captain Fletcher!" and pointed to his left. Nathan went over and found the Captain lying on the ground, fumbling for something in his pockets.

Fletcher said weakly "Tourniquet. My tourniquet." He had fished his tourniquet out of a pocket and held it out. His foot lay twisted backwards at a sickening angle, half-smashed off above the ankle by a canister ball.

Nathan took the tourniquet, wrapped it around Fletcher's upper calf, cinched it up and clamped it down. He then took the Captain's revolver, and stuffed it under his belt.

Fletcher protested feebly, but Nathan ignored him, saying "I reckon you won't be needing this Navy six, sir, but I might."

"Willie, I want you to get Captain Fletcher here back, you understand?" Willie tried to protest, but Nathan cut him off. "He's hurt bad and so are you. Now get!"

Without waiting to see if he would be obeyed by his younger brother, Nathan snatched up his musket and ran off to catch up with his company. As he sprinted, he looked to the right, in the direction of a loud, tearing racket. Rapid stabs of flame and smoke projected from under the head logs of the Yankee works, all aimed at Strahl's Brigade.

Strahl's Brigade had come before that part of the blue line manned by the Western Sharpshooters. Beefed up to almost 700 strong by successful winter recruiting and armed to a man with deadly Henry rifles, the sharpshooters threw as much metal as a battery of 12 pounders packed with double canister. They tore savagely at Strahl's butternuts, with musketry from neighboring regiments added in for good measure, decimating the brigade's first line in just a few minutes. The grey ranks buckled, and they recoiled back to the relative safety of the woods, there to wait for Strahl's second line to come up.

Nathan caught up with the company just as Maney's first line entered a swale about 100 yards from the Yankees, coming to an involuntary halt. The officers were still urging the men forward, but the Johnnies wouldn't budge from the slight shelter of the swale. Instead, they shouldered their muskets and returned fire.

Although many knelt or laid down for better protection, Nathan was among those who remained standing. He shouldered his musket and put a bullet into an enemy head log, then automatically brought his musket down, and pulled a paper cartridge from the leather box on his belt. Tearing the top off with his teeth, the acrid taste of gunpowder entered his mouth. He spat the bit of paper in his teeth away, poured the powder into the barrel, rammed the bullet down, returned the ramrod, brought the musket back up, and primed it in a quick, smooth series of motions. Reloading took less than 15 seconds. Nathan shouldered his musket and fired another shot.

He kept reloading and firing in rapid succession. At this distance and through the rapidly thickening smoke, he couldn't even see the opening under the head log, much less hit it, so instead he concentrated on putting as many bullets as he could into what he could see or knew must be there. If he put all his bullets close enough, one or two might pass through that slit between the dirt embankment and the head log.

Nathan was bringing up his musket for his fifth shot when Cleburne's line surged by on his left. They marched past at the double quick, trailing bloodied casualties in their wake. Yet they kept going, gave a piercing wolf howl, and charged the Yankee earthworks. In a matter of minutes, this first line of Cleburne's infantry was scrambling over the head logs, firing and stabbing down into the entrenchments below.

Maney appeared before his brigade, on foot and waving his sword, yelling "Cleburne's got the style, boys! Cleburne's got the style! Follow me, howl like furies, and charge in!"

Quelling his fear, Nathan stepped out of the swale after Maney, the very first of his regiment to follow. That shallow depression offered very little shelter, and as terrible as going forward was, he knew it was safer for everyone than staying where they were. There was nothing for it but to put his head down, follow Maney, and go forward, or else turn around and go back.

Nathan's face was soon sprayed with blood as Major Miller, who had sprinted out in front of him, was shot through the neck. He fell gurgling. Nathan grimaced, but continued, leaving the dying man behind and keeping his place in the ragged, advancing line. After covering half the distance, Maney yelled "Charge!" The brigade hollered a full-throated shriek, and ran forward.

Nathan leapt over the ditch, scrambled up the embankment and onto the parapet, and jumped onto the surprised Yankee beneath him with both feet. Pinning the man to the ground, Nathan stabbed down into his chest with his bayonet. Pulling the bayonet free with a jerk, Nathan spun his musket around, and swept the butt across the mortally wounded man's skull for good measure.

He could hear calls of "Fall back, boys!" and "Run!" in the familiar, flat accent of the Buckeye and the Hoosier. Stepping onto the slope behind the wide trench, Nathan took aim with his musket and put a bullet squarely between the shoulders of a fleeing man not 15 yards away. He smiled, sweet and murderous.

Nathan dropped his rifle, kneeled onto the dry dirt of the trench's back slope, and drew Fletcher's Navy six shooter from his belt. He took slow, deliberate aim, and one by one emptied the revolver's six shots into a large knot of Yankees who were withdrawing, backing out in good order instead of fleeing.

The revolver empty, he lay down, rolled over, and began awkwardly reloading his musket from atop his belly. He looked over just in time to see the neighboring Texans cheering and clearing a path for Patrick Cleburne. Never much of a horseman,

Cleburne rode a sedate old mare, and carefully walked her through a captured battery, instead of jumping his horse over the earthworks.

Cleburne's countenance was as cold as ever, but beneath his granite reserve he was brimming with pride. Yet he knew there was little time for enjoying what his men had accomplished. A brief look to the north revealed a brigade of blue infantry drawing up about 600 yards away. He could also see the fleeing Yankees were hardly broken, not really, not yet. They were drawing off in orderly groups for the most part, not running away in terrified chaos.

As he watched the northerners begin a rally around their reserve, Cleburne felt a powerful urge to go forward and smash them. He had two fresh brigades coming up in support, and felt the momentum to drive straight on. He could swiftly rout those Yankees, keep them running, chase them straight down the Military Road and all the way through Lawrenceburg.

But those were not his orders. Instead, Cleburne was to turn west, press into the woods and roll up the Federal right. He believed French was probably to come up and press the Yankee center, but that was just a guess. In stark contrast to the way things were done under Bragg, Cleburne's orders were limited strictly to what he and Cheatham were to do, and said nothing of French's Division in their rear.

The Irishman hesitated for a moment, indecisive from the temptation, but he soon made up his mind. He turned his horse and rode over to where General Hiram Granbury stood, gleefully slapping his newly captured cannon.

Granbury had his hat off, his wild, messy shock of brown hair half-slicked with sweat. "General Cleburne! Take a gander at my six new cannon. Fine Yankee iron rifles, every one!"

"Granbury, your men accomplished such a feat today as to discolor the countenance of Her Majesty's guards with spite and envy. But we have little time. I want you and General Lowery out of these earthworks. Form a line of battle and advance about a fifth of a mile. 300 yards or so. The Federals are reforming over there, and I want you to block them. I'll see about getting some guns sent up to support you."

After repeating those orders to Lowery, Cleburne rode back to hurry up his remaining two brigades and the artillery, without even so much as a backward glance. All of Cleburne's brigadiers had come up under his tutelage, and he had every confidence in them.

3:45 pm
Sweeney's Division, Army of the Tennessee, USA
Behind the Federal Center

McPherson returned to his now crumpled center to find General Thomas Sweeney, a Cork County man, riding to and fro, cussing and hollering at his men to rally. To McPherson's relief, they were, and reforming swiftly at that.

He probably is just as connipted as he seems, McPherson thought. They had called him "Fighting Tom" in the Old Army ever since the Mexican War, so Sweeney's angry, hard-driving and utterly profane style under pressure was a very familiar sight.

McPherson dealt with the crisis in a different way, hiding his excitement and anxiety behind a calm reserve. A pugnacious, short-fused character like Sweeney could afford to thunder and rant about like that, for it was expected of him. McPherson knew if he did such an out-of-character thing, it would alarm the men. So instead, he offered them words of encouragement as he made his way over to Sweeney.

"Tom, how are your losses?"

"Eh? Not bad! Not bad, sir! I'll pull the division together, right as rain and soon enough, and go straight over there and knock those Reb bastards about the head. Drive the swine right back out of my trenches."

Upon closer inspection, Sweeney seemed a little more flustered than McPherson had first thought. Beneath the braggadocio, the man was embarrassed and upset about being driven from his earthworks, even though he had brought his division out of it intact.

"Alright, Tom. Alright," McPherson said soothingly. "The boys seem more confused than scared. Now, I'm sending more artillery up to Wildcat Ridge. Those guns will shield your position here. Osterhaus is coming up from White Oak Hollow on your left. Let the artillery soften those bastards up for you, and wait for Osterhaus. When he comes up, you both go in together.

Understood?"

Sweeney nodded and went back to work. McPherson lingered and watched the Rebels. As he had been talking to Sweeney, two Confederate brigades had formed a new line just beyond the captured earthworks. Now they were moving forward.

As they did so, they came under fire from the guns on Wildcat Ridge. Thus far, the cannon on that hill had played little part in the battle, since Redding Ridge was out of range and most of the ground in-between was either wooded or out of sight. Now the butternuts were coming onto ground those cannon could hit.

4:00 pm
Cheatham's Division, Army of Tennessee, AOT
In the Captured Entrenchments

Hood was full of joy. It was all so perfect. He was under the command of a man he respected and admired, almost as much as Robert E. Lee. His corps had led the attack, gloriously piercing the Union center. What was more, Captain James Power Smith had just brought him written orders from Jackson, reiterating that Cleburne and Cheatham were to roll up the enemy line, but adding that French's Division would now move forward and exploit the breach in the enemy center. For the time being, French would operate under his command. Jackson was giving him control over one of Polk's divisions, a clear vote of confidence. It was grander than even Gaines Mill, heretofore his greatest personal triumph.

He came forward to reassert control over his corps, and discovered Cleburne's Division was already in motion. Hood turned his horse and galloped in the direction of Cheatham's brigades, trailing staff officers as he went. He felt lighter, excitement raising him out of the weariness his recent exertions had wrought on his broken body. For the first time since Chickamauga, Hood felt like a whole man.

Finding Cheatham, Hood began issuing orders. "Frank, I want you to wheel Maney and Strahl onto the Union flank and start pressing them. Bring up your other brigades and swing them around. French will come up directly, and replace Cleburne over by the road. In the meantime, keep pushing into the Federal left and rear."

"Sam, Strahl's boys are fought out. Otho Strahl himself is wounded, may lose an arm. They had to charge into the teeth of what looked to me like a brigade armed with those God damned Yankee repeaters. Got the hell kicked out of them. I reckon we ought to pull them out of the firing line for a rest."

Hood considered that. Relieving Strahl would mean a delay, but if those men really were fought out, they would be unable to make any headway in rolling up the Federal left.

"Alright. Relieve Strahl. But in the meantime you are to go on with pushing ahead and into the Yankee center. Get round that open flank and behind those entrenchments yonder."

Hood left Cheatham to carry out his orders and rode ahead to inspect the ground for himself, gleefully and recklessly jumping his horse right over the recently captured earthworks, sending his troops scurrying out of the way. They cheered him, and he waved back.

Riding out into the empty, rolling, grassy country beyond the entrenchments, Hood discovered that the area before him divided into two separate bits of ground. The Military Road ran along the tableland, or on the edge of it at any rate, making it level and relatively high. It was also devoid of cover. That was where Lowery's and Granbury's brigades were now engaged in a long range firefight with the reforming Federals. In front of Cheatham, the ridge sloped down into a wide depression, filled by a dense oak forest.

As he studied the ground, artillery fire began falling around him. An aide began imploring him "Sir, shouldn't we retire farther to the rear? The Federal cannon have found our range, sir!"

Hood said nothing. I'll leave when I'm good and ready to, he thought. At that moment, a 20-pound roundshot hit the ground nearby, bounced up into the air, and tore through both Hood and his horse, sending gristle and entrails flying, killing man and mount instantly. They fell to ground together in a gory heap.

Moments later, Cheatham came forward with Maney, to show him where his brigade was to be placed. There he saw Hood's mutilated body, surrounded by his tearful staff. Long range cannonballs still bounded through the area, tearing up turf and clay as they went, but none of Hood's people seemed to have even the slightest care for their safety.

Looking down from his horse, Cheatham blinked back his own tears, and quietly said to Hood's staff "Gentlemen, you must carry him away from here. This is no place for our gallant Hood."

He then turned to his own aides. "Send to Cleburne and Jackson that Hood has been killed. As senior officer, I'm assuming command of the corps. Maney, bring up your brigade, then turn your men over to your senior colonel and take charge of my division."

Maney returned to the entrenched line. "Boys, General Hood is dead. He was killed leading the way for us, right over yonder, and that's where we're going. Form up and follow me."

Nathan rose from the trench and stepped into line with the rest of the company. He could see clearly now that five men were gone, including Fletcher and his brother. As for the other three, dead, wounded, skulking, he wasn't sure. Oh, there were a few skulkers in the company, Nathan thought ruefully. Always eager to help a wounded man back to the rear, or run for ammunition, but taking their own sweet time in coming back.

The 41st Tennessee marched forward in line of battle, taking up a position to the left of Wright's Brigade. Nathan could see the Yankees' new line just 200 yards away. Nathan scowled. We gave them blue bellies time to pull back, refuse their line, he thought bitterly. Wasting all this time, we should a kept on them, kicked them while they was down. Now we got us a stand-up fight.

Colonel Walker from the 19th Tennessee led the brigade now. Cheatham was still in the area, having chosen to remain where he was behind the lines, until the ball was well and truly in motion. He observed with approval that despite the Yankees pulling back and refusing their flank, his line still overlapped them.

Cheatham took a sip from his flask and spoke to his division's chief of staff. "See that there, Porter? We'll get right around their flank, crush them, and get them running. You can see Stewart's Corps is moving up against their front, and French is moving up past our left, over yonder. Stewart will pin them down, and Maney will press the whole division forward and run those bastards right off this hill. Another hour, and Tennessee is as good as ours again."

Cheatham's declaration was interrupted by the crash of

musketry. Nathan looked to his left, and saw fingers of flame flickering out from behind the fat trees of White Oak Hollow. A thick blue line stepped out of the woods and into the haze of gun smoke.

Porter expected some swearing from Cheatham, and when he heard nothing he looked and saw the general bobbing in the saddle, muttering something incomprehensible as he clutched his bloody hat to his head. He snapped into action, reaching out to steady Cheatham.

Porter could hear him now. Cheatham mumbled weakly "Don't… don't let them say I was drunk."

If Cheatham was talking, his brains were probably intact. The general was soon helped away from the front by Porter and other relieved staffers.

Nearby, but unaware that Cheatham had been wounded, Nathan Grimes clenched a cartridge between his teeth, and angrily tore it open so he could reload his weapon. He felt the nervousness coursing through the ranks all around. For the last several minutes, cannonballs from that big God damned hill on the left had been ripping into the brigade's flank. Now the artillery had stopped, and those Yankee sonsabitches were moving around their flank instead.

He kept loading and firing as quick as he could, despite his whole body tensing with the anticipation that something awful was about to happen, like when he was too little to defend himself and Paw got drunk. He could almost see the kicking coming on him, a kicking he couldn't do a thing about past taking it without raising a fuss.

Colonel Walker tried to pull back the brigade's left, but there were too many Federals, who were soon slamming musketry into the Rebel flank. Nathan shuddered, part of a great, shared shudder running down the Rebel line.

The regiment staggered backwards as a group, all except Nathan, who took a step forward instead. Suddenly relieved of tension, he smoothly adjusted the sights on his Enfield, shouldered his musket, and took careful aim at the blue color bearer standing several dozen yards away. The flapping Stars and Stripes made him an easy target to find. Just aim below that flag, he thought, and I'll hit some feller in the color guard. He squeezed the trigger, but couldn't see any results. Nathan hurried backwards into the ranks, sniggering, left cheek curled up in a cruel, sneering half-smile.

Bowing to reality, Maney instructed Walker to withdraw the brigade, back into the protection of the captured entrenchments. The rest of Cheatham's Division soon followed suit. In danger of being attacked on their exposed flank, French's Division joined them shortly thereafter.

CHAPTER 11

5 p.m.
Headquarters in the Field, Army of Tennessee, CSA
Haynie Hill

After sending Hood's Corps forward, Jackson went to Haynie Hill, the best observation point of his own side. He looked on with satisfaction, eyes burning brightly, as Cleburne turned his division to attack the enemy right, Cheatham turned to attack the enemy left, and French moved along the Military Road to exploit the breach in the center. He had sent Stewart's Corps forward to attack the Yankee left as well, intending for Stewart to fix the enemy in position there while Cheatham took them from the flank.

Then he watched it all go wrong. To Jackson's consternation, the enemy still had ample reserves, and Cheatham took too long to get moving again. The enemy rallied, brought up those reserves, and counter-attacked. Stewart's attack battered the enemy in their entrenchments, but made no progress against them. Worse, there seemed to have been no coordination between French and Cheatham in the center, and he had no word whatsoever of what was happening against the enemy right, where Featherston and Cleburne were.

Still peering through his field glasses, Jackson fumed at himself, struggling with the urge to ride down there and intervene. Finally, he told himself there was no foul in going wherever Hood, Cleburne or Cheatham might be, but no farther.

"I'm going down there," Jackson announced. "Sandie, you come too."

"General?" asked Sandie. He knew of Jackson's sentiments

regarding going to the front.

"You heard me!" snapped Jackson. He spurred his horse forward and galloped down into the woods, leaving Sandie and the rest of his aides to catch up with him. So it was that he came upon Hood's staff, alone and gathered around a body resting blood-smeared shroud. In that moment, his memories flashed vividly back to Chancellorsville and being shot in the dark, and he knew instantly how his difficulties in this battle started.

Jackson blinked. "Hood dead? What happened?"

"He was reconnoitering the enemy center, sir, preparing to renew the attack."

In response, Jackson quietly mumbled "Commendable. Highly commendable." Hood has gone to God now, Jackson thought. There was no need to pray for him.

Cheatham was sitting nearby, wearing a bandage around his head with a red spot about the size of a lemon on one side. Jackson went to him.

"General Cheatham, are you hurt badly?"

Cheatham saluted weakly "A ball brushed my skull, but my thick noggin held."

"Can you return to duty?"

"Honestly, sir, I can't hardly stand up or walk straight. Doc says I ought to be better in a day or two."

Jackson nodded, left Cheatham alone, and considered his command situation. The only major general left in Hood's Corps was Cleburne, and he was off in that tangled jungle to the west. Best to let him continue as he was, since he was clearly following his orders. Polk's Corps and Hood's Corps were mixed together. He had to reestablish control over this part of the battlefield.

But there was Hood. Hood who had lost the use of an arm, lost a leg outright, and was now dead, a good, brave man who took too many chances. Jackson shuddered, despite himself, and realized that whatever he chose, if he himself was wounded, command of the army would fall to Polk. He thought the Bishop was a good man, a man of God, but no battlefield leader. Yet Polk was also the second highest ranking general on the field, and couldn't simply be shunted aside in favor of Stewart. And Jackson knew he could not do it all himself. That left only one choice.

"Sandie, I have a message for General Polk, and I want you to deliver it yourself. Polk is to assume acting command of Hood's Corps. Corral Hood's staff and take them with you. Polk will need them to assert control over Cleburne and Maney."

Sandie saluted and rode away to sort out the new command arrangement with Hood's and Polk's people. Jackson then sent for Stewart, and began thinking out a new plan for renewing the assault.

5:30 pm
Polk's Corps, Army of Tennessee, CSA
The Confederate Left

After Polk received the message that Hood would take charge of one of his divisions in the attack on the Union center earlier that afternoon, leaving himself with only Featherston, he had retreated inside the privacy of his headquarters cabin for a lengthy sulk. That was where Sandie found him, and related to him the news of Hood's demise, Cheatham's wounding, and his own temporary elevation to command of over half the army.

Polk made the sign of the cross. "Oh, our poor, gallant Hood. Colonel Pendleton, would you join me in a moment of prayer?"

Like Polk, Sandie was an Episcopalian. They kneeled and prayed, or at least Sandie prayed. Polk made a somber show of it, but inwardly he was elated by the news. The Lord works in mysterious ways, he thought, and now He had answered His servant's most fervent wish, an important command with an opportunity to shine.

Allowing Sandie to help him to his feet, Polk said "You know, Colonel, Hood asked me to baptize him before we left Tuscumbia."

"Yes, I had heard." Fortuitous that. God's will.

Polk continued "Now Colonel, if you will excuse me. There is much to do."

Sandie rode back to Jackson, and Polk set about taking the reins by dictating a written message, which was copied and sent by a gaggle of couriers out to Featherston, French, Cleburne and Maney. The messages bore orders with no substance beyond notification that Polk was assuming acting control of the deceased Hood's army corps, and that all communications should pass to him now.

When one such courier found Patrick Cleburne some time later, carrying the new orders from Polk, he decided it explained very much. The Irish general had received no word from Hood, Jackson, Polk or anyone else for almost two hours, and was out of touch with all other parts of the army. He had grown very worried and frustrated about it, as he had a fight on his hands.

After turning west off the Military Road and entering the woods, Cleburne found the Federals had already pulled back and refused their line. He attacked the new Union line at once, resulting in a regular, western army-style brawl. Both sides had plenty of rocks and trees to hide behind, so Cleburne's Johnnies came up close, to within 40 yards distance in some places, and the two sides had blazed away at each other for an hour.

Cleburne had now drawn back and was preparing to send a column around the Federal's refused flank for a new assault. He threw a saddle bag over his lap, and wrote out a message for the courier to take back to Polk:

May 5, quarter to six o'clock
Headquarters in the field, Cleburne's Division of Hood's Corps

To: Lieutenant General Leonidas Polk

Dear Sir,

Your message finds me assailing the left flank of what I believe to be Veatch's Division, of the Federal XVI Corps. As I am sure you know, the terrain here is heavily overgrown, and imposes a severe impediment to a successful attack. I will continue my efforts to drive the enemy onto Shoal Creek, as per General Jackson's orders. However, I implore you to send orders to both General Featherston and myself for a coordinated attack. If we all go in together, I am sure we can overwhelm and destroy the foe.

Yours most respectfully and sincerely,

Patrick R. Cleburne
Major General, Confederate States Army

Cleburne resumed his vigil, listening for the roar of musketry to tell him his flanking column was in contact with the enemy, and hoping for the Bishop to step in and support him.

5:30 p.m.
Headquarters in the Field, Army of the Tennessee, USA
Oak Ridge

McPherson rode behind his line with a growing sense of relief. The counter-attack mounted by Sweeney and Osterhaus had driven back French and Cheatham. That had saved Harrow and Morgan Smith from being attacked on the flank, and they in turn had seen off Stewart's assault from behind the safety of their breastworks, suffering only slight losses.

During the resulting lull, Logan had pulled his XV Corps back to a new line on the other side of White Oak Hollow. Morgan Smith was tied into John Smith's troops on the Pulaski Road from his new position, and Sweeney's Division was now astride the Military Road, only one mile from Lawrenceburg's town center.

The men cheered him as he passed them by. Good, thought McPherson as he waved back. Morale is still high. We'll hold on to this place.

"Stand your ground, boys. Stand your ground!" McPherson urged them. "The Johnnies will be back before long. You'll need to see them off one last time before dark."

The new line wasn't perfect, especially in front of White Oak Hollow, where the oak forest made artillery all but useless, and offered the butternuts a covered approach, should they choose to use it. But it was shorter, more compact, and had good fields of fire in most places.

McPherson suddenly remembered that he hadn't heard anything from Dodge yet about Veatch's Division. He went looking for Tom Sweeney, the commander of the other division in Dodge's XVI Corps.

McPherson asked "Have you heard anything from Dodge or Veatch?"

Sweeney shook his head. "Last I saw him, Dodge was fretting

about Veatch. He sent couriers, but got no reply. He went over to find Veatch himself."

McPherson's eyes widened. If Veatch was out of communication, it meant he was probably cut-off. If that were the case, there was a gap more than half a mile wide between Sweeney and Shoal Creek. If a Confederate force advanced into that gap, his army was doomed.

McPherson immediately dispatched a courier to Wildcat Ridge, to summon the brigade he had posted there. One brigade to cover ground where he previously had three. It would be a thin line, but all his reserves were already committed. It was the best McPherson could do, and even so, it would take time for them to get there. He quietly prayed that his army would be permitted that time.

6 p.m.
Headquarters in the Field, XVI Corps, Army of the Tennessee, USA
Woods Between Coon Creek and Lawrenceburg

Dodge had set out to see what was happening for himself, accompanied by his cavalry escort and a few staff officers. They cut out to the west off of Military Road, through the woods, with the intention of arriving somewhere near the center of Veatch's Division. His party came upon a clearing in the woods, stumbling right onto Govan's Arkansas Brigade of Cleburne's Division, marching past in column.

"God dammit!" Dodge cried. It was his worst fear. Veatch's Division was cut-off, or damn near it.

Dodge began turning his horse. "Don't fuss about it!" he cried. "Run, by God! Run!"

Govan's flanking skirmishers were alert, and were already firing on the men clustered around the flapping guidon emblazoned with the Canterbury cross. More Johnnies jumped out of the column and began firing at will. First the guidon-bearer fell, and then Dodge himself seconds later, struck in the cheek by a ball.

6:15 p.m.
Maney's Brigade, Cheatham's Division, CSA
The Captured Entrenchments

As he sat in the trench, Nathan Grimes rubbed fistfuls of grass on his face, trying to remove the thick grime of blood, dust and gun smoke, when he saw Willie making his way down the line. He jumped to his feet. Willie had his arms outstretched for a hug, but Nathan waved him off in favor of taking close look at Willie's face.

"Go on, Nathan. Get off a me" Willie cried, shoving his brother back.

Nathan laughed, relieved. "Aw, ain't nothing be ashamed of. The ladies like scars. Bet you get your pick when we get back home."

Willie blushed a little, and the pair sat down. Nathan asked "How's Fletcher?"

"He's alive. Sawbones ain't had at him yet. Orderly stitched me up. Didn't have to wait so long."

Nathan nodded. He pulled a flask out of his jacket and drank.

"Where did you get that?" Willie demanded.

"I liberated this here from a Yankee officer, who ain't going need it no more. Couldn't find any of them Yankee biscuits, though."

Willie looked around. Six faces were gone, including Captain Fletcher. They hadn't had any lieutenants since Chickamauga, so the company was now run by the first sergeant, Halpern. Corporal Marks was there too, so most of the old hands were still around. That was something. All except the Captain.

Nathan recognized what Willie was doing. "Major Miller got shot too. General Cheatham's wounded."

"I reckon that must have been a God awful fight."

Nathan shrugged. "Yeap. Day ain't over yet."

Colonel Tillman stepped out of the trenches and ordered the regiment to fall in. No bugles were sounded, and the officers avoided shouting. The men lined up in relative quiet. The regiment shook out a company of skirmishers to screen their advance, and then stepped off with the rest of Cheatham's Tennesseans. Now led by George Maney, the division marched in line of battle, down into the woods of White Oak Hollow, leaving the golden, late afternoon sunlight behind them.

6:30 p.m.
Featherston's Division, Polk's Corps, CSA

Featherston was contemplating his growling belly when he saw riders approaching his position. Leading them was a dark man wearing the insignia of a Confederate general.

The rider came up to him and saluted. As Featherston returned the salute, the unfamiliar general said to him in a sing-song, Cork County accent "General Featherston, I presume? We've never had the pleasure. I am Patrick Cleburne."

Featherston was nonplussed. "General Cleburne. Wha... why are you here? Why are you not with your division, sir?"

Cleburne was in a foul mood, and ignored the question. All afternoon, he had hammered away at Veatch's Division, battering their lines back into a U-shaped salient at great cost. All afternoon, he had been waiting for Polk to coordinate his attacks with those of Featherston, and all afternoon nothing had happened.

The devil take any more waiting, Cleburne thought. He would take action himself.

"Brigadier General Featherston, you are to advance your division at once and assault the Federal lines." Cleburne looked at his pocket watch. "My division will renew its attack on the enemy in 20 minutes. If we all go in together, we'll drive those people into Shoal Creek."

Featherston blanched. "General Cleburne, sir, have you seen the ground? The Yankees have turned that ravine into a death trap! Furthermore, you have no authority to give orders to me."

"General Featherston!" Cleburne snapped, his patience exhausted. "I am your senior in rank and present in person on this field. I care not even a thimbleful of dog spittle for your problems. Advance your men, by God, and do it now!"

Featherston shrank. He had been a lawyer and a politician before the war, not a solider. He wasn't sure if Cleburne's interpretation of his authority was correct, but he suddenly felt no desire to dispute the matter any further. He sent Loring's former aides scurrying forward with orders for an immediate advance.

Cleburne dismounted and went forward, Featherston following behind him. The pair found a nice spot with a good view, and watched as thousands of men poured through the gaps in the abatis, weaving their way forward through the maze of sharp wooden points. They were once again met by a fusillade of bullets and canister balls upon reaching the bottom of the ravine and splashing across the waters of Coon Creek.

After that initial firestorm, the Federal onslaught slackened rapidly. All the cannon from before were still in place, but only one regiment, Yates's Sharpshooters, remained on the line. They were armed with Henry repeaters, but had been firing all day, and were reaching the end of their ammunition. When Featherston's Division crossed the last line of abatis, the sharpshooters shot off their few remaining rounds in one sharp burst of fire, and then made ready to defend their log barricades hand to hand.

Yet several hundred Illinoisans could not hold back a few thousand southerners, not with mere musket butts. The butternut tide was held at the wall for a few minutes, and a few minutes only. At first, a handful of Johnnies jumped over the barricade, brandishing their pointy bayonets, swinging musket butts, and driving blue bellies before them. One by one or in small groups, more butternuts hopped over the wall, howling wildly. Yates's Sharpshooters faltered, broke, and ran. The bulk of Featherston's Division came over the wall in their wake.

By then, Cleburne's own soldiers were assailing the bulk of Veatch's Division. When Featherston's men appeared in their rear, the Federals turned and fought in both directions for a short time. These men were proud, tough veterans of Grant's campaigns, and for a while that pride helped them stand firm. But after some minutes, they began to crumble, in dribs and drabs at first, and then in a torrent. Many raised their hands and surrendered on the spot. A few groups of stubborn men held out to the bitter end, giving up their arms grudgingly and from cold, dirty fingers. Others ran in the only direction left open, to the west.

When Cleburne went to commandeer Featherston's Division, he left his senior brigadier, Lucius Polk, in command of his troops. A nephew of Leonidas Polk, Lucius had turned into an able citizen-soldier at the head of the Irishman's old brigade, and was Cleburne's protégé in many ways. It was Lucius who led a bayonet charge across the path of the fleeing Yankees, cutting them in two.

"Follow those men!" Lucius Polk cried, jabbing his sword at the fleeing bluecoats. "Hound them! Hound them, drive them and hound them!"

A mob of Confederates leapt at Lucius Polk's order, and chased hard after the running Yankees, who soon came upon Raven's Bluffs. Some climbed and scrambled down, finding their way to the banks of Shoal Creek. Some threw down their muskets and gave up, and others leapt from the bluffs into the creek bed below. Many of the jumpers broke their ankles or worse, but there were still dozens upon dozens of men who somehow made it down and fled across the wide, meandering bends of Shoal Creek, hoping to reach safety at the foot of Wildcat Ridge on the other side. Most of them were shot down long before they got there.

Veatch's Division ceased to exist.

7:30 p.m.
Maney's Brigade, Cheatham's Division, CSA
White Oak Hollow

After advancing about a third of a mile, Maney's Brigade found themselves in a fight with a brigade of blue belly Missourians, "homemade Yankees," at a range of about 30 yards. Men on both sides took shelter behind trees and rocks, and stood in to trade bullets for a full hour.

Nathan and Willie shared a thick oak tree, Willie loading while Nathan fired. After an hour, the front of their tree had been chewed up by musket balls, and Nathan was merely shooting in the general direction of the Yankees. A thick pall of smoke hung between the trees, and the failing light could not even begin to penetrate it.

The brothers knew from experience that fights of this kind were grappling rather than slugging matches. Given time, one side would tire or run low on ammunition, and then withdraw. Yet that took two, three or even four hours. Time was not on their side, and before long the word came to cease firing and withdraw to the shelter of their starting line.

7:30 p.m.
Field Hospital, Army of Tennessee, CSA
Bryant's Barn
Behind Redding Ridge

Fletcher had been waiting his turn outside the barn for hours, listening to the moans and screams, in his grim, private struggle to hang on to the last shreds of his courage. At least they had the merciful sense to pile up the severed limbs somewhere out of sight, he thought.

Finally, a couple of negroes came and put Fletcher on a stretcher and brought him into the barn, laying him out on a table. The interior of the barn was lit by lanterns and the day's last light. He saw that the sawbones was the army's chief surgeon, the same man who thought the regiment didn't have good enough latrines back in January.

Hunter McGuire said "Captain, how long have you been in the army?"

"Since the November of '61."

"Well, then, I don't need to tell you what I've got to do here tonight. I must amputate, below the knee. You understand?"

Fletcher nodded. He had been preparing for that obvious, terrible confirmation all afternoon.

McGuire continued "Now we need to be quick, so this will be an open amputation. We have no chloroform, so all I can offer you is some strong whiskey."

"Can I go home?" Fletcher asked, almost croaking. The army didn't keep captains who couldn't walk.

"As soon as you are well enough to travel, Captain. Your stump won't heal completely for several months, mind you, but as soon as you are well enough, you can go home. You are from hereabouts?"

"40 miles from here, give or take."

McGuire nodded, and motioned for the tin cup of whiskey. Fletcher gulped it down nervously. Already weak from blood loss, the strong spirits sent his head reeling.

A piece of leather-bound wood was placed in his mouth, and the negro orderlies held him down. Fletcher twitched a little, but he didn't push back. Instead, he bit down hard, and fought even harder not to scream. He did not need to fight for long. In a few minutes, the operation was over.

Fletcher was carried out the front of the barn, and set down beside other recent officer amputees. The remains of his leg and foot were carried out the back of the barn, and dumped onto a ghastly rubbish heap.

9:00 p.m.
Headquarters in the Field, Army of the Tennessee, USA
Confederate Post Office
Lawrenceburg

McPherson waited until it was dark and quiet, and then sent out the call for all corps and division commanders to report to the town post office for orders. The tavern he had been using was now dangerously close to the front lines, and while he would have preferred the courthouse, that building, the surrounding houses, and all the lawns in-between were crammed with his wounded. The county jail had been burned in a skirmish the previous November, so that left the post office. McPherson arrived there first, went inside, and slumped into a chair.

It had been a very near run thing. The Confederates had hammered at him up and down the line all evening, raking for any sign of weakness. On the left, Morgan Smith had a hand-to-hand fight with the Rebels. Logan put in his slender reserves, just a few regiments, but it was enough to throw them back. The right had been wide open for a time, but that gap had been plugged. There was still no word from either James Veatch or Grenville Dodge. Both men were probably lost, and Veatch's entire division along with them.

Stonewall Jackson almost certainly is in command, not Polk, McPherson thought. No way to know for sure right now, but it is beyond doubt that there are at least six Confederate infantry divisions over there. Without Veatch, I have only five, and their divisions are always bigger than ours anyway. We're lucky to have survived. Most of us survived.

Sighing, McPherson called for pen and paper. He had sent a dispatch for Sherman that morning, but much had changed since then. It was time to tell Uncle Billy that he had been beaten, and would be retreating to Nashville. He described his intentions with as much detail as brevity allowed, and then handed the message a courier.

"Get that to the telegraph office in Columbia, quick as you can. Ride that horse to death, if you have to."

That done, McPherson collected himself for the meeting to come. It was to be no council of war. His mind was made up about the necessity of his chosen course of action, and his generals were coming to receive orders, not discuss them.

One by one, McPherson's seven senior commanders arrived: Logan, Sweeney, Harrow, Osterhaus, Morgan Smith, John Smith, and Minty, the latter the only one without stars on his shoulder straps. The army's senior staff officers were present as well. McPherson started the meeting not by asking for reports, but by flatly declaring "Gentlemen, we are leaving."

No one was surprised. Every man had heard by now that Stonewall Jackson was in command of the Confederate army, an army that plainly had them outnumbered. Even so, the words weighed heavily on the gathered generals, if only because they were so unused to hearing them.

"When you go back to your outfits," McPherson continued, "you are to order your men to light camp fires, as many as possible. You know the drill. Let's put on a good show, and make the Rebels think we're all still here. Minty, beginning at midnight, your cavalry will relieve the infantry on the line one by one, starting with John Smith's Division and moving down the line, ending at Sweeney. Then you bring up the rear. Understood? Everyone understands?"

The generals all grunted in agreement. No one asked what road they would take, for there was only one road open: the Military Road, leading to Nashville.

McPherson then said to his chief quartermaster "Your job is to see all the mules unharnessed from our wagon train. We're taking the mules, but leaving the wagons. Organize a detail to thrust bags of food and ammunition at every platoon and gun crew that passes through the wagon park on its way out of town. Leave whatever we can't carry."

The quartermaster goggled. "Sir, you want me to abandon all those stores for the enemy to capture?"

"Yes, I do. If we burn the wagons, the Rebels will see the flames tonight or the smoke in the morning, and sure as the devil, they'll attack when they see it. I wouldn't put a night assault past Stonewall Jackson. And you can use those teamless wagons to block the road. Anything that buys us more time is worth it."

McPherson now moved on to the retreat's most unpleasant business. "I want the ambulances unharnessed as well. We are leaving the wounded behind."

That brought outraged protests from all around. Sweeney cursed and swore, the army's chief surgeon pleaded, and the other division commanders were aghast. Even Logan joined in. Only Peter Osterhaus remained quiet, a look of resignation on his face.

McPherson raised his hand, motioning for them to quiet down. "Make no mistake, gentlemen. Tomorrow we will be in a foot race, and the stakes are the survival of this army. The ambulances and wagons are impedimenta, and we need every advantage we can get. That is Stonewall Jackson over there, a man who made his bones training his infantry into 'foot cavalry'."

Logan asked "Can we at least bring along those less severely injured?"

McPherson shook his head. "You all know a column marches as fast as its slowest element. Jackson can afford to leave his wagons and wounded behind, with no fear of capture. He'll move fast. We have to move faster."

They can see I'm right, McPherson thought. It still leaves a bad taste in their mouth. Mine too. No one likes it. I need to buck them up.

With a wry smile, McPherson continued "Stonewall Jackson believes he is the hardest, fastest marcher in America. I aim to show him the error of that belief. I believe this army, our army, is the fleetest of foot that has ever gone to war, and tomorrow we're going to prove it. We're leaving the wagons, the ambulances and the wounded, but by sunset tomorrow, this army will straddle the Duck River."

Logan said "Mac, you can't be serious? Columbia is 40 miles away! The men will straggle by the thousand."

"No, they won't. They know as well as I do that straggling means capture, or worse, murder at the hands of some secessesh bushwhacker. Gentlemen, you have my orders. See to them.

Dismissed."

10:00 p.m.
Headquarters, Army of Tennessee, CSA
Behind Redding Ridge

Jackson had also called all his senior commanders together: Polk, Featherston, Cleburne, French, Maney, Clayton, Stevenson, and Forrest. Sandie Pendleton was in attendance, and also Frank Cheatham, although it was well understood that the latter wasn't up to resuming his duties yet.

Jackson listened quietly as each man gave his report. In addition to Hood and Cheatham, three brigadiers and more than a dozen colonels were among the casualties. Against that was the capture of two dozen enemy cannon, and thousands of prisoners from the known destruction of Veatch's Division, including General Veatch himself. More than that was not known yet.

Cleburne was the last called on to speak. Polk sat serenely, but inwardly he grew upset as he listened to the Irishman's frank admission that he had gone to Featherston and openly usurped command over a division of Polk's Corps. Heretofore, Featherston hadn't known for sure that Cleburne lacked proper authority to give him any orders. Now Cleburne was openly admitting to deceiving him, and it left him fuming.

"General Jackson, this man lied to me and committed an illegal act! I demand..."

Jackson shouted back "Demand?! You demand?!"

As far as he was concerned, Cleburne's destruction of Veatch's Division was the only real accomplishment of the entire day. He was in no mood whatsoever for a spat over how that one bright spot came about.

Jackson sighed, letting go of his burning desire to pillory Featherston. An ugly display of temper now would serve no purpose.

Instead, he said "As the only major general fit for duty in Hood's Corps, General Cleburne must assume acting command. That is final."

"But," Featherston sputtered.

"Final!" Jackson growled.

Featherston's expression soured, but he held his tongue.

"Half an hour before dawn," Jackson said "all infantry divisions are to advance skirmishers to probe the enemy lines. That is all. Dismissed."

Polk spoke up. "General Jackson, as you have heard from every one of your commanders, there is hardly a morsel of food in this army. When can we expect the wagons to catch up?"

"Dismissed," Jackson repeated flatly.

He watched as the generals filed out, waiting for Forrest to pass and seeking out his eyes. "General Forrest, a moment, please."

Forrest stopped. He had just been musing on how his first, stormy meeting with Jackson had been in the early hours of this very same day. It felt like a week ago.

"General Jackson, I wish to apologize to you for my outburst this morning. There ain't no excusing it, but..."

Jackson waved him off. "That matter is concluded. I wish to hear no more of it, but there is something else. I have heard that you personally shot men who were skulking behind the lines today. Is this true?"

Forrest nodded. "I shot at a man, sir, to put the scare in him. Just the one, he ain't wounded, let alone killed, and he was running, not skulking."

Jackson nodded. "I approve of your intentions, but under the law, even cowards are entitled to a fair trial. Arrest such people in the future, instead of shooting them."

Forrest was slightly surprised by his commander's punctiliousness. Whatever his other faults, Braxton Bragg had no such qualms. He would readily order the summary execution of a deserter or coward, if the circumstances called for it. It was one of the few things about Bragg that Forrest approved of.

"General Jackson," Forrest replied, "I can't obey your order, so if you insist, I'll have call to resign. And I'll tell you why. If that man had kept running, I would have shot him dead right where he was. I ain't shooting at them yellow bastards for punishment. I'm shooting at them to put the scare in them and get them back onto the firing line. Ain't no coward going to stand and fight just because I threaten them with arrest now and a shooting later."

Jackson considered that for a moment. When one man started running, others always followed. "You have a point. Very well. Shoot as many skulkers as you deem proper. But shoot to wound them. I want to try them later, and if found guilty, stood before a firing squad."

Forrest chuckled at that, saying "Yessir." He saluted and left.

Only Jackson and Sandie remained. Alone at last, Sandie said softly "General, don't you think the Federals will retreat during the night?"

Jackson grinned back at him. "If that is what I thought, Sandie, I dared not reveal it. But you are right, and that is why you are to prepare marching orders for the army tonight: Stewart, Polk, Cleburne and Forrest. If he is still in Lawrenceburg, I have a separate set of attack orders I want prepared too. Either way, you will have the paperwork ready for dispatch by dawn."

Jackson continued, sketching out his various plans while Sandie quietly took notes on what he wanted, for both major contingencies. When that was done, Sandie asked "What about rations? General Polk was right. The ammunition wagons caught up with us this evening, so the cartridge boxes and caissons will be full in the morning, but most of the men emptied their haversacks today. The rations won't be here until early tomorrow morning."

Jackson replied flatly "If the enemy is still in Lawrenceburg tomorrow, we can distribute rations. If not, I won't wait for them." Better they starve now than have to storm the fortifications at Nashville later, he thought.

Sandie said nothing, and went about turning his notes into formal orders, while Jackson stole a couple of hours of sleep.

10:30 p.m.
Maney's Brigade, Cheatham's Division
Oak Ridge

Nathan drained the last of his pillaged flask, and then threw it away.

Willie muttered "You ought not to drink like that, not on an empty belly."

"God dammit," Nathan spat. "It's because my belly's empty that I'm drinking it all."

Nathan slumped onto his back. It wasn't just the exhaustion and the hunger. It was the awful taste in his mouth from biting open cartridges all day. He had only half a canteen of water left, there wasn't a creek or spring anywhere near, and he knew better than to drink the rest before he knew when more might be coming.

Unlike the Yankees across the way, not a man in the regiment lit a campfire. No one had any food to cook, or anything to boil, and it was a pleasantly cool night. Willie laid out both their gum blankets, one on top of the other. Nathan crawled over and took his place, Willie lay down, the boys shook out their other blankets, and they went to sleep.

CHAPTER 12

May 6
4:30 a.m.
Main Headquarters, Military Division of the Mississippi, USA
Richardson House
Chattanooga, Tennessee

Sherman awoke sharply, his mind clear. Audenried was there.

"There is an urgent message for you, sir. From General McPherson."

Sherman rolled into a sitting position on the side of the bed. He snatched the paper from Audenried's hand, and asked for more light. He read the message, then set it aside and sat quietly for a moment.

Finally, Sherman whispered "I'll be damned."

"Sir?" Audenried asked.

Sherman jumped up. "Major, go tell the duty officer to rouse the staff. Every man. There are plans to make and papers to draw up. Then you go yourself, straight to General Thomas's headquarters. Get him out of bed and get his staff up as well. Tell Old Pap to come directly over here."

Audenried left smartly. Alone now, Sherman dressed, repeating again and in a more regular tone of voice "I'll be damned."

Stonewall Jackson in Lawrence County, Sherman thought, with Polk, Hood and Stewart. That was at least six infantry divisions, maybe as many as eight, plus cavalry. Perhaps 50,000 men, maybe more. McPherson has a little over 30,000.

Emerging from his bedroom, Sherman went immediately to his gathering staff, every one of them bleary-eyed. He lit a cigar, waved the match out, and took several hard drags before sitting down and starting to write.

Sherman's first set of orders were to the garrison commanders along the Nashville and Decatur railroad, now uncovered by McPherson's defeat, calling for a consolidation in Pulaski, Athens, Huntsville, and Decatur, if practicable. Those towns had forts and large garrisons, and might be able to hold out if a major Rebel force came calling. The rest of the railroad was held by small detachments in log blockhouses, and Jackson or Forrest could gobble those men up at will.

Sherman blotted his ink, took the paper, and held it out. "Take that to the telegraph office. It takes priority."

George H. Thomas walked in, the floorboards creaking under his bulk. A tall, erect man endowed early in life with a set of wide, powerful shoulders, which had come to be rivaled by his huge belly. Thomas had put on considerable weight over the last few years, and Sherman thought he now resembled nothing so much as a portly, aged bear.

Thomas grunted "Good morning," and shook hands with Sherman.

"What do you think of this?" Sherman asked, giving Thomas the telegram from McPherson.

Thomas spent several minutes reading the message. Sherman tapped his foot against the floor, expending his nervous energy and impatience, but saying nothing.

Finally, Thomas asked flatly "So which corps are we leaving to garrison Chattanooga?"

Sherman grinned at Thomas's implication that most of the army would go north. "None. I'm taking one of your corps, putting it on the Nashville and Chattanooga, and reforming the Army of the Tennessee in Nashville. A.J. Smith and the XVI Corps' other two divisions are on the Mississippi River as we speak, so I'm sending them on to Louisville, and then to Nashville by the trains. That ought to give me sufficient force to break up Jackson."

"You're assuming McPherson will bring his army to Nashville intact," Thomas said, quietly but firmly. "And isn't it dangerous to send troops to Nashville by train with an enemy army running loose in Middle Tennessee?"

"Yes, I am," Sherman replied confidently. "And as for Jackson in

Middle Tennessee, I'm betting he will pursue Mac right up to the gates of Nashville. Even if he doesn't, he is three or four days hard marching from the Nashville and Chattanooga line. I'll have that corps moved from here to there by then."

"Really?" Thomas asked, more audibly.

"I intend to leave the wagons, cannon and caissons for last. Men and animals go first. Nashville has an ample stock of surplus artillery, and hundreds of wagons under repair in the city's workshops. I can replace those things quickly enough. I can't replace the men as readily, and will have a damned hard time finding new horses and mules. We can move that much in three days, I'm certain of it."

Sherman had thought through the transportation problems while waiting for Thomas, his mind clicking through the details like an arithmometer. While he hadn't finished working through the details of his mental plan just yet, he had done enough to achieve certainty that he had sufficient time and wherewithal to move the essentials, and that anything that he had not deemed essential could be replaced in a matter of weeks.

Thomas folded his hands across his broad chest. "Which corps do you want?"

Sherman motioned at Thomas. "Schofield's Army of the Ohio is still in Knoxville and too far away, as we need to start putting men in the cars now. I want you to get about making it happen immediately, so I'm sorry to say, it has to be a corps from your Army of the Cumberland, one that is on hand. I was going to leave the choice to…"

"Hooker," Thomas interrupted.

Sherman was surprised at the choice for a moment, as well as the uncharacteristic speed with which it was delivered, but then thought better of it. They had been roommates at West Point, served together afterward in the 3rd U.S. Artillery, and then came together again in Kentucky during the early days of the war. He knew George Thomas very well, and Thomas had served with the Army of the Cumberland since before it even bore that name. The two corps Thomas wanted to keep were veterans of that army, survivors of Perryville, Stones River, Chickamauga, and Chattanooga. They were Thomas's boys.

Joe Hooker's XX Corps, on the other hand, was made up of spit and polish soldiers from back east, most definitely not Thomas's boys. "Fighting" Joe himself was the half-disgraced former commander of the Army of the Potomac. What made it a surprise was that while XX Corps weren't family, they were the biggest outfit in the entire western theater, 20,000 strong.

Sherman said "Very well. Get Hooker moving at once. I'll draw up orders putting Schofield under your command. You rank him anyway, and Schofield isn't the sort to make trouble, but I'll put it in writing and make it official anyway. That gives you the IV, XIV and XXIII Corps, plus two divisions of cavalry. If the reports are true, then Hardee it must be in Dalton with what amounts to one big corps. You are to go after him and push onto Atlanta."

"Now, what can you tell me about Bill Hardee?" asked Sherman. "You mentioned you served with him, last time I was here."

Thomas replied "Yes, we were both majors in Albert Johnston's 2nd Cavalry, in the Old Army." After that he was quiet for a time, but finally he grinned slightly and remarked "Able, but thoroughly conventional. He is a by the book man, which only figures, as he wrote that book. Once something is done to his expectations, he tends to take it for granted. Becomes complacent."

Sherman nodded. He could see Thomas already had some ideas on how to proceed against Hardee, but chose not to ask. Sherman knew Thomas would share his plans when he was good and ready.

Thomas asked "Is there anything further, Bill?"

"Just one thing. Your supply line might be interrupted in the coming days, but you have ample stores here in Chattanooga. I put in enough supplies to sustain an army twice the size of what you'll be left with for more than 30 days."

Sherman paused, reflecting on whether what he wanted to say was appropriate. Deciding it was, he continued. "George, this is your time. You wanted an independent field army, you waited until you could get one honestly, without the scheming and the politicking, and now you have it. Whip Hardee, but do it quickly. I'm not going to leave you stranded in North Georgia, but you need to get this done before you're scraping the bottom of your cracker barrel."

5:30 a.m.
Maney's Brigade, Cheatham's Division, CSA
Outside Lawrenceburg, Tennessee

Nathan Grimes woke with a start. By reflex, he seized the arm that was gently shaking him. Then his eyes cleared and he could see Corporal Marks.

"Get up, Nathan. We's on patrol."

"Any food?" Nathan asked.

"Naw."

Nathan's stomach growled as he sat up. He gave Willie a shove to wake him as well, and set about rolling the bulk of his gear up in his gum blanket. He was on his feet and ready in little more than a minute.

The company mustered beyond the trench line, 18 sleepy, hungry men led by a first sergeant. They spread out by groups of two and four, and advanced towards the Yankee line. Nathan and Willie formed one such skirmish group, just the two of them. The company returned to the woods of White Oak Hollow, and before long campfires could be seen flickering, standing out in the inky dark of the nighttime forest.

Then Tennesseans crept up to where they expected to find the enemy picket line, and then to where they expected to find the enemy main line. All they found were some scraps of rubbish and crackling, well-fueled campfires.

"Damn, fellas," Nathan said, in hushed, but audible tones. "They was just here."

First Sergeant Halpern gathered up the company, and dispatched a runner back to the regiment. Then he told the rest to have a look around. "See if them blue bellies didn't leave a cracker box behind or something'."

6:30 am
Army of Tennessee, CSA
Lawrenceburg

Word that the Yankees had skedaddled during the night made

its way up to Jackson's headquarters, whereupon Sandie Pendleton issued the set of detailed written orders for a pursuit, orders that had occupied so much of his sleepless night. The other, now useless set he of orders carried out to a nearby campfire and burned.

Nathan Bedford Forrest left first, leading the chase. He took the four brigades of Red Jackson's cavalry around the low rolling country and across the many shallow creeks east of Lawrenceburg, rejoining Andrew Jackson's Military Road a few miles north of town. A.P. Stewart was directed to take his corps and Abe Buford's cavalry east to Pulaski, swing around the Federals and cut them off from Nashville. The corps of Polk and the deceased Hood, now under Cleburne, would push up behind Forrest as the main body of the pursuit.

Polk yawned as he rode past French's column, his guidon-bearer beside him and a large entourage of staffers and escorting cavalry behind him. He didn't like rising early and had never truly become accustomed to it, even after more than three years of military service.

If he was more tired than usual on this particular morning, it was because Polk had spent most of the early morning hours dictating and editing a letter that was to be sent to friendly Confederate newspapers, a letter that was to be published under a pseudonym. Still, it wasn't every day he was at hand to liberate a Southern town, and he fully intended to be the first general of note into Lawrenceburg.

Thinking about it brought a self-satisfied smile to Polk's face. It was a masterpiece of political craftsmanship, giving the lion's share of the credit for bagging Veatch's Division to Polk, but not slighting the noble Featherston or the aggressive Cleburne in the process. The letter criticized no one, was impossible to trace back to him, and it would put the idea that he had been instrumental to winning the Battle of Shoal Creek in the public's mind first.

Polk led his party of several dozen riders into Lawrenceburg, and found the county courthouse, many surrounding houses and almost any open patch of grass thereabouts filled with Northern casualties. The air stank of rot, rust and feces. "There must be thousands of them," Polk stammered, surprised by the scale of the carnage. Why, they've abandoned their wounded, Polk thought. They must be fleeing in terror!

After he dispatched an aide to inform General Jackson of his discovery, Polk exchanged a few words with the surgeons who approached him. It was common for some doctors to remain with their wounded, and the custom was to allow them to return to their own side unmolested as soon as their duties were discharged.

Townspeople began to emerge from their houses. Lawrenceburg had seen a skirmish or two, as well as some lawlessness, but never a field army. All the people knew that morning was that a major battle had been fought south of town the day before.

They must not even know we've won the battle, thought Polk. Turning his horse around, he said "People of Lawrenceburg, you are free! The northerner's yoke is lifted! I am Leonidas Polk, and my gallant boys are marching the Military Road right now, marching to Nashville! Who among you will come out, and show us the patriotic spirit of God's own Tennessee?"

He led his entourage back to the main road, a crowd gathering behind him. Soon people were lining one side of the road, waving state and Confederate flags, cheering the passing soldiers on and pressing offerings of food into their hands.

Adopting an erect, equestrian pose, Polk returned the salutes of the colonels and brigadiers as they passed. Someone was playing a fiddle, although Polk could not spy who, and the march took on a parade-like atmosphere. When Featherston rode up, Polk called out to him "God bless you boys. We have a hard march ahead, but the harder you go, the faster we'll chase the invader from our sacred soil!"

North of Lawrenceburg, General French rode at the front of his division, and was the first to discover the vast, collection of abandoned Yankee wagons on the outskirts of town. Immediately recognizing the potential for trouble, French detailed his provosts and his personal escort to cordon off the wagons, discouraging potential looting. He also dispatched an aide to inform Polk of the find. When his division had passed the wagon park, French called in his personal escort, but left behind his handful of provosts to continue guarding the wagons.

Featherston's Division came up next, with Featherston near the front. Marveling at the hundreds of wagons, all stuffed with supplies, he murmured "My my. What do we have here?" and spurred off to have a closer look, trailing Loring's former staffers behind him.

He rode up to the cordon formed by French's provosts, and addressed their leader. "Major, what goes on here?"

Saluting, the major replied "On General French's orders, sir, we are to remain here to prevent looting until relieved."

Featherston blinked. Looting? he thought. By who? It isn't as if the townspeople are going to come out and raid the Yankees' wagons with an entire army marching by.

Featherston waved the man off. "Consider yourself relieved. Return to General French."

The major paused, then said cautiously "We can wait until you've summoned your own guard, sir."

"No, no. That won't be necessary. You are dismissed, Major."

Featherston waited for French's provost detail to ride away, and then set about looking for a wagon that might contain the stores of a high-ranking headquarters mess. Surely, he thought, there are some delectables here, something suitable for my table.

The first of Featherston's soldiers to march past the wagon park were the men of Quarles's Brigade, which had Tennessee men in it and were in high spirits after their joyous reception in town. Then Adams' Brigade resisted the temptation of the fat Yankee wagons as well, as their now-deceased commander had been a salty Old Army man, and had turned his Mississippians into a well-disciplined outfit.

Next Featherston's old brigade marched into the wagon park, whereupon some men broke ranks. At first they confined themselves to ransacking the contents of those wagons nearest the road in search of food, and then just as quickly fell back into the column. Yet as the brigade passed, more and more men fanned out, farther and farther from the road. When Snodgrass brought his brigade into the wagon park, much of it broke ranks and streamed into the wagon park to join in, and the looting began in earnest.

Featherston emerged from a wagon with a sackful of canned delicacies to find himself surrounded by a thousand of his men, all running amok. The sight left him slack-jawed.

"Spread out and put a stop to this riot!" he croaked at his staff. Mounting his horse, he trotted over to a nearby sergeant, busily carving up a ham with a Bowie knife, and stuffing chunks of meat into his haversack. "You there!" he ordered. "Stop this brigandage at once. You're a sergeant, by God. Help me round these men up and get them back in formation."

The sergeant sneered back "Old Swet, you can kiss my britches and take my stripes. I'm taking this here ham!"

As Featherston ineffectually demanded that his men stop their looting, Polk arrived in response to French's message. Expecting to find the fine prize of a fat Union wagon train, he instead found a riot. Broken crates were scattered everywhere, wagons had been overturned, and a few had even been set alight by toppled lanterns.

The head of Hood's Corps was marching up. Polk quickly decided the best way to avoid becoming tarnished by this catastrophe was to be the one who resolved it. He rode over to the commander of that first, oncoming regiment.

Polk barked "Major, I want you to deploy your men into a line, single-ranked. Fix bayonets, advance double quick to the edge of the wagon park ahead, and then hold fast for further orders. Do you understand?"

"Yessir!"

"Then get to it, man, get to it!"

Polk then rode into the riotous mass, trailing his escort and staffers. Adopting the style of the fire and brimstone preacher, he bellowed "Sinners! Blackhearts! You dare thieve from your brothers! Thieve and steal, while the Yankee gets away! You call yourselves Southrons? Sinners! You shame your flag! Shame your God!"

Polk continued in this way for several minutes, and most men stopped what they were doing and looked away, shamed-faced. Slowly and grudgingly, in the way of a chastised child that knows he has done wrong, but is too proud to quite own up to it, the riotous butternuts began to fall back into line. Polk ordered Featherston to get them moving. Once he was out of the wagon park, Polk sagged with relief. It had not been necessary to break up the riot by bayonet point.

Jackson galloped onto the scene. He stopped before Polk and demanded "General Polk, report! Why was my column halted? What mischief happened here?"

Polk took the last step to insulate himself from the entire ugly affair. "General Jackson, it is my misfortune to report that General Featherston lost control of his troops. Some of them broke ranks, sir, and ransacked this wagon park, looking for Yankee rations, I'm sure. It's disgraceful, absolutely disgraceful."

Polk met Jackson's blazing eyes and said "I'm afraid Featherston must be replaced. Quarles is next in line. He is the only other brigadier in the division fit for duty."

Jackson's replied in a quiet, menacing tone "No. I must suffer that fool Featherston a while longer. I would send him back to his brigade right now with the harshest reprimand, were it not for the certainty that no one under him is fit to take his place. Loring obviously allowed the entire division to deteriorate into demoralization."

As he spoke, Jackson became more determined than ever to court martial and cashier Loring. As his mind lingered on that thought, he testily dismissed Polk. "Alright, alright. That is all. For now."

11:30 a.m.
Maney's Brigade, Cheatham's Division, CSA
Andrew Jackson Military Road
Four Miles North of Lawrenceburg

Nathan Grimes took a drink from his canteen, hoping that would help make him feel a little less sick. Water wasn't the problem, though, and he knew it. Not a man in the regiment had eaten since yesterday morning, and they had fought a battle since then. The day's marching orders suspended the usual 10 minute break every hour, so they had and would continue to push on without rest. Nathan's legs and back ached and burned, he felt a little sickly, and they hadn't even been on the road that long.

He called out "Hey, Ed?!"

Corporal Marks replied "Yeap?" casting a glance over his shoulder. The regiment was marching in the free-limbed, spacious stride of the Westerner, but the officers kept them in a loose formation. Marks marched in the rank ahead of Nathan and Willie.

"Remember what them other fellers said, about coming back from Kentucky?"

Marks said "Yeap, I certainly do." The men who had been with Bragg in Kentucky were always spinning yarns about coming through Cumberland Gap and East Tennessee in the dead of winter, marching shoeless over mountains with an icy wind blowing in their face, and only a handful of parched corn in their haversacks.

"Reckon they'll finally shut up after this?"

Marks drawled slowly, affably. "They might. They just might."

Talking wasn't working. Nathan had hoped to take his mind off his plight, but each step made him feel weaker and hungrier. He whispered to his brother "Let's fall out, go foraging. We'll catch up tonight, bring some vittles for the company."

"No" Willie shot back, with uncharacteristic firmness.

"No?"

Willie became irritated, and hissed "No. You just don't get it, do you, Nathan?"

"Well, why don't you explain it to me, seeing as how you reckon you know everything now?" asked Nathan, half-amused and half-annoyed.

Willie ignored the jibe. "This ain't like before. Donelson, Raymond, Chickamauga, ain't like none of that. We got them Yankees on the run this time! Old Jack's going take us all the way. If we don't whip them and whip them fellers good, I reckon ain't going be no Pemberton or Bragg to blame. This whole thing, it's all on us."

Nathan was quiet for a time. Then they heard cheers rising from behind them, farther back down the road.

"Besides," Willie said, "I reckon them fellers in the Cumberland Gap didn't have Old Jack hounding them every which way."

As Willie Grimes spoke those last words, Jackson pounded up the road, followed by his staff officers, who were struggling to keep up. He had spent most of the middle part of the morning attending to details in Lawrenceburg, not the least among them putting his commissary chief, Wells Hawks, onto organizing the captured wagon trains, as well as to seeing that the almost 4,000 Federal prisoners were organized, issued rations, and marched off to Florence under guard. He had also personally ordered the punishment for those looters from Featherston's Division who had broken into the Yankee whiskey stores and gotten drunk, and were therefore unable to rejoin the march on any terms: they were to fell trees, so each one of them could fashion a rough post, and carry that post on their shoulders to wherever the army went to.

Now that he was on the road with his soldiers again, Jackson was stopping to cajole stragglers as he went. For the most part, he chose to ignore soldiers who were still trudging forward, trying to keep up, in favor of focusing his ire upon those who had stopped for rest or wandered off the road in search of food or water. He shouted at them, shamed them, threatened them, anything to get them back on the road and moving again.

Jackson was in the midst of such a harangue at one such hapless group of stragglers when a courier galloped up on a frothing horse. "Message from General Forrest for you, sir. With the General's compliments."

Jackson took the message and read it. Forrest was capturing enemy stragglers by the dozens, and was locked in a running skirmish with their rear guard. As of yet, he could not pin that rear guard down. Whenever he tried to make them stand, they shot their way out with repeaters.

Handing the message to Sandie, he said "McPherson is forcing the march. Forcing it hard."

Sandie said "Forrest is several miles to the front. They might be in Maury County by now. I have to say, General, I never would have counted on such good marching from the Northrons."

Jackson grunted "I do not want them good."

"No, sir."

They can keep Forrest back, Jackson thought. They can force the march with extreme vigor today, they can get ahead. But they can't keep this pace up. Tomorrow they will slow down. We'll still be on their heels, and Stewart will be out in front of them.

Jackson dismounted, withdrew his writing satchel from his saddlebag, and retired to a nearby tree stump to compose fresh orders for A.P Stewart.

Noon
Stewart's Corps, Army of Tennessee, CSA
Pulaski, Tennessee

Stewart rode forward to Pulaski in response to a summons from Brigadier General Abraham Buford, whom he had sent ahead with the cavalry to bottle up the town garrison, and to find a way around the center of town and onto the Columbia Pike. Stewart had forced the march from Lawrenceburg, and with a clear road ahead of him, his infantry was now only a few miles from town. He found Buford waiting for him on the roadside, roughly a mile outside of town.

"I've found your way around Pulaski, General Stewart!" Buford declared cheerily. "I just finished reconnoitering it myself."

Pointing off the road and to the north, Buford continued. "This here track leads through the hills, goes along Pigeon Roost Creek, and comes back out onto the Bumpass Road. That's the old frontier times name for the Pike. Now that track is rough, and it's narrow in spots, but it is solid ground."

Stewart asked "How long is your detour? Can artillery and wagons pass it?"

"Yes, they can. The trail is a little more than three miles." Buford smacked his thigh, adding "One more thing. We found that the Yankees had set up a commissary for runaways south of town. There must have been a few thousand darkies down there, all told. The darkies ran for the hills as soon as we showed up, but I captured the commissary's stores, sir."

"Outstanding, Buford, outstanding!" Stewart exclaimed. The supply wagons were back in Lawrenceburg, and he had more than 15,000 hungry mouths to feed. Now he had a large store of Yankee hardtack, bacon, beans, and coffee to do it with. Stewart issued orders to his staff to bring those stores up to the junction, where Buford's Pigeon Roost track met the Pulaski Road, and to organize an operation to hand out rations as the men marched by.

That done, Stewart turned his attention to the enemy. "What about the Union fort?"

"I surrounded it with dismounted cavalry. There are some hills north and west of that fort, in range and of equal height. Perfect for artillery."

"Really? Then let's go have a look."

Buford took Stewart up to the top of the hills west of Pulaski, their combined staffs and escorts numbering close to one hundred riders. There was little need for secrecy, as the town was already full of Confederate cavalry. Stewart made sure his guidon was in full view of any watchful eyes from the Federal fort, announcing his presence to the Yankee garrison. He saw that he could bring up guns onto this western hill unseen, and he guessed the range to be about 1,200 yards.

Putting guns on the northern hills would mean doubling back on the Columbia Pike, and there might not be enough time for his guns to make the trip.

"Bring our rifled guns up" Stewart said to his chief of artillery, "and put them on this hill. Buford, I want you to send your horse artillery around to those firing positions on the north. Keep your guns out of sight. At four o'clock, my rifles will fire some ranging shot. When you hear it, push your guns forward. Then we'll make a surrender demand."

Buford tipped his hat. "Right, sir."

Stewart returned to where the Pigeon Roost track met the Pulaski Road, to show himself to his soldiers as they marched off the road and started their detour. He was watching as his rifled cannon clattered past and rolled toward Pulaski when a courier arrived, bearing a message from Jackson.

Noon, May 6
Army Headquarters in the Field

To Lt. Gen. Alexander P. Stewart

My Dearest General,

I regret to share news that our enemy is making fast progress north by means of disciplined marches. He has sustained a lead of several miles, and unencumbered by wagons as he is, he may reach Columbia by nightfall.

In view of these developments, you are ordered to bivouac on the road tonight, and give your troops four hours rest. Upon resuming your march, direct your corps to the Lewisburg Pike, and follow this road north. You are to continue through Lewisburg, suspending all stops for rest, until reaching the vicinity of Spring Hill, Thompson's Station or Franklin. Once there, your corps will cross over on whatever road is most convenient, intercept the enemy, and impede his further advance.

Sincerely and Respectfully,

T.J. Jackson
General, CSA

Stewart smiled as he folded the message up and put it in his pocket. He knew that the typical Jackson order would specify when he was to bivouac, when he was to get up, where he was to intercept McPherson's army, and every other last detail, foreseeable or unforeseeable. Stewart had received such orders himself during the winter, but these days Jackson was leaving him with some discretion. He was Stonewall Jackson's right-hand man now, and that made him glow with pride.

He imagined a map of the region in his mind, every detail meticulously memorized days ago. McPherson was set to finish a 40 mile march in one day. Even without his wagons, it was an impressive feat, so much so Stewart involuntarily whistled at the thought. Yet the Federals would be left blasted by their own exertion. They could never set such a pace tomorrow.

My soldiers will be fed tonight, Stewart thought, and have hardtack to eat on the road tomorrow. The winter training in Georgia and the march from central Alabama had made them superbly fit. If he left behind his own wagons, he might match what the Federals were accomplishing this day, and he might just overtake them tomorrow afternoon.

Stewart checked his watch. It was half past three. He dictated the orders he wanted drawn up to his staff, left them to do the paperwork, and then rode into Pulaski.

Finding Buford, he said "General, when this affair with the garrison is over, whatever the outcome, you are to go with two brigades of your cavalry to Lewisburg. They are to ride through dark and on until they get there, understood? Leave your other brigade behind to protect our rear and the corps wagon train."

"But what about this fort and its supplies? We can…"

Stewart interrupted him. "Capturing this fort doesn't matter when there is an entire Federal army out there as a prize. We have our orders."

Stewart could see from Buford's pained expression that he didn't like the idea, and was thinking about whether to argue some more.

No proper raider would like the idea, Stewart thought, but we are more than raiders here today.

Finally, Buford said "Yessir."

Almost on cue, the Confederate guns fired a salvo. The two generals watched through their glasses as some cannonballs struck home, cratering into the fort's breastworks. Turning to the northern hills, they watched as Buford's guns were rapidly brought forward and unlimbered. The cannon in the fort remained silent.

Stewart said "We've made our impression. Time to see if those Yankees want to come out. Send your messenger, General Buford."

Buford signaled to his chief aide, who left along with an escort bearing a white flag. Before long, they returned with a blue-coated officer in tow.

Introducing himself, the northern officer said "Major Owings, 9th Indiana Cavalry. I have the pleasure to represent Brigadier General John Starkweather, U.S. Volunteers."

Stewart knew the name. Starkweather had been a brigadier in their old enemy, the Army of the Cumberland, and consequently had been at Perryville, Murfreesboro and Chickamauga. A man like that might prove a tough nut to crack.

"I am Lieutenant General Alexander Stewart, Major, and this man is Brigadier General Abraham Buford. It is my duty to inform you that our army, under General Thomas Jackson, met and defeated the Federal force under the command of General McPherson in Lawrenceburg yesterday. I am here with my entire corps, plus General Buford's division of cavalry. To prevent a needless effusion of blood, I must call upon General Starkweather to surrender his garrison immediately, and I invite him to discuss terms."

The officer hesitated, and then said "I will relay your request to the General."

"Major Owings, before you go back, I thought I might show you the predicament you and your garrison are in. Would you accompany me?"

Owings nodded, and Stewart led him out of Pulaski and onto the road to Lawrenceburg to see a long column of infantry on the march. The men on the road were Clayton's, Stewart's old division, and they waved and cheered at the sight of their former chief.

Stewart explained "This division is swinging around to the north and east of town, safely out of sight of your artillery. Behind them is another division. In the morning, I will have my entire corps and all my cannon in place and ready to assault your fort after dawn. If you force me to attack, I cannot answer for the bloodshed that must ensue."

No need to exaggerate, Stewart thought. The reality looks bad enough for them.

Major Owings swallowed. "I will relay this back to my commanding officer, sir."

Owings returned to the fort with his grey-coated minders, and Stewart settled in to wait for a reply. It was not long before those greycoats returned bearing a message.

Afternoon, May 6
Pulaski, Tennessee

To Lt. Gen. A.P. Stewart:

Dear sir,

It is my pleasure to inform you that I will not give up so fine a place to hang my hat as this fort without having made the attempt to defend it. While I sincerely regret any inconvenience my decision may have caused you, I fear if you want my fort, you must come take it.

Kindest Regards,

John Converse Starkweather,
Brig. Gen. of Infantry, USA

Stewart sighed and chuckled as he handed the message to an aide. Starkweather's bravado would pay dividends for him. There would be no assault, no siege, he thought. At sunrise, Starkweather would find his enemies all long gone. Yet this charade was not for nothing. At least now the Yankees might be scared enough to stay in their little bolt hole for a time, and not trouble my wagon train.

8:00 pm
The Atheneum
Headquarters, Army of the Tennessee, USA
Columbia, Tennessee

"Your supper, sir."

McPherson looked up from his papers to the bacon sandwich and pot of coffee placed before him.

"Thank you," he said, pouring a cup of coffee and sipping on it while resuming his work.

Confederate cavalry had found them not long after sun-up, and dogged them every step of the way. Minty did a fine job of holding them back, but he had shot off most of his ammunition by the time the running cavalry skirmish reached Mt. Pleasant. As soon as his lead division, John Smith's, crossed Bigby Creek on the outskirts of Columbia, he ordered that division to deploy in defensive positions behind the creek.

The rest of the Army of the Tennessee marched by, through Columbia, and across the Duck River. Then he withdrew Minty's cavalry behind Smith, and the pursuing butternuts found a rude surprise waiting for them: a full division of infantry backed by four batteries of artillery, all spoiling for a fight.

Minty's tired troopers were now guarding the nearer fords of the Duck River, such as Davis's Ford about four miles east. In an hour or two, he would pull John Smith's command and Columbia's resident garrison back across the Duck, and then demolish the bridges. In the meantime, McPherson had the next day's marching orders to draw up.

McPherson was chewing the last bite of his sandwich when a dusty Colonel Minty came in. McPherson immediately jumped to his feet and offered his hand. "Colonel Minty, that was outstanding work today. Well done, well done! I am recommending you to Sherman for a star and permanent division command."

Minty grinned, cheeks turning red. "Thank you, sir. Ahm, it was all in a day's work."

"What complete rot. Do you have any idea how hard it is to find a solid cavalryman in this army? The Rebs seem to pluck them from trees, but in our army, fellows like you are a rare quantity."

Minty's posture became visibly more erect, his rising pride

dulling the fatigue of spending all of that day and the last in the saddle.

McPherson continued "Now, I have something I need you to do, and I wanted you to hear it directly from me. We resume the march at 3 a.m. tomorrow. At 2 a.m., I want you to dispatch the Saber Brigade to Franklin. I hate to deprive the rear guard of them, but I don't think Jackson and Forrest will lay snugly in their beds tonight. I wouldn't be surprised if they aren't crossing a more distant ford somewhere. Franklin has some old earthworks that were thrown up there about two years ago. I don't want any Reb cavalry getting there and blocking our line of retreat. You get there first."

"That might be a tall order, if Forrest swings around and rides hard on us. What can I expect in terms of support?" Minty asked.

"I'm sending the Columbia garrison up behind you by forced march. I can't very well leave them here. It's several hundred strong. They are fresh, the only fresh troops I have at this point. I expect they will be there by mid-morning. It will have to do. The rest of us should be there by mid-afternoon."

"Yessir. Well, if there is nothing else, I need to see to my men." The two generals exchanged salutes, and Minty left.

McPherson picked up his coffee cup. The men are tired, very tired, he thought, and will have trouble keeping up even a normal marching pace. But Jackson would need to repair the bridges to use them, couldn't use the nearer fords until Minty's troopers retreated, and using the farther fords entailed a detour of several miles out and several miles back.

"I'll get us out of this yet," he said to himself. "I swear before almighty God I will."

CHAPTER 13

May 7
6:30 a.m.
Army of Tennessee, CSA
Columbia, Tennessee

"Gentlemen, forward!" Polk shouted. He rode past the fife and drum band he had ordered to the outskirts of Columbia, and led a party of mounted attendants, staff officers and escorts into the town. Nattily attired in spotless, well-brushed uniforms adorned with sparkling spurs, buttons and swords, and wearing polished leather boots, Polk's assembled headquarters made quite an impression on the residents of Columbia, who hurried from their homes to welcome the troops. Behind them marched the infantry and artillery of his corps, or the Army of Mississippi, as he still insisted on calling it.

Polk wore the smile of a man content with the world. Last night, he suggested that his troops move into Columbia in the morning, occupy the town, and repair the Duck River bridges. Jackson consented, gave the harder task of forcing the river's fords to Cleburne, and assigned his own engineers to assist in the bridge work. All Polk had to do now was liberate the seat of Maury County, the home ground of the Polk clan.

Serving under Stonewall Jackson was proving to have some rewards, Polk thought. But then again, this prize would have been so much richer if I had plucked it myself, all on my own. And I certainly would have plucked it, had not Jackson stuck his nose into my business.

Minutes later, the procession arrived at a modest brick house built in the Federal style, the one-time Columbia home of his second cousin, James K. Polk, the 11th President of the Old Union. Another band waited on the lawn, playing "Dixie" as General Polk came to a stop.

He knew Sarah, James Polk's widow, was ensconced at the Polk mansion in Nashville. That suited him fine. She was obstinately neutral regarding the current war, and he would just as well not embarrass the dear lady by using this house as his headquarters today, with her unhappy and still in residence.

"Make this our headquarters for now," Polk shouted "but do not get to comfortable gentlemen. As soon as the bridge is repaired, we will cross to the north bank of the Duck and continue our pursuit of the foe!"

As several of his officers dismounted, Polk said "Now, I'm going down to the river, to have a look at this bridge."

Several miles away, Frank Cheatham rode among his troops, who were lying down in wait just out of sight of Davis Ford. Although still foggy-headed from his concussion, he was not about to allow men from his division to make a major attack without him.

He rode hatless among the troops of Maney's Brigade, displaying his bandaged head. "Boys, two days ago I promised you Nashville. I know you are tired, and I know you are hungry. One more hard push, and we'll cool our feet in the Cumberland and feast in the Athens of the South!"

Maney's men cheered, and after a few more words of encouragement, Cheatham rode up to the top of the low hill where the command party stood. Dismounting clumsily, he joined Cleburne and Forrest, who were quietly chatting. Jackson stood apart, studying the ground through his field glasses. He didn't like what he saw.

Davis Ford lay at the end of a peninsula, formed by a sharp bend in the Duck. The elevated north bank dominated the south, and although there was a hill in the center of that peninsula, the tight confines limited how many guns he could put on it to cover the attack. Worst of all, the ford emptied into a little notch. Hasty breastworks completely enclosed that notch, making it into a veritable murder hole.

Forrest had probed the ford the night before, and found it strongly defended by enemy troopers. Whoever goes in there is going to be massacred, Jackson thought. But we must pursue. The sacrifice must be made. God's will.

Jackson nodded to the waiting artillerists. They had worked all night bringing up the guns through the throng of fleeing slaves, Unionists, and draft dodgers who clogged the back roads, and up onto line. Despite the confined space, dawn saw over 20 guns in place. The cannons fired in massed volleys at the Federal breastworks, filling that part of the Duck valley with smoke and producing such thunderous noise that windows shook in Columbia.

Nathan and Willie were lying down with the rest of their regiment, behind a line of trees in a freshly plowed field near the bellowing line of Confederate cannons. Nathan watched grimly as shot and shell tore up the small area right around the ford.

The guns stopped and the bugles sounded. Maney's Brigade rose and advanced at the quick step, General Maney on foot and leading from the front. As fagged out as his men were, quick step and no faster was the most he felt he could ask of them.

His regiments fanned out, some to each side of the ford, protecting the flanks of the main attack. The 41st Tennessee picked up the pace to a dead run, rapidly splashing across the gravel riverbed and the knee-deep water. Shots cracked out, and Willie felt a ball whiz past his cheek.

Upon reaching the other side, most of the men threw themselves down onto the sloping ground, behind trees and shrubs. The colonel and the colors kept moving forward though, and Nathan kept going too, passing everyone by. Behind him came Willie, and after getting back on their feet, Corporal Marks and Sergeant Halpern. The rest of the company followed, as if dragged along at the end of a tether, and behind them the regiment.

Nathan sprinted up the wooded slope, up onto the parapet, and over to the other side. It was only then that he realized he hadn't been shot at, that the Yankee works were deserted. Panting, he could see Yankees through the trees, mounting on horses and riding away, and couldn't have cared less. He plopped down just as the others started coming over the low dirt embankment.

Corporal Marks dropped his musket and bent over, huffing and puffing as he propped himself up, hands above his knees. Willie plopped down on the embankment. Halpern pulled his hat off, and wiped the sweat from his brow. The four men looked at each other, and started laughing.

On the other side of the Duck, Jackson watched with satisfaction. If the Yankee cavalry had held this ground, they could have delayed the pursuit all morning. Pulling out was a mistake. The hand of Providence was in it.

Now his plan could proceed. Cheatham and Forrest would cross here. Cleburne's Division, now under Lucius Polk's command, would cross by means of the western fords. Stewart's Corps was somewhere to the east, probably about halfway to Lewisburg by now. The enemy was further north, but Stewart had a clear road, and had fed his men on captured supplies. God willing, Stewart would overtake the enemy today.

Jackson mounted his horse, pulling himself up with his good, increasingly strong right arm. He knew he should return to Columbia, to see those bridges for himself. Instead, he rode down to Huey's Mill, down by the ford.

He went inside the empty mill house, and once inside, knelt in prayer, offering thanks for their progress so far, and the easy river crossing. Jackson did not mention catching the enemy in his prayers, for that was already written. A good Christian thanked his God often, but asked for little, or best still, nothing at all.

9:00 a.m.
Buford's Cavalry Division, Army of Tennessee, CSA
Franklin, Tennessee

Buford's two remaining cavalry brigades departed Lewisburg for Franklin before dawn, riding down the Lewisburg Pike. As the approached the Duck River that morning, the troopers could hear the muffled thunder of artillery firing to the west, from Columbia, and that distant rumbling lent the tired horsemen a spurt of energy. They rode on, reaching Hurt's Crossroads around 9 o'clock, where Buford sent scouts probing out to the north and west while he rested his men.

Before 11 that morning, Buford knew that McPherson's main body was passing through Spring Hill by way of the Columbia Pike, en route to Franklin. Forrest was dogging McPherson's heels, but

Stewart and his infantry were still about 10 miles behind.

Unknowingly following the example of his cousin, the northern cavalry general John Buford, Abe Buford elected to get in front of McPherson's column. He took up a blocking position south of Franklin on the Columbia Pike, astride Winstead Hill and Breezy Hill. As some Billies were already present inside the old fortifications of Franklin, Buford also posted a screening force in his rear, on Privet Knob and facing the town.

There he stayed for two hours, stalling McPherson and repulsing repeated, mounting assaults on his position until the garrison in Franklin finally stirred, moving against his rear. Buford withdrew before he could be trapped between the blue pincers, falling back to the Lewisburg Pike and on south for five miles, to Goose Creek. It was there that he finally made contact with Stewart, riding ahead of his column with a strong escort.

Stewart's blood was up, so he dispensed with pleasantries. "General Buford, your report, sir?"

As Stewart listened to Buford relate the details of his stand on the Columbia Pike, he regretted that Buford had not sent back for further instructions. He would have directed Buford to abandon any blocking effort in favor of seizing Hughes's Ford, a crossing of the Harpeth River only a few miles east of Franklin. Keeping McPherson out of Franklin wasn't half as important at this stage as securing a good river crossing and getting in front of him. Stewart knew if he could do that, he could bottle McPherson up in Franklin, and make his destruction inevitable.

So Stewart stopped Buford before he could finish his report. "Get your command turned around, General Buford, and go to Hughes's Ford. It's three miles right down this very pike. My infantry isn't far behind, and you'll have some support before nightfall."

"What if the Yankees have the ford, sir?"

Stewart spoke sharply. "Attack them. We must have that crossing."

Buford drove his exhausted men and horses as hard as they could bear, but arrived at Hughes's Ford to find the Saber Brigade already there, still in the midst of deploying. Buford dismounted his men and led a charge, which was quickly and bloodily repulsed by a hail of bullets, Buford himself coming away wounded in his sword hand. Just before dark, the first of Stewart's infantry brigades arrived, threw itself into one last charge, and that too was thrown back. During the night a truce was quietly arranged, allowing the southerners to drag their dead and wounded out of the shallow waters and off the banks of the Harpeth.

May 8
Army of Tennessee, CSA
Franklin, Tennessee

At daybreak, Jackson found McPherson's Army of the Tennessee heavily dug in on the outskirts of Franklin. Weary Billies had worked through the night, extending and improving the town's existing fortifications. Now all of Logan's XV Corps was behind thick, log-reinforced embankments, fronted by a series of four-foot wide, three-foot deep ditches and rows of sharpened stakes.

To make matters worse, Jackson readily saw that any attacking force approaching the northern half of this fortress, by way of Carter's Creek Pike, had to cross more than a mile of nearly open ground. An attack on the southern half could come up from behind the woods to within half a mile, but that end was further protected by dense hedges of thorny orange-osange, and covered by the rifled cannon jutting out of from the embrasures of Fort Granger, located on the north side of the Harpeth River and beyond his reach.

Jackson quickly concluded that any frontal assault on Franklin would be bloody and futile. Wherever it was made, the infantry would have to cross at least several hundred yards of open country under fire, go through or around two or three separate layers of barriers, and then storm the fortifications. Nor could he flank Franklin's fortifications directly, since they were anchored snugly into a bend of the Harpeth.

Anticipating this eventuality the night before, Jackson had already dispatched Forrest and all his cavalry to find a crossing of the Harpeth, secure it, and gain the Federal rear. Forrest found that Minty had already posted his worn troopers at the nearer fords, and through the morning McPherson replaced these with detachments of infantry from Sweeney's Division. Forrest did not find a suitable, unguarded crossing of the Harpeth until early afternoon, almost 15 road miles east of Franklin.

As soon as he received Forrest's message about the discovery of an open ford on the Harpeth, Jackson put Stewart's and Hood's Corps, the latter now under Cleburne, into motion. Hungry and footsore, the Johnnies arrived at the ford only well after dark, and then spent all night trudging across the Harpeth.

McPherson used that day to rest his men, and to rebuild and improve Franklin's standing railroad bridge and its demolished wagon bridge, all the while hoping that Jackson would be foolish enough to attack him. After dark, while Stewart and Cleburne were crossing the Harpeth downriver, McPherson quietly moved the XV Corps across the repaired bridges, ordered the bridges fired behind them, and marched for Nashville.

May 9
4:00 am
Headquarters, Army of the Tennessee, CSA
Harrison House off the Columbia Pike
Franklin

Jackson slept fitfully, propped up against a tree. He was exhausted, but both painfully hungry and terribly restless, and waiting anxiously for the arrival of dawn's first light. Sleep neither came or stayed easily, and upon waking one time too many, he checked his watch and decided to get up.

The headquarters was quiet as Jackson went looking for the duty officer. They stared at each other for a minute, minds thickened with sleepy weariness, unable to fully recognize each other. The duty officer's memory sparked first, and he snapped into attention and gave a salute. Jackson saluted back, and only then remembered who the man was: Captain Quintard, one of the newer aides, recruited from the Army of Tennessee, and not one of his Virginia men.

"Saddle my horse and muster an escort," Jackson said quietly. "I want to have a look around."

"Yessir," Quintard whispered back. "Shall I wake Colonel Pendleton, sir?"

"Sandie?" Jackson shook his head, looking at Harrison house, where his senior staff slept on the floors. "No, let him sleep." He needs the rest, Jackson thought, and would cluck like some fretful hen over the idea of my going on reconnaissance anyway.

The thought of a worrying Sandie gave him pause, for here he was intending to go forward, beyond his own lines, bending if not breaking his word. But Jackson couldn't stand the waiting anymore. He had to do something, to go and see for himself. So, he rationalized his choice away by saying either the Yankees would be in their works or they would not, and if they were he certainly would not do anything so foolish as to ride right up to them.

He also had no intention of putting Sandie, Smith, or any of the others needlessly into harm's way. While he lost an arm that night at Chancellorsville, several of his aides were killed in the same accident. He would go with a minimal escort, nothing more.

Jackson studied the house while he waited for his horse, a fine brick mansion with a beautiful, two-story colonnaded porch. Just north of the Tennessee River, the country had the feel of his childhood home deep in the Virginia mountains, a place of villages and crude log cabins. This place reminded him more of the place he had chosen to settle in and raise a family in the Shenandoah, a place of prosperous people, well-settled with good homes made of brick.

The South was like that, he thought. As many places just clawed back from the frontier as were genteel and showed refinement.

A small escort was mounted, and as soon as Jackson had pulled himself up into his saddle one-armed, they set out down the Columbia Pike in the early morning gloom. Once they were out of sight, Quintard hurried off to wake Sandie Pendleton. The Colonel had left strict orders with the staff that he was to be woken whenever Jackson was up, and Quintard was not about to cross the army's chief of staff, no matter what the commanding general said.

Riding over the hills, Jackson could see little in the dim light of the early morning. He hushed his escort and advanced slowly up the road, listening for any signs of Yankee pickets. There were none. As the sun crept over the horizon, they came before the ramparts of Franklin. As he had expected, there wasn't a Yankee in sight.

"Send word of this back to headquarters," Jackson said flatly, to no one in particular. "Order up the engineers, and have them meet me at the Harpeth bridges." As one of the escorts turned his horse around and galloped back to the Confederate camp, Jackson struggled to maneuver his mount through the series of earthworks protecting the opening that admitted the Columbia Pike into town, ignoring how much easier the passage was for his escort party. His horsemanship had always been subpar, much to his embarrassment.

Jackson soon found himself looking upon the smoking ruins of Franklin's railroad and wagon bridges. He knew McPherson had been thought one of West Point's most promising young engineering officers before the war, and that promise showed here. Not only were the bridge decks and superstructures burnt away to nothing, but the piers had been badly damaged by demolition charges.

The stone piers of the railroad bridge were repairable, Jackson thought, given time. The wooden wagon bridge was a complete loss. My pontoon train was behind the supply wagons, at the end of a slow column that should be in Columbia now, 25 miles away. No one would cross the Harpeth from here until tomorrow morning, at the earliest.

He scowled, despite himself. McPherson had escaped him. Even though Stewart's Corps should be on the road by now, and Forrest had advance cavalry as far as Nolensville, McPherson would reach Nashville. He was as certain of this as he was of the reasons why it had happened.

The prideful Yankees had been deceived, and he had succeeded in bringing a larger army into Tennessee than the one sent to meet him. Providence laid the prospect of a great victory before the South, a victory that would have opened the road to winning the war, to winning independence. If he had destroyed McPherson at Lawrenceburg, Sherman would have had no choice but to quit Georgia, leave a garrison in Chattanooga, and march the bulk of his army to defend Nashville.

Instead, it was all undone by wicked and worthless men within his own army. The treachery of Loring, the sloth and stupidity of Featherston, the weakness among so many of the common soldiers. The last part was especially painful. If they had caught up to McPherson yesterday, if only for a little while, Stewart would have arrived in time to smash the Federal flank. His soldiers had their orders, but they couldn't keep up, and all for a few biscuits. A third of his army was straggled back 60 miles, all the way to Lawrenceburg. Many of his men had made a valiant effort, had done their duty, but many others had not.

Bullets thwacked against the house behind him, confirming the enemy's presence on the opposite bank. Just as at Columbia, he thought, cavalry would no doubt continue to secure the crossings for much of the morning. Jackson grunted and withdrew to greater safety behind the house, a concession to his promises regarding reckless exposure, where he was met soon after by the engineers.

Leaning against a brick wall, Jackson ordered "Inspect the railroad bridge piers and begin repairs. Also, send a courier to Generals Stewart and Forrest. Halt the pursuit, withdraw to the south banks of the Harpeth, and await further direction."

Further direction, he thought. I should move right now, advance behind the curtains of the Harpeth and Cumberland, cross the Cumberland River at Clarksville, swing in behind, and cut the railroad to Louisville. The entire United States would panic, and Sherman and McPherson would have no choice but to attack me, lest every enemy soldier from Nashville to Decatur and Chattanooga starve.

Jackson's features twisted into an angry frown as he realized he couldn't, at least not yet. He needed to feed his men, just as he needed his pontoons if he was to cross the Cumberland. That meant at least two days to rest his men, regroup, wait for his bridging train, and distribute rations and ammunition. He clenched his fist and his teeth, and resolved it would be no more than two days.

"Excuse me, General, but you are *the* Stonewall Jackson, are you not?"

Jackson looked up. A wary, middle-aged civilian was standing a few yards away. Jackson wondered for a moment who the stranger was, but realized he must be the owner of the house he was sheltering behind.

Jackson's features relaxed. "Yes, yes. If I may trouble you, does your lovely town have a Presbyterian house of worship?"

The man brightened. Stonewall Jackson, here, in my backyard! "Delighted to be of service," he answered smartly. "Yes, sir, General, we do indeed. The Presbyterian Church is at Five Points, ah, that's 5th and Main."

Jackson nodded. He had ridden right past it and not noticed. He thanked the man and started for his horse.

"General Jackson! Won't you come in and have some coffee? We don't have any real coffee, mind you, but we do have a supply of Kentucky coffee."

Jackson pulled himself up onto his horse, and smiled. "No, no, but thank you." I must pray, he thought. The victory was incomplete and more battles waited for them, but that was Providence. It was also Providence that they still had a victory, if only a partial one, and with it part of Tennessee was liberated. What they had was good, and thanks were due.

Upon reaching the church, Jackson told the lieutenant that led his escort "Go find the pastor and tell him I'm here. If he is having his breakfast, insist on my behalf that he finish first. I'll wait." With that, Jackson dismounted, sat down on the church steps, put his back up against the door, and fell soundly asleep.

9 a.m.
Headquarters in the Field, Army of the Tennessee, USA
Brentwood Crossroads
Brentwood

McPherson heard the clopping and clapping of riders coming on hard from a hundred yards off, and after turning to look down the Franklin Pike, he saw a splash of red under the hat of the lead rider, far in front of the others.

That must be Bill, he thought. His spirits instantly lightened, as a feeling of relief passed through him.

He watched as Sherman thundered on fast, right up to the place he was standing. As smooth as any man in the cavalry, Sherman brought the horse up, about, and to stop on just the right spot, and then rolled smartly off the saddle.

Stepping forward with his hand extended, McPherson said "Bill, I didn't reckon you were already in Nashville, but I should have."

With a wide smile, Sherman took shook his hand and slapped him on the shoulder. "Damn, Mac, am I glad to see you. I ran into Logan on the way. Had some words. What's the situation here?"

"Well, I have Sweeney covering the approaches from Franklin

and Nolensville. The cavalry ought to arrive shortly, unless they ran into trouble with Forrest. Then I'm pulling Sweeney back."

Sherman frowned. "Jackson and Forrest. A match made in hell, right there. This fellow of yours, Bobby Minty, he seems to have done well enough against the devil in the saddle, didn't he?"

"He did, he did indeed. I'll tell you, my cavalry have taken a real kicking. Holly Grove, Lawrenceburg, covering our retreat. Not a clear win in the lot, Bill, but their morale has never been better. Minty has the style, that Irish pugnacity with a dash of British parade ground panache for good measure. He's got my enthusiastic endorsement as Kilpatrick's permanent replacement. Get him his star, soon as you can, that's my advice."

Sherman withdrew a cigar from its case, struck a match, and started puffing it alight. He muttered "I'll draw up the papers today," cigar clenched in his teeth. Taking the cigar out, he pointed away from the road. "We need to talk."

The two withdrew a short distance. "Before you get started, Bill, I just want to say… I lost at Lawrenceburg, and I know it. I haven't had a chance to write it up, but my resignation will be on your desk this evening."

Sherman was non-plussed. Even though this sort of thing was customary, that McPherson might tender his resignation was the last thing on his mind. "Poppycock. I won't accept it, Mac, and neither will Halleck or Grant. You stay right where you are."

"Bill, you and I know the press will kick up a whirlwind over this, and I don't have that many friends in Washington. Think about this. I'll be more trouble to you than I'm worth."

"You have the commanding general of the United States Army, its chief of staff, and the commander of its largest military department behind you. All three of us. Mac, if Horace Greeley, some other syphilitic newsman, or any grubby, bullying politician takes a swing at your head, he'll do it through the protests of Halleck, Grant's resignation, and my dead body."

McPherson relaxed, and out came his warm, grateful smile. "Alright, alright. You have me convinced."

Sherman took several rapid puffs from his cigar, clouding the air with smoke. "Besides, your army is about to get a lot larger, and I need you at the head of it."

"Sir?"

"XX Corps is already in Nashville, or most of the part that matters anyway, and A.J. Smith's men ought to disembark from their river transports in Louisville tomorrow. From there, they go straight to the train station and roll down here. We'll send that mean-spirited mick Sweeney to work under Smith, and reconstitute the XVI Corps. Sturgis will soon depart from Memphis with Grierson's cavalry and some others. In a matter of days, you'll have three infantry and one cavalry corps under you."

McPherson stood in silent wonder. He had known about all the different pieces, of course, but he never imagined they could be brought together so quickly. Or that they were being brought together in the first place.

"Of course, Smith and Hooker have the same problem you do, only worse: they left behind equipment to speed their journey. I have all the cannon I need to re-arm them right here in Nashville, but we still need wagons, horses, mules, and all manner of accoutrements. It will be weeks before we're ready to move out. But we will have all the manpower in just a few days. And that reminds me, I'll be accompanying you. Thomas can see to Hardee on his own."

McPherson replied flatly "Yessir. I understand."

Tapping his foot, Sherman said "No, you don't, Mac. You don't. My decision is no reflection on you. Not in the slightest bit. It's just that Joe Hooker ranks you by a year, so if I'm not here, he assumes command by default. Technically, Hooker's XX Corps answers to me, to get around that problem. *De facto*, it's part of your army. Also, it deflects some of that political lightening you spoke of before. Just keep in mind Grant's doing the same thing with Meade and his Army of the Potomac back east."

"Ah."

Still tapping, Sherman gesticulated off to the southeast. "I would have preferred one of the other Cumberland army corps, but Thomas wanted to keep them. Can't say I blame him. Remember how we felt when they broke off bits of our army after Vicksburg, piddling away detachments for this and that foolishness?"

"Yes, I do. Contemptible misuse of a damn fine army."

"That is was, that it was. Now, I have some other news for you. While you were fighting Jackson at Lawrenceburg, Grant met Bobby Lee in the Wilderness. Sorry to say, he got licked."

McPherson frowned, but said nothing, so Sherman continued.

"Yes, but do you know what Grant went out and did? Got word of it just this morning. He picked up and took off, trying to get 'round Lee's flank. You know Grant, always moving on."

McPherson brightened. Chuckling, he said "Yes, that sounds just like our man."

"Indeed. Now, you see about getting the rest of your boys into the Nashville lines, then come see me. There's work aplenty to go around."

AUTHOR'S NOTE

Keen students of history understand that while human events might be fluid, the direction those events take are limited to only a handful of potential options, in much the same way that topography dictates where and how a river might change its course. Geography, material resources, opposition, past choices, personalities, weather, and other factors often too numerous to count combine to ensure that while people have choices, as a practical matter they never have many of them.

Stonewall Goes West was likewise guided and constrained by the very real circumstances of the Civil War. To cite just a few: Leonidas Polk really did propose mounting a raid into Middle Tennessee; Joseph E. Johnston suggested changing his base and invading West Tennessee; John Bell Hood crossed the Tennessee River and invaded Middle Tennessee in November 1864. These things and much, much more shaped this story and informed its sense of realism.

Keeping these constraints in mind, the most challenging feat of all was crafting a major, fictitious Civil War battle in a place where no such thing ever took place. Putting together the Second Battle of Kettle Run was one thing, since it closely adhered to the very real events of the Bristoe Campaign and took place in a region that hosted part of several major Virginia campaigns, so the area's features were thoroughly documented.

The Battle of Lawrenceburg was a different matter entirely. The physical details for the Battle of Lawrenceburg were composed using historical records, period maps, and a thorough exploration of the town and its environs made in 2007. Wherever possible, authentic names were used to describe landmarks and topographical features. Time and modern development can markedly change a landscape, however, and no amount of research could ever describe the Lawrence County of May 1864 in perfect detail. The gaps were filled by imagination, and those gaps weren't small. If at some point in the future, someone shows me a distant ancestor's letter describing a farmstead where some important part of the story took place, all I can say is that I tried to find that letter, having it would have made my task a little easier, and ultimately *Stonewall Goes West* is a work of fiction.

Coming Spring 2014

MOTHER EARTH, BLOODY GROUND

Part Two of the Trilogy
Stonewall Jackson continues the struggle
for Middle Tennessee against
William T. Sherman

22364249R00136

Made in the USA
Lexington, KY
25 April 2013